I0742532

SLOW BURN

Also by S. L. Stoner
in the
Sage Adair Historical Mystery Series
of the Pacific Northwest

Timber Beasts
Land Sharks
Dry Rot
Black Drop
Dead Line
The Mangle

SLOW BURN

A Sage Adair Historical Mystery
of the Pacific Northwest

S. L. Stoner

Yamhill Press
www.yamhillpress.net

Slow Burn

A Sage Adair Historical Mystery of the Pacific Northwest

Slow Burn is a work of fiction. Names, characters, places and incidents are the products of the author's imagination or are used fictitiously. Any resemblance to actual events, locales, or person, living or dead, is entirely coincidental unless specifically noted otherwise.

A Yamhill Press Book

All rights reserved

Copyright © 2018 by S. L. Stoner

Cover Design by Alec Icky Dunn

Interior Design by Slaven Kovačević (slaven980@gmail.com)

Printed in the United States. This book may not be reproduced in whole or in part, by any means, without written permission. For information contact: Yamhill Press at www.YamhillPress.net.

Edition ISBNs
Softcover ISBN 978-1-7320066-0-7
EBook   ISBN 978-1-7320066-1-4

Library of Congress Control Number: 2018933939

Publishers Cataloguing in Publication

    Slow Burn / S.L. Stoner.

    230 pages cm – (A Sage Adair historical mystery of the Pacific Northwest) 1. Northwest, Pacific—History--20th century—Fiction. 2. Detective and Mystery Fiction, 3. Action and Adventure—Fiction, 4. Firefighters—Fiction, 5. Arson—Fiction, 6. Fire Insurance—Fiction, 7. Racism against African-Americans—Fiction, 8. Booker T. Washington—Fiction, 9. W.E.B. Du Bois, 10. Historical Fiction. I. Title. II. Series: Stoner, S. L. Sage Adair historical mystery.

For
George Slanina, Jr.
as Always and Forever

And in Memory of
Phyllis Sayles Stoner, Nancy Winchester Stoner
and Margaret Wickert Davie
Three Unique, Loving and Cherished, Strong Women

And in Memory of
Joey Cockatoo
Who, by His Death, Saved a Precious Human Life

And in Honor of
Portland's Firefighters
Past, Present and Future.

ONE

THE WILD GRASSES HE CRUSHED underfoot made no noise despite the heavy can he carried. Still, it conceals traps, he warned himself seconds before stepping ankle-deep into yet another hidden puddle. Freezing water flooded his shoe and wet his pant leg. "God damn it!" he yelled then froze. Had he been heard? No. The windows facing the field stayed blank.

He moved forward more cautiously. There'd be more puddles before he reached the back of the house. Damn rain. Still, this was the best time, the best weather to not get caught.

It was nearly one a.m. and the quarter moon cast light now that the clouds had drifted eastward. But, really, what were the chances anyone would be awake, let alone looking out their window? Luckily, all the houses had indoor privies—even the one he wanted. He'd made sure of that.

Then he was under the porch and waiting for his eyes to adjust to the faint moonlight shining between the boards. He glanced around. Like he'd figured, there was nothing worth stealing. At least they'd covered the firewood with a tarp. It'd be dry, ready to burn. He set the can down and peeled away the tarp. The fir pitch had dried to a milky white. It'd catch quick.

He twisted off the can cap and tossed it away. Its job was over. Carefully, he coated the wood. Like always, the odor sent shivers sparking up his arms.

Pulling a silver match safe from his pocket and hunching over it to keep the contents dry, he thumbed the lid open. Wet matches would be bad. He murmured to the snow white sulfur tips. "Which one of you beauties is willing to sacrifice?" before plucking up a sturdy looking fellow.

With perfect control, he drew the match head across the striker, sucking in its wisp of sulfur. Carefully, he touched the flame to the woodpile. It could go out. It had before. But not this time. The stove oil caught with a soft whoosh and fire raced along the glistening trail.

He breathed out slowly, then ran, heedless of any traps lurking beneath the bent stalks. Only after reaching the shelter of the fir trees did he look back. Flames were shooting up between the porch floorboards and licking at the clapboard siding. Above, the windows remained blank. Grinning, he headed away, his job done.

A screech, harsh and unearthly, sounded from behind him, whirling him around. Dumbfounded he stared at the burning house. The screech sounded again, jolting his heart and setting his feet running. Whatever made that noise, he didn't want to meet it.

Minutes later, as he tossed the empty can into a ravine, he told himself there was no reason to worry.

TWO

The saloon looked and smelled like a hundred others in the city. Gouges peppered the bar, floor, tables and mismatched chairs. The familiar odor of unwashed bodies, boot mud and years of cigarettes lay thick in the air. The patrons, too, seemed the same—as though they were actors traveling from saloon to saloon, contributing drunken laughter to the same bad jokes. The saloon's working women, their faces blurred from drink and despair, could have come from the same traveling show—with their shrieks and half-hearted swats at the same old pinches and pokes. Not that these women would earn anything tonight. It was not their allure but rather the steady rain that was keeping the men inside, nursing their beers and parsing out the few remaining coins in their pockets. No one wanted to spread a bedroll in the cold wet outside. For those who could afford it, saloon sitting was a better alternative until the sun came up.

It was one in the morning and Sage was tired. Unlike the saloon's other customers, a warm bed awaited him. But, he couldn't leave. Vincent St. Alban's cryptic letter told him to meet an "Andy Hosier" in the Cliffhanger saloon one hour after midnight. St. Alban's only descriptive clue was that Hosier'd be carrying a bag. And, since there'd been no date provided, Sage had to keep showing up until Hosier appeared. This was night three of waiting.

He stared into his beer, letting the familiar sounds lap around him. With his John Miner raggedy work duds, slouch hat and drooping mustache he was unmemorable, just another homeless man cut loose from his moorings by the downturn's economics.

He raised his head, listening for the rain. It was a wet fall. At this hour, the jail floor would be covered with people, crammed together like sardines in a tin. According to Sergeant Hanke, the city councilors were squawking at having to pay $750 a month to feed their homeless guests each morning. Doubtless those councilors would rather spend that money on pet projects carried out by their relatives, friends and business cronies.

Except for Fred T. Merrill, of course. The thought of that colorful contrarian made Sage smile. Merrill was the Council's conscience. His latest crusade was that of opposing more oil tanks on the Willamette's east bank. Thought of that particular battle spurred another smile. It was just like Fred to defy one of the country's most powerful corporations—Standard Oil, no less.

"You John Miner?"asked a voice at his elbow. Sage's start sent his chair scooting backward. He looked up at a clean-shaven stranger of about twenty-five with fine dark hair and alert brown eyes. It was the type of face that would look youthful well into middle age.

"I might be. And, your name is?" Sage said, in his best Appalachian drawl, ending their mutual appraisal. He gestured at the vacant chair.

"Andy Hosier," came the answer as Hosier plopped down. He was huffing slightly, as if he'd been running. His pant legs were soaked almost to the knee.

Hosier reached down and tugged a large canvas bag closer to his foot. A slip knot of heavy twine kept its top tightly closed. He noticed Sage studying the bag.

"That's my turnout gear," Hosier said. "The city fire bell might ring and I'll need to run. That's why I asked to meet here at the Cliffhanger. We're only a block from Fire Station 1, on Fourth Avenue. That's my firehouse," he added proudly.

Seeing Sage's confusion, Hosier gave a half smile. "I see that Mr. St. Alban left you in the dark. I'm a part time firefighter, what's called an 'extraman'. Us extramen are paid only if and when we fight a fire. Otherwise, most of us work at other part time jobs. Me, I do handyman work wherever I can. Only firefighters assigned to fire equipment get paid full time. Us extramen have to run for the nearest firehouse when the big bell sounds.

His boot nudged the bag on the floor. "My turnout bag holds my helmet, boots, canvas jacket and pants. I always carry it when I'm away from the firehouse in case I have to catch the fire engine on the run. It'd waste time, going back to my firehouse just to fetch my gear."

"All the Saint wrote was that I was to meet you. He usually doesn't say much—too many management spies around," Sage said.

Hosier scooted forward to lean over the table and say in a low voice, "Exactly. That's why St. Alban said I should meet with you in secret. You see, I'm trying to start a firefighters' union. We need to get rid of the volunteers and the extramen. Go to a full time, professional fire department—one that pays all of us enough to live on."

Sage sat back, mystified. What kind of help could he give the firefighters? He wasn't a volunteer. He'd never even entered a firehouse. "What kind of help do you need?" he asked.

Hosier opened his mouth to respond but froze before twisting around to stare at the door. Then Sage heard it too—the deep, rolling boom-boom of the city's fire bell sounding in the fire station tower a block away. There was no mistaking its summons.

The saloon quieted as everyone strained to hear a second round of booms. When they came, Hosier snatched up his bag and ran for the door. "Come on," he called over his shoulder though Sage was already at his heels.

Outside, a horse-drawn fire hose cart rattled past, a spotted white dog running alongside the horse. The rain had stopped and the clouds had cleared. The driver's cap badge and his jacket's brass buttons glinted in the light of the quarter moon.

"Where's the fire?" shouted Hosier, raising his turnout bag in the air.

"11th and Market," the driver yelled, his words nearly drowned out by the steel wheels clattering over the cobblestones. At block's end, the driver half stood to haul back on the reins and send the horse trotting around the corner.

In quick succession, two more pieces of fire equipment followed—a ladder truck with men clinging like barnacles to its sides and a steam fire engine. The driver of the steam engine waved at Andy who waved back and began following it—Sage at his side.

As the fire engine rounded the corner, its nickel-plated dome shone beneath the gaslights. Hosier breathed, "Isn't she a real beauty?"

Sage glanced behind them. The only women in sight were the saloon gals who'd run outside to see the excitement. Somehow, he doubted one of them had inspired Hosier's admiration. "She?" he prompted.

Hosier shot him a puzzled glance. "Our steam fire engine. She's brand new. The very latest in topnotch engineering. Come on, we need to catch them."

Not waiting for agreement, Hosier increased his speed. Sage hesitated before running to catch up. "No way I'm going into a burning building," Sage declared upon reaching Hosier's side.

Despite their brisk pace, Hosier had breath enough to chuckle. "Don't worry," he said. "Chief Campbell never lets volunteers enter burning buildings." It was with pride and admiration that the young man said the fire chief's name.

Hosier continued, "But, you can help by stoking the boiler, provided you don't mind getting a few ember burns. The ladder truck carries spare turnout gear for volunteers. That'll help protect you."

Ember burns. Like most Portlanders, Sage'd done his share of fire scene gawking. Usually, the police herded spectators far away. He looked closely at the young man. Sure enough, there was a nasty red mark on Hosier's neck between collar and hairline.

St. Alban's really tossed me into it this time, he mused. What he said aloud, however, was, "So, if you don't see the firefighters on their way to a fire, how do you know where to go? The bell doesn't give locations."

"The big bell sends volunteers and extramen running to the nearest firehouse. Folks there know where the fire is and if our station's been sent."

"Sounds like it could delay getting to some fires," Sage observed.

Hosier gave a derisive snort before saying, "You don't know the half of it. First, someone has to see it, then find the nearest fire alarm box and read the tin plate that says which house or business has the box key. Next he has to rouse them folks, get the key, unlock the box and yank the lever to send a signal to the central station which orders the big bell rung and alerts the firehouse nearest the alarm box. That firehouse crew races to box. From there, they can usually spot the fire. 'Course, nowadays, if someone has a telephone, they call in the exact address. That's lots faster," he explained.

Sage mulled that information over for a few strides before saying, "I suppose that's why there's so many alarm boxes around the city."

"Yup. But, we're still way short. There's not enough of them. Especially on the eastside." He shifted his bag to his other hand and kept explaining, "Right now, we got over five hundred fire alarm boxes. We need three times that number. And, the circuits jam when more than one alarm lever gets pulled. Then, all we know is that there is a fire but darned if we can figure out where. So, we just head in the general direction of the jammed boxes." Nearing 11th Avenue, they picked up speed until there wasn't breath enough to talk.

A minute, and many puddle jumps later, they saw orange flames shooting into the black sky, sending twinkling sparks into a strong wind blowing from the north.

"Damn, I hate the wind," Hosier said as he began running full out, his boots splashing through rain puddles that Sage carefully skirted. Hosier probably doesn't care about his trousers, since they're already wet, Sage thought.

Soon both men were leaping over empty fire hoses stretched toward a wood frame house that sat on a steep slope. It was two stories high in the front and three stories high at the back. Flames engulfed the entire back half of the building.

As Hosier ran past the ladder truck he snatched up a bulky canvas bag and tossed it to Sage. "Get over by the engine, put on that gear and wait for me!" he yelled over the whinnies of horses and the shouts of men.

Sage ran to the fire engine. Using its side to steady himself, he yanked on canvas pants and jacket. After strapping on the hard leather helmet, he looked for Hosier and spotted him standing beside the ladder truck, talking to a man who appeared to be in charge. Even as he talked, Hosier was rapidly donning his own gear. Then he turned and pointed at Sage. Receiving a nod from the other man, Hosier ran toward Sage. "The station chief says for you to go ahead and stoke the firebox. But, he doesn't want you anywhere near the fire or handling any hoses. You do know how to tend a coal fire, right?"

Sage nodded, relieved he'd get no closer to flames than those in the steam engine. And, he was also relieved to note that the wind was carrying the embers away from the engine.

Hosier gave instructions, "Open that metal door. Lay the coal in just a little at a time. Keep the grate nicely covered, but not thick—say no deeper than three inches. Take your orders from the engineer. His name's Ollie. He'll tell you when to stoke once he's calculated the pressure needed for each hose."

Sage nodded, retrieved a small shovel from the engine's fuel bin, scooped up some coal and stood ready to toss it in. It was only then that Sage noticed the smooth-coated Dalmatian curled beneath the steam engine, warm, dry, and out of the way. She raised her head and studied Sage with calm, dark eyes before dropping her head back onto her paws.

Meanwhile Hosier checked the hose connections at a nearby hydrant before running back to tighten the fire engine's output connections. That done, he ran between the men who stood braced against the coming kickback of water and the engineer who was monitoring the engine gauges. A minute later the engineer shouted, flipped a lever and the two water hoses swelled and lengthened like boa constrictors before shooting water onto the burning house's peaked roof. The engineer waved a hand at Sage who opened the firebox door and threw in his first shovel of coal.

In the hour that followed, the engineer kept his fingers and eyes on the gauges, signaling Sage whenever he needed more coal. Hosier ran to and fro, lending a hand everywhere. As he passed the chugging engine he'd throw questions at the engineer. Once the fire began to slacken, the engineer had Hosier step in to monitor the gauges, remaining the entire time at the young firefighter's elbow. A few minutes later, he patted Hosier's shoulder before edging him aside and taking over once again.

Sage watched the firefighters whenever he wasn't adding coal. Their teamwork was impressive. He also couldn't help but smile when he saw Hosier pause to fondly pat the engine.

He understood Hosier's admiration. The gleaming red and chrome machine was a marvel. Though relatively small, it created enough pressure to send arcs of water two stories high.

Once the fire was out, Hosier returned to Sage's side. "You did real good. Ollie says you kept the temperature nice and even. She ran like a top. She sure is a beaut," he added, patting the boiler yet again and missing Sage's flush at hearing the engineer's praise.

Sage nodded, straightened and, for the first time, turned away from the smoldering house to see the horses bunched together about a block away. As usually happened at fire scenes, young neighbor boys had led the fire horses off to walk them cool and keep them calm. Nearer to hand, a man and woman in sleeping clothes huddled in a corner of the yard, wrapped round by blankets. Both were consoling a little girl sobbing in the man's arms.

Hosier saw where Sage was looking. "Those folks are lucky. The little girl's pet bird 'Joey', a cockatoo, screeched them awake so they got out in time. Otherwise, the smoke alone could have smothered them. The bird didn't make it. His cage was on the first floor, right near where the fire started."

"They know what caused the fire?" Sage asked.

Hosier shrugged. "Naw, not yet. It's still too hot to tell. Though it looks like it started outside, in the back. That means it's probably arson." He nodded toward the family. "It's a rent house so no insurance. They'll have a tough time getting back on their feet if everything they own burned up."

Around them, the activity slowed. Firefighters began rolling up the hoses, weariness slowing their movements. Soon, they had the horses maneuvered into position with their harnesses cinched tight.

Just as the equipment started to roll out, the city's fire bell boomed once again. Hosier and Sage exchanged looks. "Think you can go another round?" Hosier asked. "We still have some talking to do but firefighting's gotta come first."

THREE

This time a one-story, dry goods store was burning. Heat had already blown out its window glass, sending flames roaring out the openings and shooting high above the roof line. There's no way to save this building. The poor shopkeeper has lost his business, Sage thought. Although Mozart's Table was a ruse created to conceal his real purpose in town, he'd hate to see the restaurant burning like this.

Fire Chief David Campbell and another firehouse's crew were already on the scene. Sage recognized Campbell from newspaper photos. Stern faced and clad in turnout gear, Campbell ignored the sparking cinders raining down on his helmet and shoulders.

Apparently, he also believed the building was a lost cause because he gestured the first crew toward the buildings on either side. Within seconds, those men were climbing ladders to soak the neighboring walls and roofs.

Hosier ran ahead and greeted another firefighter with a shoulder hug. Turning to Sage, he said, "Meet my brother-in-law, Jimmy Baldwin. He's married to my only sister, Violet." He playfully punched Baldwin's shoulder and added, "This here's the crazy galoot who talked me into taking this job. He's also the best damn carpenter in town, if you ever need one."

The other man flashed a toothy grin from beneath a bushy mustache before returning his attention to the hose nozzle just as the first glut of water shot out. "Glad to see you here helping us smoke eaters," he said over his shoulder.

Sage quickly stepped into place at the steam engine's firebox. Minutes later Ollie threw a lever that sent water streams shooting onto rooftops. A scruffy dog started barking and making as if to attack the busy firefighters. In a flash, the Dalmatian was out from under the fire engine and charging at the interloper. The other dog ran off, tail between his legs. The fire dog scooted back into her sheltered place but not before pausing to look at Sage. He could swear she was smiling. "Good dog," he told her. She wagged her tail and disappeared beneath the engine.

Hosier passed by, looking glum. "What's the matter?" Sage asked.

"That damn Jimmy, he thinks he's some kind of monkey. He promised Violet he'd stay off roofs and now the fool is running up the ladder."

Sage looked but couldn't distinguish Hosier's brother-in-law from all the others. A collective gasp turned him toward the onlookers crowding the sidewalk across the street. The store's roof had fallen inward, sending up a huge column of sparks. Firelight showed some spectators were worried, others frightened, and, still others twitching with excitement.

It was four a.m. before they could safely leave the scene. Hoses tucked away, Sage and Hosier climbed up beside the engineer for a ride back to the firehouse. Once there, Sage saw that the ground floor served as both garage and stable for the fire apparatus and horses. A sturdy brass pole gave the firefighters a fast descent from the second floor.

Once they were inside, Hosier made the formal introduction. "This here is Sadie, our fire dog. Her job is to keep other dogs away from the horses and us. That's why she runs alongside the curb. Me and her are great pals. I've been promised that she'll be mine when she retires from her firehouse job next year." Andy reached down and scratched the dog's backend, sending her hind leg to thumping. "Course we have to find us a real place to live, don't we girl?"

Sage admired the animal's intelligent eyes, jet black ears and dramatic spots. Not for the first time, he regretted that he lived in a third floor apartment. "Hey, Sadie," he said, "we're already pals, aren't we?" Hearing her name, the dog looked up and Sage scratched behind her ears. She accepted his attention with a single thump of her tail before turning to gobble up the meat Andy tossed into her bowl.

Hosier led Sage up the narrow stairs into the firefighters' living quarters. There the two of them tiredly shed and stowed their gear before sitting down with coffee. It wasn't private enough to discuss the St. Alban matter so Sage asked questions about firefighting.

It was a short session because just thirty minutes later, the firehouse bell shrilled. This time the blaze was in the Canning and Wallace wholesale drug depository on the waterfront, between Ash and Pine. The fire station chief told them that a messenger boy spotted the flames and ran to alert the nearby police station. Hosier and Sage looked at each other and shrugged. For the third time that night, Sage donned the stiff canvas trousers, coat and leather helmet.

The fire was immense. Another crew was already on scene, pumping water to little effect. Chief Campbell was also there. He immediately gathered the Station 1 firefighters around him, acknowledging Sage's presence with a nod. "This is going to be a bad fire," he told them, shouting to be heard over the roaring flames. "The owner says he's got oil and alcohol stored on all three floors. I don't want any of you in that building or on top of it. Is that clear? We've got to let her burn and focus on saving the nearby businesses. That one on the south is full of brooms and wooden matches. The one to the north, is full of turpentine, linseed oil and varnish. If either of them catch fire, we'll lose the whole waterfront." Soot-filled lines on Campbell's face emphasized the fact that he was seriously worried.

Suddenly, a nearby fire horse let loose a high-pitched, ear-piercing scream. Its front hooves pawed the air before slamming down onto the street. Then it and its mate bolted, the empty ladder truck bouncing along behind. At first, Sage thought falling embers had seared the creature. But then he saw electricity's unmistakable blue spark. As the wagon headed into the dark, a live wire dropped off the vehicle, onto the wet cobbles. The men nearest the downed wire scooted backward before circling around it to chase after the wagon.

Simultaneously, near disaster struck from another quarter. The horse's scream had startled a hose man. His jerk at the sound sent his water stream against a firefighter standing two stories up a ladder. The blast knocked the man off the rungs, swinging him to the ladder's underside where he clung like a baby possum. Another firefighter raced up the ladder to rescue him.

The chaos increased as fire apparatus from other firehouses filled the street. Campbell had summoned more help. Sadie abandoned her place beneath the engine and moved near the bunched horses, trotting a perimeter around them, her tail high in the air. She was on guard.

Spectators were stepping on hoses and getting in the way until policemen arrived and began pushing them back.

Sage returned to filling the firebox. Having become familiar with his stoking task, he observed the scene as he worked. Campbell stood eyeing the building's front. Suddenly, the fire chief ran forward, waving his arms and shouting at two men who'd begun advancing toward its entrance with the obvious intention of shooting water through its front door.

Campbell shoved them aside just as a plaster cornice fell. The falling ornament hit Campbell, knocking him to the ground. Men rushed forward and pulled him clear just before the building's plaster front crashed down.

Seconds later, Campbell staggered to his feet and shrugged the men off. His leather helmet sported a deep gash from a blow that would have killed him but for its protection. His shouted instructions soon sent ten streams of water shooting onto the building from neighboring roofs and the street. That proved to be enough. By seven a.m., the men were once again rolling the hoses up and stowing them on the cart. The building they left behind was a total loss but they'd managed to save its neighbors.

Sage and Hosier walked the ten blocks back to Fire Station 1. There they found the firehouse chief, Ray Faden, dishing up eggs, toast and coffee. He'd apparently left the fire early because his clothes and his light brown hair were clean and his attitude jaunty. The exhausted firefighters, stinking of sweat and smoke, ate before flinging themselves onto the cots that lined the walls. Mingled scents of horse manure and feed wafted up from below turning the room odiferous.

Soot still blackened the smoke eaters but relief lightened their laughter. No one had died or been hurt in any of the night's three fires. Even the runaway horses were uninjured, though the men discussed whether the one shocked by the electrical wire would ever again pull a fire wagon.

Sage and Hosier ate but then parted outside the firehouse's big doors after agreeing they were too tired to talk further. Instead, they would meet later that day. Sage had taken but a few steps, however, when the city bell boomed yet again. Sighing, he reversed course and was soon clinging to the side of the ladder truck alongside Hosier. "Hang on real tight," Hosier shouted, "You can get thrown off rounding corners. Two fellows been killed that way. And, pray we don't hit a trolley 'cause that happens too. They seem to think they have the right of way."

Sage tightened his grip, his booted toes uselessly trying to clutch the narrow wooden slat underfoot. "I had no idea Portland had this many fires every day," he shouted to Hosier.

The extraman shook his head. "We don't. If we did, I wouldn't have to work as a sometime handyman. I'd earn the same pay as a full time firefighter."

Sage looked up at the gray clouds scuttling fast across the sky. "Maybe it's the wind we're having," he shouted.

Hosier also looked up but then shook his head and shouted back, "The wind makes it worse alright but it looks like someone's setting fires. Sure wish it'd start raining."

The ladder truck rumbled toward the Steel Bridge, only to find it raised for ships fleeing the conflagration consuming the Victoria dock. The firefighters' cavalcade diverted to the Burnside Bridge, crossed it and rumbled up Larrabee Street and onto the railroad embankment that rose behind the burning dock and warehouse. A suddenly gusting wind began driving flames up its slope, forcing spectators to turn and run.

Further uphill, Larrabee Street residents were evacuating. A few callous gawkers perched on the evacuees' piled furniture as though watching a play. Other people raced to help their neighbors save endangered possessions. Onto the scene came a phalanx of helmeted police who began chasing the spectators off the furniture and herding them away.

As the Station 1 crew ran toward the fire, cinders rained down and sizzled in the embankment's long grasses. Sage focused on stoking the firebox and lost sight of Hosier. This was definitely their worst fire yet. The dock, warehouse and its surroundings were an inferno thanks to years of oil and creosote coating the dock timbers. Though they tried, the firefighters couldn't reach to the warehouse's river side with their hose water. All they could do was frantically wet down the back of the building, the grass and neighboring structures. Additional fire crews arrived just as the smoldering embankment roared to life, sending spectators fleeing and the arriving firefighters running forward. Within minutes the fire crossed the railroad tracks.

Sage glanced up from his stoking and saw two firefighters shoving each other until a stream of water, directed by a third firefighter, ended the dispute.

Hosier passed by and, seeing the fracas, paused to say, "Damn volunteers. They only take direction from each other, never agree and ignore our fire chief. Fights happen all the time. Campbell's trying to make us a professional fire department, but the Council won't leave go of having volunteers. Cheaper, you know," he added, sourly.

With that, Hosier hustled off, leaving Sage to mull over all he'd learned in the last nine hours. Certainly it was clear to him why Hosier wanted a firefighters' union.

Three hours later, the men were again rolling up hoses and stowing ladders. The Victoria dock and its warehouse were smoldering ruins. The fire had also charred the railroad embankment, twisting the steel rails out of alignment.

Still, it hadn't been a complete rout. The firefighters had saved all but one home on Larrabee street, along with a sash and door company, the Irving and Columbia docks and the brigantine *Amazon* that had been endangered by its captain's refusal to move it from the nearby Irving dock.

Chief Campbell paused by the steam fire engine to reach a hand toward Sage. As they shook, Campbell said, "Mr. Miner, I'm David Campbell. I want to thank you for the good job you've done all this night and day. Ollie says you kept the temperature steady and never flagged. We can use more volunteers like you."

"It's been an education, alright," Sage said, using his Appalachian accent to color his words while returning the handshake. "I surely do hope you don't have many days like this."

Campbell only nodded, cuffed him on the shoulder and strode off, his stride as vigorous as if he'd just crawled out of bed. Sage shook his head and felt a smile tug at his lips. He could see why Hosier liked the man.

Leaving an eastside crew on the scene, Station 1's firefighters and equipment headed out. Ollie had an injured firefighter riding with him, along with a very tired fire dog that Andy insisted needed a ride. So, Sage rode the ladder truck back across the river. When they reached Second and Burnside, Sage called it to a halt. Saying goodbye to Hosier and waving at the other firefighters, he dropped off and limped toward Mozart's.

FOUR

His stumble up Mozart's hidden staircase seemed endless. Reaching the third floor, Sage pushed aside the concealing tapestry over the stairway's entrance and staggered into his well-appointed bedroom.

Food and a carafe of coffee sat on the small alcove table. He dropped down into a chair and began unlacing his boots.

"My goodness, why are you sooty black? And, what are those red spots on your hands? I thought you were just going to meet that Hosier fellow. I didn't think you'd be gone all night," his mother said as she charged into the room, her voice hectoring as it often was whenever she was weary, worried, irritated or all three—like now.

Glancing up, he saw fatigue lines in Mae Clemens' face and realized she'd lain awake, waiting for his safe return. Damn, not once had he thought she might be worried.

He roused himself because she deserved an explanation. She put up with a lot. Whenever he disappeared on one of St. Alban's missions, she was the one who kept the restaurant running. Besides providing cover for their clandestine activities, the posh Mozart's Table was also an excellent source of intelligence about the dodgy schemes of Portland's rich men.

The extra work meant more silver glinted in her dark hair than when he'd last noticed. And, his missions for the Saint were partly to blame as well. Anyone would worry during those absences but their history intensified her fears. She'd already lost him once when he was nine. It was after he'd nearly died in a mine explosion and the mine owner had taken him away to be fostered because he'd saved the mine owner's grandson. She hadn't a choice—it was either surrender him to be raised and educated in wealth or send him back down into the coal mines. Long years passed before she'd seen him again.

He started to apologize, but she waved away his words, avid interest sparking in dark blue eyes identical to his. She had already forgiven him. Still, he owed her so he pushed on anyway. "I'm sorry but I couldn't get word to you, Ma. Did you wait up all night?"

A wry smile twisted her lips. "Don't worry son. It's not like a body could sleep with that damn city fire bell going at all hours. I started thinking the whole town must be ablaze." Her eyes widened as she put the bits and pieces together. "Lordy, you were fighting those fires, weren't you?"

"Take a seat," he said, gesturing to the other chair. "And, I'll give you a blow by blow." As he drank and chewed that's exactly what he did.

"So, you still don't know what you are supposed to do for this Andy Hosier fellow?" she asked.

"No, but if he wants to start a union, I'm going to help. Those firefighters risk their lives every time that bell sounds. They throw themselves into one danger after another—they slide down the brass pole and their ankles fracture. Riding on the apparatus, they die by falling off or getting thrown off in a collision. At the fire, wires electrocute them. Climbing ladders, they fall to their deaths. Hell, a few hours ago, a water hose nearly blasted one man off a ladder and an exploding ember blinded a second firefighter. They all carry burn scars. Even Ollie, the steam engineer, has scars although he works farthest from the fires. Then, there's the fire itself. They rush into buildings that fall on them or they catch fire or the smoke smothers them. Andy says some firefighters wear big mustaches so they can put them in their mouth to help filter out the smoke."

Sage paused to pour himself a whiskey and saw that his hand was shaking. Taking a gulp to calm his anger, his next words were mocking as he said, "And do the city's fine citizens reward their bravery? They damn well don't. Andy says most firefighters can't afford to get married because they make so little money. And, they're lucky if they get a half day off a month. They've got no pension even though many of them get a lung sickness and can't work at anything again. Others drop dead from heart attacks while fighting fires or right afterwards, back at the station."

He knew he sounded bitter but she understood. She shared his outrage over how working people got treated. He never had to hide that outrage from her like he did from so many others. Sometimes, when hearing Mozart's rich patrons' heartless remarks, he clenched his teeth so hard behind his smile that his jaw ached the next morning. Because they considered him to be one of them, Mozart's patrons seldom held back—especially after he served them free glasses of wine. That stratagem was one way he learned of their money-grubbing schemes—some of which he'd been able to stop.

"'Anyways,'" he continued, deliberately emphasizing her trademark word, "After what I saw last night, whatever Andy needs, he's going get it—if it's within my power to give it."

She studied him for a moment. "I've heard that Fire Chief Campbell is a pretty good guy," she said.

He nodded and smiled. "Yup, I met him. He even thanked me. He has to be exhausted. Andy told me that lately Campbell's been turning up at nearly every fire. Still, he went around and thanked each one of the volunteers. Last night, I watched him almost lose his life saving two of his men. Andy told me Campbell wants to improve the firefighters' working conditions and pay. Apparently, the Common Council's mighty stingy when it comes to the fire crews."

"Sounds like you're already fond of this Andy fellow," she observed.

Sage thought about the young man's passion for his colleagues' well-being, for firefighting and for that shiny new steam engine. He smiled. "Yup, I guess I am."

Six hours later, Sage sat in the OK Coffee House and Bakery, reading the *Daily Journal* as he tried to wake up. The OK had few tables and simple fare but was close to Station 1 where Hosier had a sleeping cot. Again, as when they first met, Hosier was late. Every time the café's entry bell tinkled Sage looked up, expecting to see Andy's stringy figure and wide smile. He was impatient when it came to waiting, especially when he was full of questions.

After half an hour, Sage finally gave up. Stepping out into the street, he breathed in November's crisp chill. He didn't particularly like the dense haze of burnt wood and coal but he realized its necessity. As a child, he'd warmed his fingers and toes before pot-bellied stoves that struggled to heat Appalachia's drafty shacks. Later, he'd done the same in crowded Klondike cabins where prospectors burned wood year around to melt the permafrost and warm hands that ached from sluicing in frigid creeks.

He headed toward the firehouse, certain he'd find Andy there since the fire bell hadn't rung. Probably he was still asleep along with the other firefighters—the full timers and the extramen who couldn't afford to live anywhere else.

Andy had said that his dream was to become a full time steam engineer. "Ain't nobody can put out the fire unless the engine is pumping. It's the most important job of all. You gotta learn to fix the equipment and be real mechanical. At fires, the engineer's got to calculate how much pressure each hose needs to reach its target—how far and how high the water needs to reach determines the numbers. Those are tricky calculations. I know because Ollie's teaching me how to do them," he said with pride.

Reaching Fire Station 1, Sage entered through the small door next to the barn doors fronting the street. On the ground floor, harnesses hung from the ceiling, open horse stalls lined one side and the center space was full of fire equipment. Today, the only sound was the soft chomp of hay-eating horses.

He climbed the wooden stairs quietly, not wanting to disturb any sleeping men. In the big room most of the men lay on narrow iron cots behind mosquito netting—some reading, some dozing. According to Hosier, the netting kept off the flies that hatched in the manure below.

Four men sat around the kitchen table talking with quiet intensity. He recognized all of them from the night before. These were some of the full timers—the hose cart driver, the ladder truck driver, the steam engineer, Ollie, and the fire station chief, Ray Faden.

When he saw Sage, Ollie raised a welcoming hand and called softly, "Step on up Mister Miner, we're just jawing about last night's fires. You're welcome to throw in your two cents."

Sage sat, feeling pleased at the acceptance implied by Ollie's invite. "Thank you," he said while nodding his thanks to the ladder truck driver who put a mug of hot coffee before him. "That was my first time as a volunteer and let me tell you, it was a real eye opener. I had no idea what a hard job ya'll have." As he had the night before, Sage spoke in his "aw shucks" hill country drawl.

The men chuckled. "Most folks don't," said the hose cart driver. Despite the grueling hours he'd just spent, the bright-eyed man's uniform was spotless with its buttons shiny as mirrors.

The truck driver spoke up, "That damn city Common Council sure don't have no idea what we do. Too bad one of their houses don't catch fire." The station chief, Faden, didn't try to squelch the rebellious talk.

"Say, I'd hoped to find Andy Hosier here. Is he still asleep?" Sage asked only to see his question make every jaw tighten.

"You a friend of Hosier's?" the cart driver queried. There was no missing the caution in the man's voice.

"Well, I just met him yesterday for the first time. Still, I'd surely like to think he's my friend," Sage responded, as worry immediately took hold. "Is he hurt? Has something happened to him?"

"I'll say," Ollie said. "He's been arrested. They claim he started that house fire up there on Market. The first fire you worked."

"But he was with me when that fire started," Sage protested.

That straightened their backs and one asked, "How long was he with you before you heard the fire bell?" The fire station chief jumped in, asking, "And where were the two of you?"

"We'd been talking about five minutes or so at the Cliffhanger saloon, about a block from here," Sage answered.

The men at the table exchanged looks and Faden said, "That doesn't get him off the hook. The fire was burning at least thirty minutes before we reached it. There was time enough for him to light it, run down and sit with you a spell."

Sage remembered the young man's enthusiastic ramblings about double-acting pumps, churn valves, pounds pressure per square inch and a host of other mysterious mechanical parts and terms. And, Andy'd been equally fervent when talking about the firefighters' hardships. Sage shook his head and said, "Naw, I don't believe it."

Faden studied him with narrowed eyes before saying, "Well, I find it hard to believe myself. But he's always begging me for more work. Hell, he's desperate to go full time. No better way to make that happen than to light more fires."

Ollie shot a grateful look at Sage before saying, "I don't believe it either. Problem is, a witness described someone who looked just like Andy running away from the fire, carrying his turnout bag."

Sage thought back. Andy had arrived with wet pants, a turnout bag and seemed tense when they'd met. But that might only mean he'd splashed through a puddle on his way to the saloon, not that he'd been in that swampy field behind the burning house. And. maybe his being tense was only because he was late. "Nope, I don't believe it," he repeated, though this time, there was a tad less conviction in his voice.

Faden stood up. "It wouldn't be the first time an extraman's turned firebug," he said. "If that's what he's done, I hope he burns in hell. I'm going to check on the horses," he added, heading for the stairs. The other men stared into their cups and said nothing.

FIVE

"Angus, I can't thank you enough for accompanying me," said the man at his side.

Angus Solomon glanced down at his companion. "I appreciate your thinking that I might be of assistance," he replied.

"It's not like I couldn't do this on my own, of course I could. But, I figure that together, the two of us might lessen any," here B.J. paused, searching for the word, ". . . difficulties."

Angus shot another glance at his friend who was staring straight ahead, chin held high. B.J. Cooper was a very proud man. It had cost him to ask for help. Fortunately, common sense prevailed over pride. What did that Austrian mental doctor call it? "Ego" that's it. The situation was too serious to let ego get in the way. B.J.'s son was in danger.

The two men climbed the police station's steep steps. Once inside, they crossed the lobby to stand before the desk officer. He glanced up before to returning to his paperwork. Angus cleared his throat. The man still didn't look up. Angus finally said, "Excuse me, Officer. We wish to inquire about a young man, James Cooper. We believe he is being held here."

The desk sergeant sighed and raised his head to study both men. His watery blue eyes widened slightly as he registered their well-cut suits—garb that matched the elegant diction of the black man who'd just spoken. Then his eyes widened even more. Angus could tell that he'd been recognized. As the Portland Hotel's maitre'd and owner of the New Elijah Hotel, he was one of Portland's well-known Negroes. Tall, broad-shouldered, with burnished brown skin and Indian-high cheekbones, Angus Solomon was one of the few black men frequently recognized by Portland's white folks.

That recognition didn't bring the desk officer to his feet but at least his attention remained off his paperwork. "You boys take a seat over there," he said, pointing to the wooden bench against the lobby wall. "I'll be with you once I'm done here,"

Angus didn't move. He wouldn't be put off. For one thing, his companion had a reputation for impatience. Already, the tightening of Cooper's hands into fists meant his anger was building. And, more importantly, James Cooper was only fifteen. It was not safe for him to stay jailed amongst white criminals. Particularly, since B.J. and Frances had raised James to believe he was equal to anyone.

"Perhaps," Angus said, "you would be so kind as to inform Sergeant Hanke that Mr. Angus Solomon is here to see him?"

That request gave the desk officer pause. Sergeant Hanke was both well-respected and a rising star in Chief Hunt's department. The man sighed and rose, saying, "I'll see if the sergeant is available. He's pretty busy."

The officer left and returned in less than a minute. "The Sergeant said to escort you to his office." He unlatched the half-gate and gestured them through. They followed him down the hallway to a small office.

Sergeant Hanke stood as they entered. He was as tall as Angus but hefty with a broad, bland, Germanic visage. "Please close the door, O'Leary," he instructed their escort.

Once the door was shut, Hanke reach his big hand across his desk to shake Angus' hand. "It is always good to see you, Mr. Solomon, though I suspect this is not a pleasant occasion." He glanced toward B.J., his eyebrow raised.

Angus smiled faintly, "No, I'm afraid not." He turned toward his companion saying, "This is Mr. B.J. Cooper. He is the editor of the *New Era* newspaper. We're here because you have his fifteen year old son in custody. We'd like to find out what happened and return him to his family."

Hanke reached across the desk to shake Cooper's hand. "Pleased to make your acquaintance, Mr. Cooper. Gentlemen, do take a seat," Hanke said before settling back down into his own chair. "As it happens, I was just reading that arrest report."

"What does it say happened?" Cooper demanded, his tone a trifle too sharp for politeness. Angus put a restraining hand on his friend's forearm.

Hanke remained impassive as he flipped open a folder to read, "At approximately 4:45 p.m. this officer was approached by a man who said assistance was needed at Drucker's sweet shop. Arriving at Drucker's, this officer observed an altercation in progress on the sidewalk outside the sweet shop and subsequently broke up a physical fight between Edward Orpin and a black boy named James Cooper. Took Cooper into custody and charged him with assault."

B.J. Cooper leaned forward, every line of his body taut with anger. "Let me guess. This Edward Orpin is white," he growled

Hanke looked uncomfortable, glanced at Angus and then answered in measured tones, "It doesn't say that he is but I suspect that you're correct."

Cooper stared, momentarily taken aback by Hanke's abashed admission.

Angus decided they'd learned all they could. The boy needed rescuing from the dank cells beneath their feet. "What is young Cooper's bail for this offense?"

Hanke flipped open the file once again, ran his finger down the page and stopped. "It says the standard, ten dollars. Of course, he'll have to appear in court. In the meantime, I will speak to the patrolman to find out why Orpin wasn't arrested and why they both weren't charged with the lesser crime of disturbing the peace."

"Why was that Sergeant Hanke so helpful?" Cooper asked quietly, after they had paid the bail and taken seats in the lobby to wait for James' release.

"He's sympathetic to our situation here in town. He agrees with what you've been alleging in your editorials; that Negros are arrested in situations where whites are not."

"He's actually said that?" Cooper was incredulous.

"More than once. But no, he won't say it to you and have it printed in the newspaper. He does that and his ability to help us out once and awhile would vanish."

Cooper frowned. "How come you know so much about what a police sergeant is thinking?" There was suspicion in his question.

Angus studied Cooper. He knew the man's suspicion came from his frustration and fear. He also knew that he could not reveal that he and

Hanke were both members of what Angus like to think of as "Adair's Irregulars"—a name inspired by the Sherlock Holmes tales. So, he simply said, "We've had dealings in the past. I've always found him fair and agreeable to reason."

Before Cooper could push harder, the basement door opened and a grinning James Cooper stepped into the lobby. Angus moved back, not wanting to intrude on the meeting between father and son. The boy's relief vanished the instant he caught sight of his father's stern glower. There was no hugging between the two, just a snapped, "Let's get out of here," from the older Cooper before he turned his back and strode out of the station doors.

Once they reached the street, the sidewalks were too narrow for them to walk three abreast so Angus dropped back, though not far enough to avoid hearing the exchanges between the two Coopers.

"What in God's name were you thinking of—fighting a white boy?"

"I fought a jackass." The boy's matter-of-fact words carried a hint of defiance.

"Don't act ignorant with me. You knew that you'd get the short end of the stick in any fight with a white kid or hey, maybe he was sitting in the jail cell next to you?"

James didn't reply but Angus could see the light brown of the boy's neck darkening. He'd apparently inherited some of his father's temper. Sure enough, his next words were accusatory, "You haven't even asked me if I was justified. You don't even care what we were fighting about. You don't care what happened."

Cooper spat out, "I know all I need to know. My black son got into a fight with a white kid." Then Cooper took a visible, calming breath and continued with palpable restraint, "So tell me, son. What happened for you to get into a fight and land yourself in jail?"

James snicked a glance at his father before answering, "Sarah, the white girl who works in the candy store, knows me from school. We were just talking over the counter about English class. Orpin tried to interrupt and she told him to get lost. She doesn't like him—most folks don't. Anyway, when I came out of the store, he was waiting. He punched me without warning and then called me a 'nigger buck'. I hit him back, that's all."

"Obviously there was more since you were still fighting when the police officer arrived."

"Well, he just wouldn't shut up calling me that."

"Damn it James, I've told you more than once. You have to turn your back and walk away. Being called ugly names is part and parcel of being a black man. You won't change someone like that by hitting them. Every time we get into a tussle with them, we confirm their prejudices. We're the ones who get called 'ignorant' and 'violent' and 'subhuman'. You fighting and getting arrested is what will be printed in the newspaper tomorrow, not that the Orpin kid started it."

James turned sullen. "I'm just as good as he is. In fact, I'm better. I'm still in school. He dropped out because he's so dumb he can't even read a baby book."

The three of them walked in silence. Angus was thinking about the boy's last words. Portland was unique in that white and black kids attended school together. Originally, they'd been in separate schools but the school district decided that, given the city's few Negro children, it was too expensive to maintain separate institutions. Even today, 1903, the city's black inhabitants numbered fewer than twelve hundred. Still, James had a right to be proud of his continued school attendance. With widespread poverty, no black teachers and little kindness from classmates, most black children dropped out of school after the sixth grade.

James shot an accusatory question at his father, interrupting Angus's thoughts. "How long are you going to put up with it, Father? You're refused service in their restaurants and saloons. You're forty years old and you have men younger and far less educated than you, calling you 'boy'."

The weariness with which B.J. responded signaled that this was an old argument. "We've made progress in Oregon. Black men can vote, they can sit on juries, they can join some unions, own businesses, homes. Mr. Solomon, who has taken time out of his busy day to come get you, even owns a hotel and he has a prestigious job at the Portland Hotel. He earns more money than most white men. You're lucky we live here and not in the South. Down there, they hang black men just for being 'too uppity'. Down there, you could have been hung for today's little fiasco."

"Yah, yah. I've heard that all before and I appreciate Mr. Solomon coming down to get me, I do." He half turned to nod at Angus before facing his father again. "But, can he rent a room in that fancy Portland Hotel? And if some white jackass decides he wants to pound on some black man's head, is Mr. Solomon safe?"

Cooper didn't answer the questions because all three knew James was right. In a calmer voice his father said, "You need to tone it down,

James. Do your homework, help around the paper and respect your elders. Stay away from white folks. And if you have to be around them, you just be polite and agree with everything they say."

"And when do I get to be a man, father? When do I get the respect? I don't want to kowtow to ignorant fools. I think Booker T. Washington's "proving we deserve respect" is bull crap. We will never get that respect until we demand it and refuse to settle for less!" The boy's anger was building. People on the street were glancing in their direction.

Cooper noticed their interest because he hissed his next words. "You listen here, James Cooper. As long as you put your feet under my table, you will speak respectfully of Mr. Washington. And, you will speak respectfully to me!"

The young man gave a derisive "huh" but said nothing more.

As the three continued in silence toward the Cooper house on Northwest 21st Avenue, Angus pondered the conflict he'd just witnessed between father and son. It wasn't the first time he'd heard those arguments. Lately, grown men shouted them at each other. Booker T. Washington counseled self-improvement, education in a hands-on trade and faith in the idea that, by demonstrating they were worthy human beings, blacks would eventually win respect and fair treatment from whites.

Washington was the race's shining example of that strategy. Born a slave, he'd educated himself and won great stature with some in the white community—so much that he dined at the White House as President Roosevelt's guest. The uproar over that invite had a Southern senator declaring they'd have to "lynch 1000 niggers" to undo the harm caused by that single invitation. And, the senator wasn't just barking. Lynching of black men was on the rise in the South. Worst of all, Roosevelt was doing nothing to stop it.

The last few years had brought a challenge to Washington's views. Young James was repeating the arguments of W.E.B. Du Bois. Born a freeman in New England, Du Bois was educated alongside whites in some of the nation's better schools. In fact, he was the first black person to receive a PhD from Harvard University. Du Bois' writings increasingly rejected Washington's hat-in-hand approach. He argued that blacks needed to celebrate and expand their own culture while demanding equality as their right.

The two viewpoints were clashing in black communities across the country. Even in Portland, people were arguing. Some Portland Hotel waiters had pooled their money to start their own newspaper, *The Advocate*, because they thought Cooper's *New Era* was too docile in a time of growing white racism.

If Angus hoped that the silence had calmed his two companions, he was disappointed when, after mounting the steps of the Cooper home, B.J. gestured for James to open the door. With that irritating contempt common in youngsters, James responded by stepping away from the door and saying, "Oh, you should open it, Father. After all, the republicans made you their very own "doorkeeper."

Angus's breath caught. James was referencing the fact that, after Cooper shamed the republicans into making him a delegate to their state convention, he'd gone further and demanded an official position. With exquisite contempt they'd created the position of "doorkeeper." He wasn't given the sergeant at arms position he'd sought—the man who verified credentials and kept the peace. No, they put Cooper in charge of opening the door to admit convention attendees—just as if he were the butler in a southern plantation.

The barb hit home because Cooper's hand flashed out to cuff his son's ear, sending the boy reeling into the porch post. Both Coopers froze. Fortunately any further conflict was forestalled by Mrs. Cooper's throwing open the front door and rushing onto the porch to throw her arms around her son.

Rather than witness additional family conflict, Angus quickly took his leave. Walking back to the Portland Hotel he thought about the clash between father and son. Cooper senior knew death closely stalked black men every single day. He reasonably feared for his son's life. He wanted James to survive, to thrive as a black man. He was doing his best to teach James how to do that. Young Cooper, on the other hand, was insisting that without respect and equality, there could be no manhood, no end to Negroes being treated as subhuman. The painful, grievous truth was that both Coopers were right.

SIX

"Oh Katy, bar the door!" exclaimed Philander Gray when he answered the knock and found Sage standing in the hallway. "What crazy scheme do you have going on now?" he asked as he opened the door wider to let Sage inside.

"How about I treat you to an early supper and tell you about it?" Sage asked, slyly targeting Gray's weak spot. Despite being what Mae Clemens called a "string bean," the lawyer could tuck away more food than a cook shack full of lumberjacks. An exaggeration, sure, but the man had a huge appetite.

Gray groaned. "My dear wife promised me pork chops, milk gravy and applesauce tonight," he said even as the tilt of his head and sharp gaze signaled that the lawyer's curiosity was aroused. Usually, that's all it took.

Sure enough, Gray shrugged, picked up the telephone handset and jiggled the lever for the operator. Giving Gray a bit of privacy, Sage walked over to study the framed diplomas on the far wall which told him that the lawyer graduated, *cum laude*, from an exclusive eastern law school. Having used Gray on a number of matters, Sage knew that honor was deserved.

Once the lawyer hung up the ear piece, Sage remarked, "I didn't know you'd acquired a telephone instrument."

Gray donned his coat and chuckled. "Darling Amanda gave me no choice. Either I installed one here and at the house or she was moving in mother—*my* mother, God forbid. Can you imagine having two hens pecking away at you? Amanda said too many dinners burned while she waited for me. And, she's right—hence, the new telephone. Have to say, it's already sped up my law practice. I don't have to fuss with messaging back and forth when all I need is a quick answer."

Sage grinned. "I'm glad you're making Miz Amanda's life easier." Sage liked Gray's wife who was an excellent cook.

Outside, rain pounded down. As he walked, Sage eyed the telephone, electrical, fire and police wires running from the poles and across roof tops and wondered how many lacked protective insulation. Andy had said, "We never know which company owns a particular wire. We got to one scene and had to call ten different electric companies. We reached all but one and, of course, that's the one we needed to reach. Anymore, Campbell won't send a man with a hose up a metal fire escape or onto a roof if there's wires hanging too close."

Gray's neighborhood restaurant fronted a narrow alleyway and sported a bright yellow interior and large windows framed by blue gingham curtains. Given that Sage was wearing his John Miner guise, it was a wise choice for their supper. Once Gray had ordered double helpings, Sage told the lawyer about his involvement with the firefighters.

"You know, I've never thought too much about firefighting," Gray mused. "Of course I worry about fire, any sensible man would. But I've never pondered what their lives are like or what dangers they face." He was silent for a beat, looking thoughtful, then he said, "So, I take it you're convinced this Hosier fellow isn't the arsonist?"

"I could be wrong of, course. He does want more work and he sure is enthusiastic when he's fighting a blaze. But, I'd swear on Ida's apple pie, that he'd never deliberately set a fire."

"Miz Ida's apple pie? That's a serious endorsement," Gray said with a grin. It was his oft declared opinion that, when it came to cooking, Ida Knuteson ranked second only to his own wife. The lawyer shoved his cleaned plate aside and stood. "Guess we best head on down to the police station. See if we can corner Sergeant Hanke and then visit with Hosier."

After a brisk walk through the chill rain they found Hanke at the police station. The sergeant escorted them into his office and shut the door before shaking both their hands with a friendly vigor. "Good to see you, Mr. Gray," he exclaimed. "It's been awhile. Since you're both here and, since Mr. Adair's wearing his Miner disguise, I suspect there's something 'afoot.' Which means," here he winked, "there's tricky footwork ahead for both of us."

Sage grimaced. Now even the police sergeant was quoting Doyle's fictional character. Newspaper serials were always popular, but Doyle's were phenomenally so, even Sage read the stories as soon as they appeared.

"I'm afraid you've nailed me on this one, Sergeant," he said, shaking hands. "Something is definitely 'afoot,' though what it is, I can't say. We are hoping you can enlighten us regarding a recent arrest. The fellow's name is Andy Hosier."

Hanke gestured them into the chairs in front of his desk and took his own seat behind it. "Well, now, this must be my day for helping out members of our…" he searched for the word, "let's say, 'family,' for lack of a better description. Angus Solomon was just in here. His friend's son got into a spot of trouble."

"Nothing serious, I hope," Sage said. The hope was sincere. If Solomon needed help, he'd be Sage's first priority. But, at the same time, another task would add complications since Sage was already knee deep in sorting out Andy's problems.

Hanke's headshake reassured. "Naw, just minor fisticuffs between boys. I'm going to see if I can get the charges dropped. I suspect the white kid started it. Of course, I haven't told Mr. Solomon and his friend that. I'm still waiting for the final report. My patrol officer did a damn shoddy investigation. He's new, so I sent him back out with my best man to do a proper job."

"Well, we're hoping that a failure to fully investigate is also the problem with Hosier's arrest," said Gray. "He's apparently being held for arson. John, here, believes he's innocent of that charge."

Sage always twitched a bit at being called "John". The name never felt like it fit. Still, here in Portland, only his mother, Fong and one other called him "Sage."

Hanke's questioning eyebrow spurred Sage into quickly recounting all that had occurred during the previous hours. He ended by declaring, "Andy would never endanger other firefighters by setting a fire. Sure he wants to work full time and he does obsess over the fire engine, but that's just because he loves the mechanics. I'm certain he'd never set a fire."

Hanke silently absorbed everything before heaving a sigh and standing up. "I don't have that file on my desk. I think someone's copying it for the prosecutor. Let me see if I can round it up." He left the office.

As they waited, Gray said quietly, "We need to be careful not to ask the sergeant to do anything that could get him into serious trouble. He's too valuable to us in this position."

Sage chuckled and waved a hand to brush aside the warning. "Don't worry, I agree with you but Hanke is scrupulous when it comes to not crossing what he calls 'the line.' He'd refuse if we asked him to do something clearly illegal or against the interests of his boss. Necessity has forced me to ask him to bump against that line only once or twice. Each time he has, he's been able to make what he calls 'a good arrest.' We're lucky he's befriended us. Despite his woefully low pay, Hanke's one of the few honest cops in town. We need him to stay that way," Sage added just as the door swung open.

The subject of their conversation edged back into the small room and made his way around to his desk chair. For a few minutes he paged through the papers, moving his lips as he silently read. Once finished, he shut the file and looked at them, "I don't know, Adair," he said. "You might be riding the wrong horse this time. Looks like we've got him dead to rights. A fire station chief says a confidential witness described Hosier as the fellow running from the house fire . . . just minutes before it was discovered.

"And," here he held up a finger to silence Sage who'd begun to protest, "And, it looks like he is also going to be charged with setting fire to a dry goods store." Same thing—a different fire station chief says a witness came forward claiming he'd seen a man fitting Hosier's description lurking near that building. Other evidence links the two fires, the nature of which I can't share with you at this time."

"But, that can't be. I was right beside Hosier the entire time between the house fire and the store fire."

"Yup, in his interview, Hosier gave 'John Miner' as a witness to his alibi. So far, we haven't been able to find that fellow," Hanke's lips twisted ruefully after saying Sage's oft-used alias. "As you know, our Mr. Miner tends to shy away from attention, especially if it means he'll have to show up in court."

Sage's shoulders slumped. Would this be the situation that finally forced him out into open? Expose the fact that he masqueraded as a wealthy restaurant owner while secretly helping people as the itinerant John Miner? If so, he and his mother would have to uproot and start all over somewhere else.

He shrugged his shoulders in resignation. "Well, if I have to testify to save Andy, then I will. Hopefully, we'll prove his innocence before he ever goes to trial." He leaned forward. "I don't understand, though. Lots of people saw Hosier going from the house fire to the store fire. They have to know he couldn't have set the store fire."

Hanke shook his head. "The fire marshal says that it looks like the store fire was delayed—that it was rigged to start after the arsonist was long gone. Something about candle wax at the ignition spot. His theory is that Hosier first set up the store fire, then fired the house and then ran back to Station 1 or thereabouts just so people would see him far from both fires. So, your testimony probably wouldn't help."

While Sage mulled over Hanke's information, Gray asked a few more questions and then stood up. "I'd like to see my client now," he told Hanke. "Is there a chance we could talk to him in private rather than down in the cells?"

Hanke also stood. "I'll have him brought upstairs to one of the interview rooms," he said and exited. Returning, the sergeant said, "I'll take you to him. It would be best if you kept it short. The fewer people who notice "Mr. Miner" meeting with Hosier, the better."

They left Hanke's office and entered a drab interview room where the plaster walls sported cracks radiating from head-sized dents. Sage tried not to think about how they'd gotten there. Instead, he focused on Andy who entered and looked confused when his eyes landed on Sage. "Mr. Miner, how the heck did you get in to see me?" he asked while settling onto a chair and nervously glancing at Gray.

"Never mind that now. We have very little time to talk. This gentleman is Philander Gray. He's consented to act as your lawyer."

"But, I can't afford a lawyer," Hosier spluttered, both hope and fear in his brown eyes.

"Don't worry about that. His fee is taken care of. Did you set those fires?"

Hosier reacted to Sage's blunt question with a vigorous shake of his head. "No, Sir. I definitely did not. I would never do that. Fires kill people. My friends have died fighting them. The last thing I'd do is set a fire."

Sage sent Gray questioning glance. The lawyer cleared his throat. "All right, then. My job is to make sure the prosecutor can't prove his case."

"And," Sage interrupted, "the best way to do that is to find the person who set the fires and framed you. Does someone hate you enough to do that?"

Hosier's forehead wrinkled in thought. "Well, not the fire marshal. I don't even know the fellow. My fire station chief, Ray Faden, don't like me much. I think that's because he knows I've been talking union to the fellas. He takes it personal. He's tetchy that way. I don't criticize him. I just talk about pay and job security. Still, he probably thinks it's about him but other than acting unfriendly, he hasn't done or said anything mean to me."

"What about Chief Campbell? What's he think of your union activities?" Sage asked, thinking that the fire chief was in the perfect position to influence the evidence.

For the first time, Hosier's openness closed down, his voice tightening. "No, it definitely ain't Campbell."

"How do you know that?" Sage pressed.

"I just do. It ain't Campbell." Hosier's tone was mulish. He pushed back in his chair and crossed his arms over his chest.

Sage and Gray exchanged a glance. Obviously, Hosier was withholding something but Sage didn't press him. There'd be time enough for that later. "Okay, Andy. For sure, we need to find out who set those fires because, right now, there's damning evidence against you in the form of two eye witnesses."

Hosier's mouth fell open and shock propelled him to his feet. "Two witnesses? How can that be? I wasn't anywhere near either place except when we were fighting the fires. You know that, you were with me."

"It's a bit more complicated, Andy. The evidence indicates that someone rigged one fire to delay its start. The house fire burned for half an hour before the fire trucks got there. They think that means you could have set them both and still met me before the fire bell rang. We've got to find those witnesses and discover who put them up to it. Framing you by burning down buildings suggests someone feels extreme hate towards you." Sage tried again, "Are you absolutely certain you've done nothing to rile someone up?"

Hosier's eyes darted to one side before he slumped back down onto his seat as if someone had just yanked out his backbone. He cleared his throat and mumbled, "Even if my union work has made someone mad, I can't believe that a person would start fires to get at me. Heck, all they need to do is drop a ladder or live wire on me at a fire scene. Or, trump up a reason to get me fired from the department. I don't have a life outside my sister, Jimmy and the fire department. There can't be any civilian mad at me."

Sage had to agree. He'd seen a lot of union busting during his undercover work. Murdering or severely beating a unionist, yes. But, burning down a third party's property was a step way too far. "Andy, is there someone at your firehouse we can go to for help? Someone who might believe that you're innocent and will give us truthful information? Someone you'd trust with your life?"

"Oliver Banning. Ollie, the steam engineer. He's spent hours teaching me how to run the engine. I think he'd be truthful and help."

Sage was relieved when he heard the name. Banning seemed fond of Andy. And, he was favorably inclined toward Sage, given his recent praise of Sage's efforts at the fires. Also, he seemed an intelligent, thoughtful man. "Okay, then. We'll talk to Ollie."

Hanke stepped into the interview room. "Sorry but, you'll have to leave now. I need to escort Hosier back to his cell."

As they trailed Hanke and his prisoner toward the front of the building, Gray spoke quietly into Sage's ear, "That young man is holding something back."

Sage could only nod. He'd noticed it too. Hosier was definitely doing something that could have riled someone up. It was there in that sideways flick of his eyes. But how could they get him to say what it was?

When they entered the lobby, Hanke was in the lead with his prisoner. Suddenly, a thin young man with a beaky nose and buck teeth leapt up from his seat on the bench. He pointed at Hosier. "That's him! That's the fellow I saw at the house. He was running hell-bent through the back field."

Hanke merely nodded and, as he pulled a stunned Hosier toward the basement door, said, "Thank you, Sir. You may go now."

Sage couldn't help himself. "You set this identification up, Sergeant?" he asked, in a voice tight with anger.

Hanke paused. "I still have a job to do," he responded in clipped tones thrown over his shoulder. He herded Hosier down the stairs, the door swinging shut behind them.

SEVEN

It was a bright morning beneath a clear sky of washed winter blue. Inside the firehouse, Ollie was polishing the engine's nickel-plated dome. The city fire bell hadn't rung overnight and the engineer looked rested. Sage hoped he'd be in the mood to talk.

"Howdy!" Sage called as he entered. The horses shuffled their hooves and nickered in response. Sage paused to pat the nearest one on the forehead. He didn't like to ride or drive a horse. But they were a useful animal and he'd even felt fond of one or two of them. A searching glance assured him that, other than the horses and Ollie, no one else was on the ground floor.

Ollie turned to look at Sage, climbed down and shook his hand. "Howdy, yourself," he said with a friendly smile.

"Good morning, Mr. Banning. I was hoping that you could spare a few minutes to talk with me."

"Why, sure," the engineer responded. "But, you'll have to call me Ollie. Everyone does. You want to go upstairs? Maybe grab a cup of coffee?" He gestured toward the stairs.

"Actually, I was hoping for a private conversation with you. Can I buy you a cup of coffee and something to eat in that café down the street?"

The man considered Sage before nodding. "It's about young Andy, I suspect. Let me get my coat." He walked over to a wall where coats hung on hooks. After donning a coat and the hat sitting on the shelf above it, he headed for the door. "Let's go. Though, if the bell sounds you're liable to be left sitting by yourself. Unless," here he looked hopeful, "you've a mind to help with the firefighting. I'm sure gonna miss Andy's help. He's a crackerjack at babying our engine," he said as he gave the engine an affectionate pat.

That's where Andy got that habit, Sage realized.

Once in the café they grabbed the farthest table and both ordered coffee and pie. It was mid-morning and the place was nearly empty.

Sage studied the man across from him. His weathered features and the stoop of his shoulders said the engineer was past fifty—older than most firefighters. But then, this man didn't have to climb ladders or run into burning buildings. As the mechanic who kept the water pumping, he'd only gain more skill as he aged.

Ollie was staring back at him, his faded blue eyes equally appraising. "You gonna help the boy?" he asked.

"I'm going to try. I don't believe he set fire to the house or to the store."

Ollie's mouth fell open. "Store? What store?"

"They're saying that he also set fire to the dry goods store that same night."

Ollie was shaking his head. "Nah, ain't no way. Yah see, that dry goods store is in Station 3's district. That's Andy's brother-in-law's firehouse. Andy thinks the world of Jimmy. He'd never endanger him. What the heck is going on?" For the first time Ollie looked angry. "Who is doing this to him?"

His question relieved any concern Sage had about Ollie's loyalty. The engineer knew which side he was on. "I intend to find out who really set the fires and why. Andy said you could tell me things about the fire department. To be honest, until the other night, I never gave it much thought."

"Most civilians don't, until their house is a'burning," Ollie said before straightening to become all business. "What exactly do you need to know, Mr. Miner? I've been fighting fires in this city since 1885—eighteen years."

"First, does the fire station chief, Faden, know that Andy has been talking about starting a firefighters' union?"

"Boy howdy, does he ever," said Ollie. "He called me into his office and asked me about it. He turned madder than a soaked hen when I told him 'yes.'" Obviously worried that Sage would think poorly of him for tattling on Andy, Ollie rushed to explain. "He already knew, of course. Everybody was talking about it and Faden has his favorites in the ranks. One of them would have told him for sure. I told him that Andy only wanted to see a pay raise and more full time positions—exactly the same thing Chief Campbell keeps asking for from the Common Council. I said that Andy really respects him."

"Did that work?" Sage asked.

Ollie's headshake was rueful. "Nah, he's one of those fellows who has to feel in complete control. He stomps down any man who steps forward with a new idea. Matter of fact, all it did was make him suspicious of me."

"Is control so important to him that he'd frame Andy by setting fires?"

This time the man's headshake was a vigorous denial. "Hell no. Faden's an ornery cuss but I can't think he'd do something like that over a union. Besides, he was in Station 1 the whole of that night. Only left it when the firehouse bell sounded."

Sage peered through the foggy restaurant window while casting about for another question. Turning his attention back to Ollie he asked, "Have you heard anything else about the house fire or the dry goods store fire?"

"Well, I know that Faden is heading up to both scenes today. He'll do a survey and then make reports to the fire marshal and insurance folks."

They parted outside the restaurant with Ollie promising to quietly ask around and keep his ears open for anything that might help Andy.

Twenty minutes later, Sage stood across the street from the burned-out house. Its rear half was destroyed, leaving charred timbers to glisten black in the pale sunshine. Hard to tell if it could be rebuilt.

People were roaming about. He saw the householder, his wife and child in the yard's far corner. As he watched, the father set aside a shovel he'd been using and placed a small wooden box in the hole he'd dug. The little girl was in her mother's arms. She alternatively looked down as her father filled in the hole or buried her face in her mother's shoulder.

That'd be "Joey" the hero cockatoo, Sage thought, feeling a pang of regret at the bird's death. Funny how so many different kinds of animals could have loveable personalities—just like humans. Then he corrected himself—only like "some" humans. If it came to a lovability contest, many other animal species would probably win out over humans.

A wagon rattled up just as the burial ceremony ended. The man and woman began loading boxes of possessions into the wagon's bed.

Sage rushed to help—partly because he wanted to but also because he needed to move closer. He wanted to study the other two men walking around the yard.

One was clearly a fire station chief because he wore the dress uniform complete with cap and polished fire badge. But, he wasn't Faden. The second man was in a decent suit. Both men were looking at the front of the house and talking.

"Looks like you were able to salvage quite a bit from inside," Sage commented to the father as they hefted a big box onto the wagon bed.

"That was my wife Bessie's doing. She's a right quick thinker. She had us tossing stuff onto the bed blankets and sheets. Soon as one was full, she knotted it up and tossed it out the window. Saved everything in the bedrooms—all our clothes and trinkets and such. And, thanks to the fire department, the stuff in the front of the house only got real wet. Our neighbors helped us dry things off and gave us some of their extra things. We're going to be fine."

"You have insurance to cover your losses?" Sage asked.

"Nope. But then, it ain't our house. I think the landlord's got insurance. That man over there with the fireman is an insurance man."

Their meager belongings loaded, the little family climbed aboard and rolled off, heading to their new home. It was only then that Sage saw the paper flower posy decorating Joey-the-Cockatoo's grave.

Sage walked about half a block before turning to watch the station chief and insurance man. They didn't look to be searching for evidence. In fact, they appeared to be simply socializing, chatting and laughing as they strode around the property.

Sensing movement to his side, Sage stiffened. The house fronts on his side of the street were aligned so that, when he crouched down beside one, he had a view down their open-sided porches. Four houses away, a man wearing a heavy coat and a hat pulled low, stood half-concealed behind a porch pillar. He appeared to also be watching the two men across the street. Maybe he's a curious neighbor, Sage thought, quickly stepping behind the house corner before the other watcher noticed him.

The two men had apparently finished their survey because both quickly departed in a buggy. Sage started to follow only to pause when he saw the man on the porch rapidly descend to the sidewalk and head in the same direction as the buggy.

Shrugging it off as mere coincidence, Sage decided to head toward Fire Station 1 because he'd thought of another question to ask Ollie.

The engineer was still polishing equipment, only this time focusing on the brass nozzles of the connecting hoses. "Why, yes." Ollie responded. "Our fire station chief meets with the insurance man whenever there's an insured fire. He's the one who signs off on the paperwork saying how much destruction the fire caused. That's so the owner can collect. Don't matter if the fire starts by accident or otherwise. 'Course, the fire marshal conducts his own investigation to decide the cause. Don't know why another fire station chief was there, maybe he was doing a favor for Faden."

Despite figuring it would be a waste of time, Sage next headed off to view the dry goods store that Andy had supposedly set afire. Just as he reached it, Faden and a different insurance man climbed into a buggy. After they'd driven away, Sage decided to conduct his own inspection and started to cross the street only to veer off when he saw someone lurking between two neighboring buildings.

That figure stepped out into the sunlight. It was the man from the porch and he was scowling at the departing buggy. Sage ducked into a doorway recess and waited until the man turned and headed towards the city's center.

"Well, this is interesting. The stranger could be a police detective but he's wearing an expensive coat and hat. Detectives don't make that kind of money," Sage murmured and began to follow.

Sure enough, the stranger didn't head toward the police station. Instead he kept walking until he entered the Sherlock office building on Second Avenue. Sage watched through the glass doors as the man mounted the lobby's open staircase. Once he was out of sight, Sage entered the lobby and crossed to the building directory. Scanning the listings, his eye snagged on the entry, "Board of Fire Underwriters of the Pacific, Dist. D, J.C. Stone Mgr." He quickly scanned the rest of the listings but none had anything to do with fire.

Half an hour later, Sage was again in Philander Gray's law office. It being midday, he encountered a secretary, a legal clerk and a wait. "Mr. Gray is a busy man, you should have made an appointment," he was told though he doubted she would have been so snippy had his mustache been waxed and had he worn his John Adair duds.

When the secretary returned after delivering Sage's message, Gray was right behind her. "I have a client in my office, so let's talk in my clerk's office," he said as he shook Sage's hand. After shooing the clerk out of his own office and closing the door, Gray turned to Sage. "Did you discover something helpful?" he asked.

"No, I don't think so. But I did encounter something odd. What do you know about the Board of Fire Underwriters of the Pacific?"

Gray's forehead wrinkled and then relaxed. "I know the organization's involved in setting insurance rates. Some of my business clients have mentioned them. Not favorably I must say. But, other than that, I only know they lecture the Common Council on occasion."

The lawyer's response wasn't very helpful but it did give Sage a lead to pursue. Departing under the disapproving eye of Gray's secretary, Sage set off for Mozart's. He had to change his outfit if he was going to pay a visit to Portland's Bicycle King.

EIGHT

Once in his room, Sage quickly donned his prosperous-appearing John Adair garb. As he did so, he felt his stomach knot. A part of him could not believe someone would use such a monstrous crime to frame a union organizer—and arson was monstrous. It wasn't just that a building burned. That little family could have died, and would have died, if not for their pet bird. Had the wind been stronger or the fire department slower or less competent, the fire might have jumped to neighboring homes. People still talked how the 1873 fire leveled twenty-two city blocks.

Arson also put every firefighter at risk, starting from the minute the fire bell sounded. Who so lacked a conscience that they'd risk harming so many, just to frame an innocent man?

That was the question knotting his stomach because whoever the arsonist was, his lack of conscience made him an extremely dangerous foe. Sage briskly waxed his mustache ends into neat curls, turned from the mirror and donned his coat. He needed to hit the street and ask questions, starting with Councilman Fred T. Merrill. He had to find out why the Underwriters' man was skulking around the fire scenes.

He looked forward to seeing Merrill again. Portland's bicycle king was a lively character who boosted his business by engaging in antics like days-long races between horses and him on his safety bicycle. Yet, despite his showmanship, Merrill was also an effective thorn in the sides of his fellow council members. His district was home to many working class folks and he represented them well. Besides opposing more oil storage tanks on Portland's east side, he'd managed to stop crony grants of city franchises. And, to the consternation of the city's monied elites, Merrill incessantly tried to legalize prostitution. His annoying argument was that while Portland's rich men profited most from the city's nearly five hundred houses of ill repute, it was the prostitutes who paid the fines. That was because the rich owned most of the buildings and usually took a cut of the proceeds. Sage wished more Merrills sat on the Common Council.

Reaching the restaurant's door, he paused to survey the dining room. It was an elegant place with its dark walnut wainscoting, green plaster walls and gilt framed copies of old master paintings. In the evening, classical music issued from the musicians' balcony while the gas-fed crystal chandeliers twinkled above the diners' heads. Then realization dawned. Every table was full with noon time patrons and a waiter was missing. His mother was trying to greet and serve guests at the same time. Wisps of hair had come loose from her normally tidy bun. When she whizzed past the entry where he stood, she shot him a tight smile. He hung his hat and overcoat on the hall tree. The Merrill visit would have to wait.

Soon he was greeting and seating, pouring water, clearing and otherwise making himself useful. Mae sent him more than one grateful smile over the next few hours. At two o'clock, Sage locked the front door behind the last customer. There'd be a breather before Mozart's re-opened to serve the four o'clock tea favored by city's society women.

After Sage fetched two cups of coffee, he asked his mother to sit. They were alone since the other waiter was in the kitchen prepping for the tea. "What happened to Horace," Sage asked. A remarkably reliable man, their headwaiter's absence was unusual.

Mae sipped her coffee and sighed before saying, "He came to work with his cheek puffed out from a bad tooth. I made him go to the dentist to get it pulled. He didn't want to go but I gave him no choice. My cousin died from that."

Sage could imagine the scene. The frog-faced headwaiter confronted by the implacable Mae Clemens. No contest. Off to the dentist Horace went.

"I better tell you all I've learned last night and today."

Fifteen minutes later, she knew everything he knew and was shaking her head. "I sure hope you can catch whoever's behind this fire business because he ain't fit to wallow with hogs."

"Don't worry, I will," he said with more confidence than he felt. "I'm going to go out, rattle a few doors and shake a few bushes. Something's bound to drop out."

Mae shook her head. "You are such an optimist. Keep in mind that, just because you make thunder, it don't mean it's going to rain."

Sage laughed knowing it was yet another one of her little sayings that would snag in his head only to pop out unexpectedly. "Don't worry, Ma. I intend to make damn sure it rains buckets on whoever's setting those fires. I even intend to avenge Joey Cockatoo's murder. I know he was just a bird but his death broke that little girl's heart," he said. "And, what do you mean 'optimist'? I'm not the only optimist in the family. You are too. Otherwise, you'd be lounging around that house I offered to buy you, sipping tea and eating crumpets instead of working your tail off in this restaurant and spending your nights worrying about me."

She greeted his declaration with a dismissive sniff. "Pshaw. I don't even know what a crumpet is, so I'm sure not going to eat one. Besides, someone's got to keep an eye on your doin's." Then she turned serious, reaching across the table to cover his hand with her own. "My bones tell me solving this one is going to be like licking butter off a sharp knife."

Sage didn't laugh this time. He couldn't because he had the same feeling.

The bicycle emporium was empty of customers. Probably because rain didn't inspire thoughts of bicycle riding. The lone salesman was listlessly polishing chrome handle bars while Merrill sat in his small office at the back of the showroom, reading a newspaper. Seeing Sage, he jumped to his feet, brown eyes alert. "Hoo-boy! John Adair!" he exclaimed with an exaggerated waggle of his bushy eyebrows. "Tell me you're looking to buy ten bicycles! Business is slower than a tortoise traveling through tar."

"Well," Sage drawled, "for certain you must be needing sales. Your ears have gotten lost in that mop of yours. Trying to send your barber to the poorhouse?" It was a fair jest. Merrill's curly gray hair was a wild nest atop his compact body.

Merrill laughed heartily as he reached across the desk to shake hands. "Naw, my barber's in the hospital getting his appendix extracted.

I figure I'll just wait till he gets out and pay him extra for the trim. Besides, it's winter outside. Keeps my ears warm."

"Surely you're not still wheeling around on that bike of yours?"

"Why the heck not? It's no worse than riding a horse or walking or waiting around for a trolley. Besides, I got plans for next spring. I'm going to put on a big bicycle extravaganza. Can't get flabby before that to-do."

He peered closely at Sage. "Something tells me you're not here for chitchat." He gestured toward the visitor's chair, "Take a load off, Adair." Merrill hollered for his salesman who came running. "Gallop next door to the café and bring back two coffees. And grab one for yourself. Tell them to put it on my tab. I'll settle up before closing. Put it in gear, we're thirsty."

While they were waiting, Sage asked, "You going to run for re-election next time?"

"Nah, ain't no point. Since they're changing the city charter from district elections to city-wide elections I'd have the proverbial snowball's chance. You've got to have a lot of money backers to pull enough votes city-wide. Today, I know practically every voter in my district. Come election time, I just start visiting and, Bob's your uncle, I win by a landslide." His smile at the memory quickly disappeared as he said, "Mark my words, ordinary people will lose their voice with citywide elections. You're only going to get money men or fellows the money men like. That sure the hell won't be me."

Not good news, Sage thought. In fact, it was very bad news. He couldn't think of anything consoling to say other than, "It's a damn shame. Yours' is one of few honest voices in city politics." Merrill just lifted his shoulders and dropped them, clearly having given up the fight.

The salesman returned and once they were both sipping hot coffee, Merrill got to the point. "Okay, Adair. What is it you need to know this time? Don't tell me it's another crooked city engineer. We got rid of the last one for you."

"Nope, no problem with a city employee—far as I know. But I was wondering what you could tell me about the National Board of Fire Underwriters. Like, what exactly does that organization do?"

"Oh, you want another civics lessons, do you? Well, the short answer is that they do a heck of a lot. And, it just so happens I'm the right fellow to ask." Merrill took a long sip of coffee, folded his hands on his desk and leaned forward, obviously relishing his role of instructor.

"First of all, the fire insurance companies foot the bill for the Board which has branches all over the country. They send teams of experts into cities to evaluate fire danger. Then they give the city a score and the insurance companies use that score to set the cost of insurance premiums."

"All insurance companies follow the lead of the Board?"

"Only the ones you'd want to insure with. You remember the Chicago fire?" At Sage's nod, Merrill continued, "Well, most insurance companies went bust in that one. Hurt a whole lot of people who'd counted on having insurance only to find out they didn't. The Underwriters don't want that happening again."

"So, the Board must be pretty powerful."

"Boy howdy, that ain't the half of it. Powell and Milwaukie Avenues are going to be planked this year. You know why?"

Sage shook his head.

"Because of the Underwriters." Glee turned Merrill's lips into a grin as he continued, "Nowadays the Underwriters are taking on the owners of the waterfront warehouses and docks. They say the city has to buy a decent fireboat. Otherwise, they're threatening a big jump in premium costs."

"Will their threat work?"

"It's worked in every other city. Municipalities are buying fireboats all around the country. The Council even sent Fire Chief Campbell on an expense-paid junket to look at fireboats last year. Though, 'junket's' not fair. He did a fine job, turned in a thorough report. Accounted for every penny he spent."

"Sounds like you have a good opinion of Campbell."

"I do. He's the best department head we have in the city. He's competent, hardworking and honest. What I like best about him is that he cares about the welfare of his firefighters. You ought to hear him arguing on their behalf in some of our closed door Council meetings."

"How come you know so much about the Board of Fire Underwriters?"

"Well, that little brouhaha over the Powell and Milwaukie roads opened up my eyes. When the Underwriters spoke, the Council listened. Folks in my district worry about an oil tank fire gutting their homes and businesses. The last thing they want to see is more tanks on the east riverbank. So, I got myself a meet with J.C. Stone, the Underwriter's local manager and discovered that our interests coincided perfectly. Once the Underwriters started questioning the wisdom of siting more oil tanks across the river, the knucklehead Council suddenly adopted my position."

"Congratulations," Sage said and meant it.

Merrill rolled his eyes. "I suspect even that isn't the real truth of the matter. I'm betting the Underwriters told Standard Oil that their proposed tanks would be uninsurable. That's a safe call for the Underwriters. There's already too many tanks over there as it is. The Union and Standard tanks sit side by side. One of them catches fire and explodes, we stand to lose blocks of buildings. You can bet that the insurance folks weren't keen on increasing that danger.

Sage thought about Merrill's words. He wanted to ask another question but he needed to word it carefully. Much as he liked and admired Portland's Bicycle King, the fellow tended to inadvertently blabber all he knew, regardless of the consequences. It made him a great source of information but a terrible keeper of secrets. "So, does the Board of Fire Underwriters have anything to do with investigating the causes of fires?"

Merrill nodded. "You bet they do. They track causes nationwide and it's paid off. Stone told me that, in the late 1890's, the Underwriters noticed an increase in fires. They traced it down to the spread of electricity. That's why they pushed our Council into adopting a city electrical code. They also pushed the Council into designating fire limit areas."

"What exactly are those? Mozart's customers complain about them all the time."

That question got a grin from Merrill. "I'll surely bet them rich buggers are squealing. Anything that shrinks their profits sets them off. But fire limit areas are the right thing for the city. They're pretty simple. If you're an owner and want to build or remodel a building situated in one of the fire limit areas, you have to install all sorts of fire prevention measures—no open stairways, brick enclosed elevator shafts, fire escapes, sprinklers, things like that. And, you can't construct any new wood-framed structure within a fire limit area. Let me tell you, that's ruffled the developers' feathers. The Council gets weekly requests for exemption from the fire limits. So far, it usually rejects those requests. That'll probably change too." Merrill's lips pursed with frustration.

"And, finally" he continued, "the Underwriters also track arson. Stone's said there's more and more arson fires every year."

A surge of excitement jolted him but Sage tried to keep his question casual. "Arson? Why, I heard there were a couple of arson fires just the other night."

Merrill narrowed his eyes at Sage. "That's supposed to be kept quiet. The Council doesn't want folks knowing there's a firebug on the loose. Though, now that they've made an arrest, that danger is over. Who'd you hear that from, anyway?"

Sage decided the less said the better. "Oh, I know a fireman. He told me about it."

Although Merrill scowled, he continued talking. "Well, for sure, arson's a serious problem. Stone says our arson rates are way higher than in Europe. Many different reasons for that. But for sure, some of it's insurance fraud and some is crazed firebugs. The Underwriters are offering a pretty hefty reward to anyone who turns in an arsonist."

Their cups drained, Sage could think of nothing more to ask. So, after thanking the man and exchanging a few more jests, Sage headed back to Mozart's, certain that the man entering the Sherlock building was investigating the arson angle. That made sense, given what Merrill had said. Still, why was the Underwriter's man still skulking around—especially when, as Merrill noted, Andy had been arrested? That was strange. Or, as his mother would say, "Sorta like seeing a hoppy toad in a sunbonnet."

NINE

When Horace turned up to wait tables at suppertime, they sent him home. Mae told him a pulled tooth needed rest and refused to let him stay. It turned out to be a long night for Sage because his head barely hit the pillow before the city fire bell rang out. As he listened to its basso voice reverberate across the rooftops his mind's eye saw firefighters jumping into turnout gear and running for the brass pole. He imagined the excited horses standing beneath their harnesses while the drivers buckled their belly bands and saw the big doors spring open and the barking Dalmatian charge out into the night.

It was the second sounding of the city's bell that did it. "Ah, hell," he said aloud. "I might as well get down to the firehouse in case Ollie needs help with the firebox.

The firehouse was empty. But the lone station tender told Sage which fire alarm box had sounded and urged him on his way. This time it was up near the Chinese hill gardens and Sage took off at a trot. He knew those vegetable gardens and some of the gardeners who lived in the adjoining shacks. Arriving at the scene, he saw that a telephone pole was ablaze and sending fire down a number of overhead wires. Running to the engine he found Ollie flinging coal into the fire box. Sage grabbed the shovel from him as he asked, "What happened?"

"Damn crossed wire up above set the pole off. That got the other wires involved and sent fire running down to the buildings. Luckily, someone had a telephone and we got here in time to knock the wires down and wet the buildings. Watch where you step. Them wires on the ground bite. Go to the ladder truck and get yourself into rubber boots."

After picking his way around the live wires to the ladder truck and donning fire gear, Sage felt safer. Returning to the engine, he began stoking. Campbell was again on the scene. Although they quickly brought the fire under control, Campbell wasn't his usual celebratory self. And, as soon as he could, he climbed into his buggy and set off north.

"Where's the fire chief going?" Sage asked.

"I suspicion he's heading back to a photography shop fire in District 3," Ollie said and explained further when he sensed Sage's unspoken question. "Yup. It looks like it was another arson. Started in back but the extraman who spotted flames was just one block from his firehouse. Campbell says he smelled stove oil 'round the outside dustbin. That's what was burning. It'd just started a'running up the back wall."

As Sage helped coil the hydrant hoses, he considered what Ollie had said. Maybe this new arson fire would cast doubt on the idea that Andy was the arsonist.

Ollie's mind must have been galloping down the same track because he said, "I think Campbell went back to study things a bit closer. If the method is the same, Andy can't be the firebug."

"Surely, the fact stove oil was used in all three fires should be enough to clear Hosier," Sage said.

Ollie paused, removed his helmet and rubbed at the groove it had pressed into his forehead. "Nah," he said, "fire bugs like stove oil. There's lots of it around and it catches fire good." After glancing around, he leaned closer to say, "I'm thinking Campbell's gone back to look for the cap 'cause he don't believe Andy did it either."

Seeing Sage's wrinkled brow, Ollie tugged him closer to the engine and explained in a low voice, "This firebug's been around for awhile now. Them two fires the other night weren't his first. Campbell told me it has to be the same fella who's setting the fires because he always takes the can with him but tosses the cap away at the scene. If Campbell finds a cap back of the photography store, then our Andy can't be the firebug." Ollie frowned, tapped Sage on the chest and added, "You keep that info about the cap to yourself, you hear?"

By the time Sage trudged up the secret staircase, the city lay underneath the solid gray of a rain-soaked dawn. Dropping his smoky clothes on the floor, he climbed into bed. Two hours later, he awoke as his mother placed a tray of toast and coffee on the table. "I heard you go out," she said, seeing his opened eyes. "And, I smelled you come in," she added as she picked up his Miner duds and tossed them into a wicker basket. "How much longer are you going to be running off to fight fires?"

He pulled himself up and to the edge of the bed. "Depends on whether Campbell finds a cap," he said. He explained about the missing can and tossed cap.

"So, what's the next step?" she wanted to know.

"Head down to the police station and talk to Hanke soon as I've eaten."

When Sage mounted the police station stairs, he did so as John Adair. His tailored overcoat and suit were of the finest wool and his waxed mustache was precisely curled. It was change enough that David Campbell didn't recognize him when they passed on the stairs. Campbell, wearing his somber chief's uniform beneath a rubber slicker, looked both preoccupied and grimly determined. Still, Sage turned aside.

Hanke looked up from his desk and frowned at Sage's entry. Sage studied the sergeant before saying, "Am I to assume that your lack of delight in seeing me this fine morning has something to do with the fire chief who just stormed out of here and nothing to do with me personally?"

"Shut the door," Hanke responded.

Sage did as instructed and took a seat.

"It seems you may be right. Maybe Andy Hosier isn't our firebug. Campbell insists he isn't. Something about finding a can cap at an arson fire last night. Says, it's a little bit of information he's been holding back. So, don't you go blabbing it about."

"This means you'll be releasing Hosier?" Sage heard the relief in his own voice.

Hanke held up a hand to stop him. "Whoa, like I told Campbell, a dropped cap isn't enough to make that happen." Hanke squinted calculating eyes at Sage. "Can you keep something to yourself? Not even tell Gray?"

"If that's the condition, I will," Sage said.

Hanke leaned forward across his desk. "After you left the other day, I got to thinking about that witness who identified Hosier in the lobby. You know, when you got mad at me?"

Sage nodded slowly, wondering where Hanke was heading.

"Well, it seemed a mite suspicious, him turning up like that. So, I asked the desk officer about it. He said the fellow had come in, asking if Hosier was still in jail. The officer made the mistake of saying I'd just taken him to an interview room. After that, the fellow just hung out in the lobby."

"So, you didn't arrange that encounter out there?" Sage asked, realizing he should have trusted Hanke—the Sergeant was never underhanded.

"Heck no. I was as surprised as you were when the desk man came and told me he was there. But, don't feel bad about thinking otherwise. I would have thought just like you did. And, I did take advantage of it, after all." Hanke raised a finger as he said, "But, anyway, that little encounter got me wondering. We'd just trusted these were good witnesses. But what if they weren't? So I sent my best man around to find out something about the one in the lobby."

Hanke paused and the silence seemed to stretch on. Sage slid forward in his chair, eager to hear what Hanke would say next.

"My officer got to the house and lo and behold, the fellow didn't live at the address he gave us. No one's ever heard of him."

"What about the second witness?"

"My officer's out there checking on him now."

For a minute or so, the two men just looked at each other trying to puzzle out the meaning. Their contemplation was interrupted by an urgent rap on the closed door. Without waiting for Hanke's response a smartly uniformed officer, who was clearly excited, thrust the door open. He started to speak but paused when he saw Hanke had company.

"Go ahead man, tell me what you found out," Hanke ordered.

"Sarge, it's just like we thought. That address doesn't even exist. The house numbers go right past it." I knocked on every door in the block. No one's ever heard of the second witness either. And, when I asked the station chief, he said the fellow was a total stranger who just walked in off the street."

Hanke shook his head in disgust but he said, "Good job, Officer Bryant. That'll be all for now".

The officer turned to go and then turned back to ask the question Sage wanted answered most of all, "We gonna let Hosier go, Sir?"

"That's not my decision but, I suspect so."

Once the man was gone, Sage and Hanke went back to their respective contemplations. Sage was the first to break the silence, saying,

"This isn't making sense. Why frame Hosier using such flimsy evidence? Whoever set it up had to know you'd discover the witnesses were phony."

"Yup. It doesn't make sense. What if," Hanke narrowed his eyes as a thought struck, "the idea was simply to get Hosier out of their hair for awhile but not send him to prison?"

"But, if that was the case, why expose the scheme so soon by sending that one witness to the station, asking about Hosier?"

That stumped Hanke until Sage came up with an answer to his own question. "Maybe it was a mistake. Maybe that witness in the lobby got over zealous. Maybe he thought whoever put him up to it would be pleased at his making a firmer identification."

"Well, he didn't strike me as too bright."

"At least not bright enough to realize you might think his behavior suspicious. Of course," Sage added with sincere admiration, "most police would have been grateful for the visual confirmation and stopped there. He couldn't know what a sharp mind lurks behind that calm exterior of yours."

A dull flush ran up Hanke's neck. Sage decided to save his friend with a question. "What's going to happen next?"

"Next, I go talk to the prosecutor. Tell him the case against Hosier has collapsed and that we need to let him go. In the meantime, don't tell Gray. It's better if he hears it first from the prosecutor. That way, our legal beagle won't wonder if I've been talking out of school."

Sage walked back to Mozart's with a light heart, so great was his relief. Once Andy was free, they could meet and get down to the business of carrying out their unionizing work. Although, he reminded himself, Andy still isn't safe. After all, someone went to the trouble of framing him. And, the fact they resorted to arson, means they are both conniving and determined. They might attack Andy in another way if he continues unionizing. There's no way to protect him at every fire scene, the firehouse and all points in between.

Then another thought hit Sage with enough force that he froze at the curb's edge. What if Andy's union work has nothing to do with it? What if it is something else? That idea gripped tighter the longer Sage thought about it. He'd been doing union undercover work for nearly five years—in the Kentucky mines, with the New Orleans workers and the last few years here in Portland. No question but that company thugs were quick to thump heads, kidnap and even murder. But their actions never threatened entire communities like arson did. What would be the point?

If it wasn't the unionizing that sent someone after Hosier, then what could it be? Sage could think of nothing except—this time it was recollection halting him in his tracks—there'd been Andy's little eye snick when Sage had asked him that very question. Andy knew of something, Sage was certain of it. The trick was getting the young firefighter to say what that something was.

TEN

THE MESSENGER ARRIVED JUST AS Mozart's last noontime customer exited. Sage stood in the restaurant's foyer reading Philander Gray's note. Hosier was to be freed within the hour. The lawyer wanted Miner there.

As before, they began with a meeting in Hanke's office. Fatigue slumped the big sergeant's shoulders. Still, he smiled when he saw the two men standing in his doorway.

"Guess it turned out to be a mighty short case for you, Mr. Gray," he said as they shook hands.

"Can't say I mind that," Gray responded. "I understand from the prosecutor that your witnesses turned out to be unreliable. He seemed a bit peeved."

Hanke chucked. "You've got that right. He must have yelled for five minutes straight."

"Are you in trouble?" Sage asked.

Hanke shook his head. "Nope. I told the prosecutor and Chief Hunt at the time I thought we were jumping the gun. It seemed too coincidental that we'd have two witnesses turn up at the same time talking about two different fires. But, since the prosecutor's the one who pushed for the arrest . . . well, his yelling is only him spitting into a wind that's blowing right back on him. That's what I say and so does the Chief."

In short order Gray, Andy and Sage were heading down the police station's steep stairs to the sidewalk. At Gray's suggestion, the three of them turned toward his office. Andy chattered the entire three blocks.

"Did you fight any more fires? Anybody hurt? How's the fire engine running?" were his first questions to Sage. Sage assured him the fire engine was running just fine. He also told him of the last night's fires and how Campbell found evidence near the photo shop fire that helped prove his innocence.

Once settled in Gray's office, Sage got down to business. "Andy, you realize that you are not safe yet?"

Hosier looked surprised. "I thought they found out the witnesses were bogus. You mean they're going to arrest me again? I sure wouldn't like that. The jail walls got water seep and, come night, there's so many folks sleeping on the floors that a fella can't get a wink of shut eye for all the snoring and coughing. And, boy oh boy, 'cause they don't have money to take a bath, or get their clothes washed, the stink is enough to make your eyes smart."

Sage raised a hand to stop the flow while wondering how someone as naïve as Andy made it safely into adulthood. "Your arrest is the least of our worries. Whoever went to the trouble of setting fires to frame you, might try something worse the next time."

His warning seemed to penetrate because Andy just blinked, looking from one to the other. Gray backed up Sage's warning with a grave nod.

Finally Hosier said, "Whew. I guess I was just thinking about how good it felt to be out of jail.

"So, exactly what have you been doing to unionize your co-workers?" asked Sage.

"Well, I've talked to the fellas at the firehouse. And, I've met with a few folks from other firehouses."

"How have people responded to the idea?" Sage asked.

"They want better pay and steady work. And, some of the firehouses are falling down around their ears. Heck Station 5 puts buckets all over the second floor to catch the rain. If it's a heavy rain, they have to pack up their bedding and sleep down with the horses. They want the darn roof fixed. And, everybody's fed up with having to fight volunteers at the same time they're fighting fires."

"What do you mean, 'fight volunteers'?"

"Oh, we get to the fire scene and we're following orders and they're not. And, they don't know what the heck they're doing 'cause they ain't been trained proper. Half the time, we'll be racing to do something and run smack dab into one of them. Even worse, we get blamed for their thieving."

"Thieving?" Sage echoed.

"People run out of their house when it's afire. We go in the house but so do the volunteers. Sometimes, people's valuables go missing."

"The volunteers steal?" Sage prodded.

"Ah," here Hosier looked shamefaced. "well, I seen paid men steal too. That's because they're only making about two dollars a day. Some of them have families. Not that thieving's okay, it isn't. I'm just saying . . . but yah, the volunteers steal more."

"Okay," Sage said. "So, one strange thing I've been wondering about. That is why both phony witnesses went to a fire station chief. You'd think they'd have gone to the police direct."

Hosier was nodding. "That's peculiar, alright."

Gray shifted forward in his chair. "What about the Fire Chief himself, David Campbell?" he asked.

Hosier turned mulish, lowering his brow and tightening his lips. "What do you mean, 'what about Campbell'?"

"Well, does your unionizing make him mad? Would he frame you to stop what you're doing?"

This question brought a vigorous headshake from Hosier, "No, Sir. Like I told Mr. Miner here, Chief Campbell's a good guy. Everything the men want, he wants. In fact, I 'spect he's telling the Council to treat us better or they won't have no firefighters. What I'm doing helps him. Now he can say we're starting a union to get what we need. Some of them hate unions." Hosier raised an admonishing finger. "Whatever you're figuring, you're wrong. It ain't the Chief who's causing me problems."

Sage and Gray exchanged looks. Sage probed a bit more, "Look here, Andy. We're just trying to help. I know the men think a lot of Campbell but we don't know him. We have to suspect everyone who's in a position to harm you."

Hosier, looking somewhat mollified, said, "Okay. I understand. But, for certain sure, it is not Chief Campbell." His adamant tone made Gray and Sage exchange looks yet again but they dropped that particular inquiry.

Stepping outside into the early fall dusk a few minutes later, Sage said to Hosier, "We still need to talk about St. Alban and what I can do to help you."

"You mean besides springing me from jail?" Andy asked with a shy smile.

Sage led the way to a nearby coffee shop where they were able to select a table away from others. Once seated, Sage said, "Andy, I'm willing to help you with the firefighters' union. But, right now, I think you have to stop organizing until we find out who was behind your arrest."

Hosier shifted uneasily in his seat, his eyes flicking away from Sage. "Okay, I'll tone it down a bit," he promised.

Something wasn't feeling right, Sage realized. "What did St. Alban think I could do for you?" he asked.

"Introduce me to other union folks. Help me get their support. Advise me what we should do if the men vote to strike. Things like that."

"That's easy enough," Sage said but he continued staring at the young man, finally saying, "Are you certain sure there is nothing else you are doing that might be making someone mad?"

That question brought a quick shake of the head and, again, that evasive, sideways look. Sage gave up. Whatever Hosier was up to, he wasn't ready to tell Sage about it.

Minutes later the two parted with Hosier heading back to Station 1, eager to get a lesson from Ollie in how to change engine gaskets.

Mozart's had a busy supper hour and Sage was tired as he climbed the stairs. Maybe he'd sleep better now that he didn't have to worry. Hosier was out of jail and willing to slow his organizing efforts, giving Sage time to discover who'd framed him.

Around two a.m. the city's fire bell boomed across the roof tops. Sage sat straight up in bed, his heart pounding. Before meeting Andy Hosier, he'd just roll over and go back to sleep whenever the bell sounded. Now the bell's call triggered mental images of firefighters on ladders, roofs and stepping into flames. Sleepless he lay with his eyes wide open, puzzling over the rash of arson fires. Those thoughts lead him back to the strange behavior of the Board's man.

Another hour of sleeplessness and the city bell sounded again. Since he was still wide awake, he decided he might as well head to Station 1 and see if they'd been called out. If so, he could help Ollie and keep an eye on Andy.

The night's second fire was in a waterfront storage warehouse. Andy greeted Sage with a wide grin, gestured to the firebox and ran off to help with the hoses. Minutes later, after scooping coal into the firebox,

Sage glanced up to see Andy walking the hose nozzle toward the building's front. Fire engulfed the building, with flames leaping out roof and windows. Something about what he was seeing seemed wrong. Then he realized what it was. Andy was handling the hose on his own when usually there were at least two men.

Then he froze. Because the fire engine sat away from the fire and to one side, Sage could look along the front of the building and see the wooden struts holding the huge company sign. They were on fire. From where Andy was, he couldn't see the struts—just the sign's front. He was steadily advancing, dragging the heavy hose. In just seconds he'd be under that sign.

Sage slammed shut the firebox door and took off running. He had a good hundred feet to cover. As he jumped hoses he hollered but between the fire's noise and the helmet mashed down over his ears, Andy couldn't hear him. As Sage ran, he kept his eyes on the sign. It was starting to tilt outward. Andy had reached the doorway and was standing directly under the sign. His back was to everyone else as he peered into the flames he was trying to douse. Sage couldn't reach him in time.

The sign sagged, pulling away from its struts. If it had been quiet, Andy would have heard the ripping sound of its detachment. As it was, the young firefighter would never know what hit him. Gripping the hose, his legs anchored in a wide stance, Andy's sole focus was the fire before him.

Sage kept running despite knowing it was hopeless. The roaring fire and the tilting of the sign above Andy was a hellish nightmare happening right before his eyes. Then Sage dove for Andy's hose. Landing atop it, he grabbed with both hands and scooted as far backward as his flaying feet could push him. He yanked, praying that Andy's grip was tight enough, that the hose wouldn't simply slide through his hands. There was a jolt as the hose pulled taut and he yanked at it with every bit of strength he had. Then Sage was falling flat on the ground as the hose suddenly slackened.

Momentarily—wind knocked out of him—Sage lay on his back, staring up at embers sparking against the night sky. Then the ground shook as the heavy sign slammed down. He heard other men shouting, running past him toward Andy but it was too late. Muscles suddenly weak, Sage struggled to sit up. All he could see was the canted sign on the ground and the backs of the firefighters' coats as they bent over something at their feet. Sage knew what they were seeing—the horror of the hose snaking out from beneath the fallen sign—maybe the soles of Andy's boots.

Sage got to his feet and staggered over to help. Glancing at the engine, he saw Ollie quickly shutting off the water to Andy's hose. Turning back, Sage saw the men step away. Between their legs he saw Andy, sitting on the ground, head in his hands.

Sage ran forward and squatted down. As the young man looked up at him, his skin pale beneath streaks of soot. Sage asked, "Are you okay, Andy?"

"You the one who pulled on my hose?" At Sage's nod, he said, "You saved my life."

"Why the hell did you get so close to the building?"

"I thought it was safe. The fire station chief told me to get water into the building through the front door."

A voice spoke from behind them, "That's right, I did. I just didn't realize the idiot would get that close to the building." Faden reached down and pulled Andy to his feet as he asked him, "Can you still work the scene or do you need to leave?"

"Nah, I'm fine," Andy rushed to say. "It scared me but I can still work." He turned to Sage. "Hey, Miner can you help me free the hose? Sure hope that sign didn't punch holes in it."

ELEVEN

B.J. Cooper lay beside his wife, staring at the ceiling. Outside, fitful wind gusts rattled the night's chill silence. A single thought kept circling through his mind: How would he support Frances and James once the Portland Hotel men published their rival publication? There were only so many businesses willing to advertise in a Negro newspaper.

A clang, like metal milk cans hitting together, came from the backyard. B.J. sat up, straining to hear. Were those footsteps squishing across the flooded backyard? Who was out there? Fear shot through him. There'd been that arson story in the newspaper. They said they'd caught the firebug but the police could be wrong. What if someone was trying to set fire to their house?

B.J. swung his feet out of bed and hurriedly donned robe and slippers. As he sped from the bedroom, his wife called after him, alarm in her voice. He paused and hissed, "Shush. Somebody's in the backyard."

At the kitchen door, he pulled aside the curtain and peered out. Shadows of naked tree limbs whipped across the yard. He squinted. Had a figure just slipped out the side gate? He waited, watching for movement but saw only dead leaves tumbling before the wind. Easing the door open, he stepped onto the concrete steps. He sniffed but smelled neither gas nor oil. The tool shed's door was shut and neither flames nor smoke were shooting out. For five minutes, he shivered on the top step. He debated going to check the shed but the backyard was so swampy, his slippers would never recover. Besides, the shed held nothing of value.

Back inside, he moved to the front of the house and peered out the window. The street was empty. He opened the door and stepped out. No one had done anything to the covered front porch or the tiny fenced yard. Forehead wrinkling, he headed back to bed. Must have been someone checking the tool shed. Nothing much in there—just old paint cans, used paint brushes, a rusty wheelbarrow and an old push mower. Nothing worth stealing. He'd check tomorrow. He climbed back into bed.

"What was it, B.J.?" his wife asked.

"I thought I heard someone in the backyard but everything looks alright. No one's out there." No sense mentioning the tool shed. She'd insist he put on his shoes and go check.

Next morning, the three of them sat at the kitchen table eating breakfast. The silence was thick with unspoken words. Frances heaved a sigh, got up, crossed to the back door, opened it wide and returned to her seat. Cold November air spilled in. B.J. and James both looked at her.

"Well, you two seem to like a cold atmosphere while you eat. Thought I'd do my bit and make it chillier," she said before digging into her bowl of oatmeal.

Her husband and son gaped at her, exchanged looks and laughed. B.J. got up and closed the door. Turning back to James, he said, "I'm sorry son. I shouldn't have cuffed you on the ear like I did."

"Ah, Pop. I was wrong in what I said. I'm proud that you're my father. I was just mad that Orpin can start the fight but I'm the one who goes to jail," James laid down his spoon and leaned forward over his oatmeal, bleakness slowing his words. "Sometimes, I don't know why I even bother to stay in school. Darnell Jackson got his high school certificate and when he applied to be a fireman, they just laughed at him. Except for volunteers, there hasn't been an African-American firefighter in Portland since 1895."

B.J.'s dark eyes softened as he looked at his son. "James, you're going to attend the Tuskegee Institute with Mr. Washington once you graduate from high school. You will obtain an advanced degree. You won't need to be a fireman," he said.

"That's fine for me, but what about my friends who don't have the money or whose fathers aren't Mr. Washington's personal friend?"

Frances, sensing a growing tension, said, "Can I get you both some more bacon?"

Before either could answer, urgent pounding shook the front door.

"What the heck?" B.J. said, jumping to his feet. "You two stay right here until we know what this is about."

He opened the front door and found his porch crowded with brass-buttoned police officers. Before he could speak, he was strong-armed against the front door by policemen rushing past him. "Where's your son, James?" one of them snarled as he leaned close to B.J.

"We got him!" came a shout from the kitchen. Seconds later they were shoving a handcuffed James, still in his shirt sleeves, out the front door.

"What? What is he being arrested for?" B.J. asked, forcing calm into his voice despite the panic tightening his throat.

"He's the damn firebug," spat the last policeman before he exited the front door and banged it shut behind him.

B.J. and Frances stood in the hall, staring at each other in stunned silence. Outside a hard rain began to beat down.

"A messenger from Mr. Solomon is at the kitchen door," Mae told Sage as she took his place at the entrance podium.

Angus Solomon sending a message was unusual. Yet, there was Solomon's nephew, whom Sage'd recently met, standing outside the kitchen door. "Hello, Nathan, come on in," he said.

Nathan shook his head. "Can't. I've other messages to deliver. My uncle asks whether you will come to the Portland Hotel as soon as possible. He can't leave work but needs to see you."

"I'll get my coat and head right over," Sage told him. The young man flashed a grateful grin and ran off.

Sage arrived at the Portland Hotel in record time. Spotting him, Solomon immediately led the way to the table behind the palm, next to the kitchen door. Their purposeful passage caused the other diners to glance up from their plates.

"Thank you for coming, John. A friend of mine is in a bit of a fix. Or, rather, his son is the one in trouble."

"The black kid they arrested for fighting? Hanke said he thought he could sort that out. Get the charges dropped."

Solomon went momentarily silent but he didn't bother to ask how Sage had learned of James' earlier arrest. Instead, he said, "Lord, I wish that were the problem. No, they've arrested James for arson. They claim he's the firebug who's been setting the fires."

"Oh crap," Sage said as two reactions collided in his head: sympathy for the boy's parents and frustration because he'd thought he was temporarily done with the firefighting business. Now here it was again. "What do you need me to do?" he asked.

"I was hoping you would prevail on Mr. Gray to help us out," Solomon said. "I'd ask but I don't know him nearly as well as you do."

"I am happy to do that but wouldn't your friend want to use Mc-Cants Stewart? I've heard he's an excellent lawyer."

Solomon gave a rueful headshake. "Ordinarily, my friend would prefer Stewart, trusting in his own kind, so to speak. But unfortunately Stewart has chosen to assist a group opposed to my friend and his newspaper," he said.

Sage tried to puzzle out what Solomon was saying.

Solomon saw the confusion because he explained further, "My friend is B.J. Cooper. He's the editor of the *New Era*. Some of the folks here at the hotel have pooled their money and plan to start up a rival newspaper, *The Advocate*. McCants Stewart is acting as their legal advisor."

"Two black newspapers in town? Just for twelve hundred black people and half of them kids?"

"There's two political factions in town. The people wanting to start *The Advocate* think Cooper is too old school, too favorable to Booker T. Washington's hat-in-hand approach to ending white racism. They side with W.E.B Du Bois' more militant stance and want to put his viewpoint forward in their newspaper."

Sage sat back to absorb that information which was new to him. He'd seen *Gazette* articles about both men. The *Gazette*, owned by the city's rich white men, definitely favored Washington but that's all he knew. He seldom read the *New Era*. "Okay, I see why Mr. Stewart is not an option," he said. "I'll go see Philander Gray immediately. When was the boy arrested?"

"First thing this morning. Sergeant Hanke sent word to me so I went over to B.J.'s house. He and his wife are frantic with worry. I told them to not do anything until I contacted Gray."

Sage stood, waving away the waiter who was approaching with coffee. "I better go find Gray right now. He might be in court or, more likely, chowing down somewhere knowing him."

Sage got lucky. Gray was in his office and the two of them immediately set out for the jail. Sage stopped a messenger boy and sent word to Solomon that Gray was on board, heading to the jail and that he and B.J. Cooper should meet them there.

When Solomon arrived, the three of them asked to see Sergeant Hanke.

The sergeant didn't look surprised when they told him they were there for the Cooper boy.

"Before we discuss the situation, can we wait for the boy's father to arrive? Mr. Solomon has sent him a message," Gray said.

Hanke grimaced. "That won't be necessary. We got a confession."

Gray exploded. "Do you mean you've questioned a child about such a serious matter without either his parent or his lawyer present? That's outrageous!"

Hanke flushed crimson but his voice remained calm. "No, Mr. Gray, we questioned no one. Mr. Cooper turned himself in about an hour ago. He's the one who confessed."

Solomon, Gray and Sage exchanged confused glances. Finally, Gray spoke, "Well, then, I guess I am representing both father and son until this situation gets straightened out. Other than the father's confession, what evidence do you have?"

"Three empty stove oil cans were found in Cooper's tool shed. Each one lacks its cap. And, an anonymous letter points the finger at the Cooper boy. We also found a witness who says the son has been spouting off about how the fire department discriminates against black applicants for firefighter positions. Apparently, a friend of his was turned down for a job," Hanke replied.

"What? Another witness with a phony address? Come on, Sergeant Hanke. We ran around this flag pole a few days ago," Sage said.

Hanke was shaking his head. "Nope this was a school teacher who overheard the conversation. Very reputable and well-known."

"Where's the son now?" Sage asked.

"In a cell around the corner from his father," Hanke said. "We think the father's trying to save his son with a false confession. The son isn't talking. He's clammed right up."

Satisfaction thinned Gray's lips into a tight smile. "At least one of my clients knows to keep his trap shut." He stood and picked up his hat. "Looks like I have my work cut out for me. I will need to see my two clients, separately, in private," he said.

Nodding, Hanke rose from his desk. "I'll arrange it."

Sage and Solomon waited on the lobby's hard bench for over an hour. They said little, only exchanging looks as the jailer escorted the father and then, the son, to and from the interview room.

Once James was returned to his cell, Gray appeared and slapped his hat on his head. "We better discuss this in my office," he said and headed toward the outer doors.

The three of them trooped to Gray's office and settled into chairs. "Mr. Cooper's confession isn't going to fly," Gray told them. "He knows nothing about the fires. He says he just tossed the caps to the cans any old where. Hanke tells me the caps were all found at the ignition point for each fire."

Sage nodded. That fit what he'd already learned from Ollie. He leaned forward, "What about the boy? What about James?"

"James is adamant he had absolutely nothing to do with any fires," Gray took a deep breath. "And, I believe him." Gray turned intent eyes on Sage, "You know what this means, don't you?"

"That I will be paying your very expensive fees to sort things out?" Sage said, his grin taking all sting from his statement.

Gray smiled. "Well, that too," he agreed. He cleared his throat, studied both men and said, "What it really means is that you two, along with your friends, better find the real firebug before one of the Cooper fellows goes to trial because I seriously doubt it will be fair. As you know, our prosecutor always strikes black men from juries where the defendant is black." Gray's lips twisted. "He claims they can't be impartial. Hah. What he means is he wants the opposite kind of partiality so he can keep his conviction numbers up."

TWELVE

"Well, hey there Mr. Miner," Andy Hosier said, straightening and tossing his polishing rag into a bucket. He stepped forward to shake Sage's hand. Sadie followed, trotting over to nudge Sage's other hand for a pet. Her tail wagged her whole back end and her dark eyes closed with pleasure as he scratched around her ears. Once Sage gave her a final pet, she returned to leaning against Andy's leg.

"That dog sure seems fond of you," Sage observed.

"She's a sweetheart," Andy said, reaching down to gently tug the canine's velvety ears.

Glancing toward another firefighter tossing hay to the horses, Sage said to Andy, "How about we step outside for a breath of fresh air?"

An afternoon downpour sent the two men quickly scurrying into the nearby café. Once seated with coffee before them, Sage wasted no time. "Andy, how have things been going for you? Any more close calls?"

The other man hesitated. "No, close calls but I think someone did take my boots out of my turnout bag and cut loose the soles."

"Why would they do that?"

"Well, if I was running to help Ollie or stumbling around inside a burning building, the soles could part company from the boot and send me flying. Might not kill me but I could be hurt."

"You've stopped trying to unionize, right?"

Andy nodded vigorously but, once again, there was that sidewise glance. He was holding something back. "Are you certain that you are doing nothing else to make someone mad at you?" Sage prodded and heard exasperation in his own voice.

Andy waved a dismissive hand. "Aw the boot thing is probably nothing. Maybe the last fire, I got too close and the glue melted. Hey! Did you hear they caught the real firebug?" he said eagerly.

Andy was too keen to change the subject but Sage played along. "I heard that. There wasn't any suspicious fires last night?"

Andy's brow knitted in thought. "There was one. Except, someone said the evidence was different at last night's scene." He perked up. "That's got to mean they caught the right fellow for all them other fires."

Sage leaned across the table and asked softly, "What if they didn't? What if he's being framed just like you were?"

After taking a moment to mull over Sage's words, Andy said, "Criminy, I didn't think of that."

They were both quiet for a moment until Sage asked. "Exactly how was last night's fire set?"

"Don't know for sure what caused it. The fire marshal hasn't said. Us firefighters thought it suspicious because it started against an outside wall. Plus, one of the fellows found an empty jar that smelled of gasoline. When we looked behind the building we found a trail of dry straw across the ground. Like maybe somebody brought straw to pile against the wall," Andy said.

He leaned forward. "Do you really mean it? Somebody might have framed the fellow just like they did me?"

"I'm willing to bet they did. He's a young black kid, still in high school. He says he didn't have anything to do with it and I believe him."

"A kid, huh? They got him in a jail cell? That's not good."

"Afraid so. What I don't understand is why the scoundrels are framing a second person. Especially someone who has nothing to do with firefighting or the fire department. Plus, I wonder whether the original firebug has simply changed his modus operandi."

"Modus what?"

"The method he uses to start the fires." Sage stood, clapping his hat on his head. "I better go take a look at the scene. Where is it?"

The boarding house's blackened ruin lay beneath a lowered sky fat with rain. Half a block away, Sage stepped into a narrow opening between two houses so he could observe unseen. Faden, the firehouse chief, was walking the scene alongside a man dressed in a suit. The two shook hands, then the man climbed into a buggy and drove away leaving Faden on the curb.

Sage was going to step out to talk to Faden but paused when another buggy rolled up. It halted in front of the burned out building and another well-dressed man climbed down to shake the station chief's hand. They also walked around the site, Faden talking all the while. Their circuit complete, both men climbed aboard the buggy and departed.

As Sage pondered his next step, a man appeared on the sidewalk, as if from nowhere. He must have been concealing himself somewhere down the street. The stranger advanced on the burned boarding house, heading toward the side where the fire looked to have burned the hottest. There he squatted down and using a stick, he poked through the rubble. After a bit he stood, removed his hat and scratched his head. Sage recognized him as the fellow he'd seen enter the Sherlock building.

When the man left, Sage followed and, sure enough, the stranger again strode into the building's lobby. That made three times that he'd seen the Fire Underwriters' man at the scene of an arson fire. Would he still be investigating the fires if he believed the police had the real arsonist behind bars?

A small coffee shop with big windows sat across the street from the Sherlock building. Sage grabbed a seat and three cups later, the fellow exited the building. Throwing money on the table, Sage left the coffee shop and was soon trailing only half a block behind his mystery man. They crossed the Steel Bridge as an arriving train on the lower deck vibrated the steel plates beneath their feet.

When the stranger reached the river's other side, he strode up Holladay Street, pausing only to pat a wandering dog and drop a coin into an old woman's begging can. Then he glanced at his pocket watch and picked up his pace. Sage began to fear that he was wasting time by simply following the fellow home. But, no. The stranger stepped into a small café that Sage entered a minute later. Inside there were only a few tables and a four-stool counter. Sage sat at the counter, his back to his quarry. When the café owner approached, Sage ordered coffee and pie.

He heard the café owner cheerfully address the stranger as "Mr. Roberts". Just as Sage's pie arrived, another man entered the café. When Sage glanced at the newcomer, he nearly spat out his coffee. Fire Chief David Campbell stood in the café doorway, his frame backlit by a sinking sun.

Fortunately, Campbell immediately crossed to Roberts' table, seemingly without noticing Sage. Remembering the close attention Campbell paid to his firefighters, Sage hunched over his pie, keeping his back turned toward the two men.

They immediately began talking in voices too low for Sage to overhear. Afraid Campbell might look in his direction during a conversational pause; Sage dropped coins on the counter and quickly exited the café.

"When the heck is Fong going to get back? I need him here!" Sage felt both frustrated and irritated.

His mother turned from the cook stove, a wooden spoon in the air, an eyebrow cocked in exasperation.

"Whoops! I mean we need him here," Sage corrected. "But really, have you heard anything?"

"Yes, as a matter of fact. His wife sent word this morning that he's arriving on tonight's train. He's finished the San Francisco job," Mae said, before turning back to stir the huge pot. "Funny how a person notices what someone does when they're not around to do it," she muttered.

Sage wasn't sure exactly who her observation was aimed at so he pretended he hadn't heard it. "I need to go over to the firehouse and talk to Andy for a few minutes. But, I'll be back by supper to help."

Mae twisted around, "Go ahead on but it would sure help if you made it back. Supper starts in an hour. Fong not being here is nearly as bad as when Horace was gone. It's running me ragged."

As he headed for the firehouse, Sage thought about Fong. Almost four years it had been since Fong rescued him from a terrible beating. In that amazing flurry of arms and legs, Fong had gone from being Mozart's mild-mannered busboy into being their full partner, Sage's martial arts teacher and his closest friend.

When he entered the firehouse's ground floor, the only sound was the soft thud of horses shifting in their stalls and murmuring voices drifting down from the living quarters overhead. Then a soft cursing sounded from the workbench behind the engine. Sage made his way there, expecting to see Andy. Instead, it was Ollie who stood at the bench, trying to loosen a clamp around a small tube that kept rolling from his grasp. Sadie lay under the workbench. She looked up eagerly but dropped her head back on her paws with a huffing sigh when she saw him.

Sage stepped forward. "I'll hold the tube while you unscrew the clamp," he told the engineer.

That was all it took. Soon Ollie had the clamp off. "Thanks for the assistance," he said. "This tube has a hairline fracture and could bust at the wrong time. Usually, Andy's Johnny-on-the-Spot to help but he's not come back.

"Come back?" Sage echoed.

When Ollie turned to look at him there was a worry crease between his eyes. "I figured he was with you. Abner said he left kinda quick. I was up napping and never saw him at all this afternoon. He didn't take his turnout bag."

Unease pricked Sage's spine. "Nobody knows where he is?"

The other man shook his head. "Matter of fact, folks are a bit upset 'cause it's his turn to cook supper. Looks like that's not going to happen." Ollie laid down his screwdriver, his attention fully on Sage. "You know, that isn't like Andy at all. With him, the crew always comes first. You don't think something's happened to him, do you?"

Sage could think of no way to ease the other man's concern. So many peculiar things had happened to the young firefighter in recent days that it made this new disappearance ominous. So he simply said, "I'll go look for him."

Sage started by going into every place of business around the firehouse. Evidently Andy had made friends with all the neighbors. They knew him but none had seen him—with one exception. A produce seller had seen him heading north at a brisk pace, just before it started to turn dusk.

"Did he seem upset? Was anyone with him or following right behind him?"

The man eyed him thoughtfully. "You know, now that you're asking, it was kinda funny."

"What was?" Sage prodded, hearing the urgency in his own voice.

"Andy looked worried. It was like he was trying not to run. He didn't give me a nod or a smile, which sure isn't Andy. He always has a cheery word. I figured he'd gotten worrisome news about his pregnant sister or something. He kept his eyes straight ahead."

"Did you see him turn off the street, head east or west?"

The man shook his head, "Nope. He stayed walking north, like he was heading into the North End."

Sage spent the next hour in that rough neighborhood. It wasn't the first time he'd searched its crowded, rundown streets for a missing friend. His dread grew as he went in and out of storefronts and saloons. Something told him the search was hopeless. If Andy had been kidnapped, he'd be imprisoned in a seedy rooming house or derelict building. Or, worse, he could be under Sage's boots, trapped in the city's enormous underground.

Damn, he needed Fong. In the past, they'd found missing people, thanks to Fong's army of tong men—men Fong called his "cousins." They knew the North End and the underground better than the backs of their own hands.

He gave up and was near the firehouse when the fire bell sounded. He reached it just as the doors sprang open and the fire horses trotted out, the apparatus bells clanging. A barking Sadie ran alongside, between curb and clattering hooves, her paws seeming not to touch the ground.

He scanned the vehicles as they sped past. Andy wasn't there. That's when he knew for certain that the young firefighter was in serious trouble. Andy would never ignore the city's fire bell.

THIRTEEN

Soft thudding slipped into his dreams and woke him gently. For a moment he just lay there, savoring the familiar sound, grateful his friend had returned. Finally, Sage got up, donning baggy pants and a soft shirt before climbing the narrow attic stairs into candlelight.

Fong's black clad body moved with a grace that Sage had seen turn deadly in a fight. He paused in the doorway, unwilling to break the concentration that flowed through the other man's sinews, muscles and bones.

His caution failed. "Ah, you here," Fong said and ceased moving. A toothy grin split his long face, squinting his black eyes. "I think you maybe not practice while I gone. Dust on floor," he said.

Sage gave a guilty shrug saying, "You caught me. I know I should have but things got busy. I just didn't think of it."

Fong smiled. "Never too late," he said, before turning and readying himself by breathing deep and lowering his shoulders. "Raise hands," he intoned.

Sage knew the drill by heart. As he raised his hands, his spirits lifted.

"This Andy fellow, he is young?" Fong asked over the rim of his cup.

Sage nodded as he poured more coffee. They sat at the small table in his room, having spent an hour practicing the Snake and Crane. "He's about twenty-four and lively. I'll check again today but I don't have much hope he'll be at the firehouse.

"Maybe he decide to take break," Fong suggested.

"Mr. Fong, if you'd seen him fighting fires, you'd know he'd never abandon his job or the other firefighters. And, for sure, he'd never walk off without telling the engineer. Even the engineer fears something bad has happened to him."

Fong sighed. "Okay, I talk with cousins. I plan to relax for few days but that not going to happen."

"How was San Francisco? Were you successful?" Sage asked. In his youth, Fong had been a fierce tong warrior in that city. Now, in his late fifties, he acted as a counselor to the tongs, all his efforts aimed at forestalling fights between them. He'd traveled to San Francisco to do just that. Given the growing anti-Chinese sentiment among whites, Fong wanted unity.

Fong's smile was tired. "Think now cousins try to get along until next small thing overturn cart of apples."

"I'm sorry to interfere with your well-earned rest," Sage said. "I wouldn't, except I'm certain Andy's in danger."

"No problem. I must meet with cousins 'anyways' . . . as Lady Mother says."

After his friend left, Sage felt hopeful. If anyone could find Andy, it was Fong's cousins.

Ollie was polishing chrome when Sage entered. His back straightened with hope only slump when Sage shook his head.

"I ain't heard nothing from the boy," Ollie said before Sage could ask. "We had two fire callouts last night and he didn't turn up for either one. Nobody's seen hide nor hair of him."

"I was afraid of that. I came by to tell you that I have some people out looking for him. Ollie, were either of last night's fires suspicious?"

The engineer's brow wrinkled but he answered readily enough. "Aye, an old umbrella factory burnt up. The owner showed up. He said it was closed and he'd planned to tear it down anyway."

"Was it another one of those straw and gasoline jobs?" Sage asked.

"How'd you know?"

"Andy told me the technique had changed."

Ollie quietly studied him. "You're thinking it's the same firebug as before? The one who used stove oil and left the caps behind?"

"I think there's a chance. What's the location of the umbrella factory fire?"

"It was just half a block north from that boarding house what burnt a few days ago."

"Same owner as the boarding house owner?" Sage asked, hoping the answer was "yes". That would at least give him a direction in which to look.

"Nah, different fella altogether."

The scene was familiar—charred rubble beneath a misty rain. Heavy clouds pushed down, giving the day a monotonous gray cast. No one was in sight. Sage didn't know if the burnt building could help him find the missing Andy or prove James Cooper innocent of arson, but lacking any other idea, he'd poke around.

After waiting a few minutes to ensure he was alone, Sage crossed the street and stepped gingerly through the blackened doorway. Broken glass crunched underfoot as he moved deeper into the building now mostly open to the sky. Slowly, he picked his way amongst the rubble and pools of water hidden beneath a dusting of ash.

Reaching the building's center, he paused. There'd been an odd sound. To his left, a pile of fallen timbers shifted slightly. Moving closer he held his breath and thought he heard a faint exhalation. Then silence. Why would the firefighters pile up burnt wood? It wasn't their job to clean up the mess. And the pile was too helter-skelter to have been there before the fire. As he studied the pile, it shifted slightly. Was that rats or some other critter?

Curiosity drew him closer as the mist overhead turned into pattering raindrops that drowned out every other noise. Reaching the pile, he listened hard but heard nothing. Glad he was dressed as Miner and, feeling a bit foolish, he picked up and tossed away one of the boards. Two more pieces went flying before he saw the shoe, attached to a leg, encased in a trouser.

A minute later, he had the body completely uncovered. The man lay face down, dark red blood matting the hair on the back of his skull. Squatting, Sage gently turned him over. It was the man from the Fire Insurance Underwriters—the man he'd followed yesterday, Roberts.

He was deathly pale and his chest wasn't moving. Sage stared down, awash with sorrow. From what he'd seen, this had been a good man. Then Roberts' eyelids twitched.

Sage quickly pulled off his coat and laid it across Robert's torso. Leaning down he said, "Sir, I'm going for help. Don't move, I'll be right back." The man made no response nor did he move.

Sage ran pell-mell for the street, leaping over rubble and splashing through puddles. Fortune must have been looking down because, when he exited the building, Sage spied a policeman at the end of the block. Two minutes later the officer was racing to a telephone and Sage was running back into the building.

As the rain strengthened, all Sage could think to do was get on his hands and knees over the man's head, his back serving as a roof. For what seemed an eternity, Sage arched over the unconscious Roberts.

Finally, help arrived. Roberts was loaded onto a stretcher and carried to a waiting wagon. Sage's coat was filthy but he donned it before slipping away.

Minutes later he stood outside the Sherlock building where those exiting gave him a very wide berth for good reason. His clothes were black from head to toe and dripping wet. Climbing to the fourth floor he opened a door and stepped into the modest office.

"I need to see the manager, Mr. Stone," he told the clerk sitting at a desk just inside.

The young man promptly stood up and left the room. When he returned he was followed by an older man whose gray eyes swept Sage from head to toe before he said, "I'm Jasper Stone, the manager. How can I help you? Is it about a fire?"

"It's Mr. Roberts. Someone hit him over the head and hid his body inside a burned-out umbrella factory. He's on his way to the hospital."

Blood drained from Stone's face. "I don't understand. He was checking on that last fire. Why would he be attacked? Is he going to be okay?"

"I don't know if he's going to make it. He was unconscious when I found him and never came to before they put him in the wagon."

The young man slipped from the room at Sage's first words. He quickly returned with a coat and hat that he gave to Stone. The other man put them on. "Which hospital?" he asked.

"St. Vincent's."

"Will you go with me a ways? I don't want to waste time." He turned to the clerk. "Hurry, Roger! Find a cab, send it to Mr. Roberts' home to pick up his wife and take her to the hospital," he ordered. The young man ran from the office, followed by Stone and Sage.

When they reached the ground floor, Roger was already speaking to a cabbie. Stone hailed another hansom and seconds later the two of them were heading toward the hospital.

Stone turned to him. "Who are you?"

"Name's John Miner. I'd shake your hand but I'm a bit grubby at present."

"How did you come to find Roberts? Were you scavenging at the factory?"

"No, not scavenging. Looking for clues."

The other man's brow knotted. "Maybe you better explain yourself, Mr. Miner."

Sage told him about hunting for Hosier and his belief that someone had framed James Cooper for the arsons. When he finished talking, Stone stared at the horse trotting ahead of them. Then he turned to Sage.

"I didn't know Andy was missing. If someone's attacked Roberts, it's hard not to imagine the worst. Roberts is one of my inspectors. He's been on special detail. I've had him investigating those arson fires. Folks think it's some kind of deranged firebug but we're not so sure."

"Who is 'we'?" Sage asked, his question triggering another thoughtful gaze forward by Stone who finally turned to him, his lips a narrow line. "It's not my place to say. At least not right now. I need to get to the hospital and see about Wally. Take care of his wife. They're new in town and she has no one here. How can I reach you?" Stone asked.

Sage gave him Gray's name and address, knocked to halt the cab and got down. As he watched the vehicle roll away he smiled grimly. He didn't know all that the Fire Underwriters were up to but he intended to find out.

He walked up the street until a thought stopped him. He'd never mentioned Andy Hosier's first name, yet Stone already knew it. Why would the manager of the Fire Underwriters' Board be familiar with the first name of a mere extraman?

As Sage stood on the curb, he had the sudden sense that he was, at last, on the right track. The arson fires, Andy Hosier's disappearance and the attack on Roberts were connected. At least, he hoped so, because it meant he was one step closer to finding Andy and freeing James Cooper.

FOURTEEN

"Yesterday morning you were feeding the horses when I came in to talk to Andy. Do you remember that?" Sage asked.

Abner, one of the full time firefighters, tugged on his sweeping mustache as he fished around in his memory, then he nodded. "Yup, as a matter of fact I do because, before you came in that day, me and Andy was having a discussion."

"About the union?" Sage asked.

"Maybe," the man said cautiously thereby confirming that Andy hadn't entirely stopped his organizing work.

"Was anyone else down here in the garage, anyone who could have overheard the two of you talking?"

"Nah, Andy's real careful about that ever since somebody messed with his boots." The fellow stood there, looking expectant.

"Do you remember when Andy and I left?"

"Sure, I remember."

"Did Andy come back to the station after that?"

"Yup, he was in the middle of tinkering on the engine. He wanted to get a part cleaned and re-installed quick like."

"Do you remember when he left again?"

The man scratched his head. "You know, that was kinda strange."

Sage's heart leapt. "What was strange?"

"Well, a messenger came with a note for him. A kid on a bicycle. Andy read the note and got real excited. Wiped the grease off his hands and skedaddled. Luckily, he'd finished up the work on the engine or else Ollie would have been mad."

"Why?"

The fellow gave an aren't-you-ignorant smirk before saying, "Well, you sure can't push out water with an engine that's tore apart."

"Did Andy ever come back after that?"

"Nope, never saw him again. It's worrying. Andy wouldn't run off and leave Ollie to run the engine without help."

Sage took off his hat and ran his fingers through his hair. Another dead end. "Is Ollie around?"

"Yup. He's upstairs. You can go on up if you want."

Ollie's look was glum as he sat alone at the table. Sadie was at his feet, her ear cocked toward the top of the stairs. Both man and dog came alert when Sage entered the room. Seeing their looks of hopeful expectation, Sage slowly shook his head.

Ollie sighed and Sadie's head dropped back down onto her paws. "Gol durn it! Where's that boy got to?" Ollie whispered once Sage had taken a chair.

"Still working on it," Sage answered just as quietly. "I wondered. Can I look at Andy's turnout bag and other belongings? Maybe something in there will give us a clue about where he went."

"Why sure. He wouldn't mind. Even if he did, it's his fault for making us worry." Ollie strode over to a cot and pulled the canvas bag from beneath it. He tossed it on the bed, undid the drawstring and dumped the turnout gear onto the blanket. Reaching under once again, he pulled out a small cardboard box.

Sage snatched up the boots to examine the soles. The boots were brand new. He cast an inquiring look at Ollie.

"We all pitched in and bought him new boots. It was the least we could do since one of us must have ruined them. Seemed fitting to make the culprit pay something to replace them, even if we don't know who he is."

"You never figured out who did it?"

Ollie just shook his head and carefully lifted the lid on the cardboard box. Inside there were a few trinkets and a small green book.

Sage picked up the book and read the author's name aloud, "'Horatio Alger.' Andy was a reader?"

"Every spare minute. That book there was his bible. Only book he owned. The rest he borrowed from that new public library. He acted like he'd died and gone to heaven when that library opened last year."

Sage turned the worn book over in his hands. A blank slip of paper served as a bookmark. Opening to that page he read aloud the underlined words, "The dying man's last words to his son were 'To get ahead in your life, my son, work hard, be honest and respectable.'"

"Why does he have so few possessions?" Sage wondered aloud.

"Wahl, like the boy in that book, Andy is an orphan. Folks died of typhoid. He and his sister grew up at the Hillside Poor Farm out Jefferson Road way. That's probably why he saves practically every penny he earns. Always talking about them owning their own home. Big dream of his."

"I seem to remember him saying that his sister lives here in town." Sage said.

Ollie nodded sadly. "She was here early this morning, asking about him. It wasn't an easy trip for her. She's about to have a baby."

"What did she say?"

"She's upset. He was supposed to eat supper at her house last night. He never showed up. She said he never misses her suppers unless he's out fighting fires."

Sage wore his John Miner-Sunday-best outfit when he entered the big Victorian that someone had chopped up into cheap apartments. The front door was unlocked, so he climbed the elaborately wood paneled staircase to the second floor. The apartment door opened immediately at his knock. A very pregnant young woman looked inquiringly out, her eyes red from weeping.

"Excuse me ma'am. I'm looking for Andy Hosier's sister, Mrs. Violet Baldwin?"

She paled and her knees buckled. Sage quickly grabbed her forearms so she wouldn't fall. "Excuse me," she mumbled as he helped her inside. A quick glance showed a single room, one window, a small kitchen area and a bed against the wall.

She sat in one of the two chairs then looked up, with alarm, at the stranger she'd allowed through the door. "Thank you, Mister . . . ?"

"My name's John Miner. I'm a friend of Andy's. I'm trying to find him."

Her eyes filled with tears. "I don't know where he is. I went to the firehouse. They don't know where he is either."

Sage handed her a handkerchief. "Yes, I know. I have people out looking for him," he told her.

She straightened and her strain eased. She gave him a weak smile. "I'm sorry. I'm not usually so missish. The baby's due soon and . . ."

"And you are worried about Andy."

"More than I can say. This isn't like him. We were orphaned when I was twelve and he was ten. We didn't have any relatives so they declared us paupers and sent us to the poor farm. All those years we only had each other. Even now, it's just me, Andy, and Jimmy, my husband. He's an orphan too."

"You've heard nothing at all from Andy?"

"No, and he is always so careful to stay in touch. Last night, he was supposed to come here for my birthday." She glanced at a half eaten cake that sat on the counter beneath a glass dome. Eyes wide with worry, she looked at him. "He'd didn't show up or send a message or anything."

The tears seemed about to start again, so Sage spoke quickly, "Like I said, we're definitely searching for him. If he wanted to get away, is there some place he might go?"

She shook her head. "Just here," she said in a small voice.

"Does he have any friends besides you, your husband and the men at the firehouse? Someone he might stay with?"

"No, that's what has me so worried. And, I . . ." she broke off and stared at the sky outside the window.

"What?" Sage prodded.

"It was hard at the poor farm. We worked constantly and were hungry all the time. The farm manager believed in whipping us kids. Me and Andy, we took care of each other. After a while..." She fell silent.

"'After awhile', what?"

She gulped in some air and looked at him imploringly. "Please don't think I'm tetched in the head but, after a while, it got so we could tell what the other of us was feeling, even when we were apart."

"You're saying you can sense Andy?"

She nodded. "Yes and he's in big trouble. He's hurt and he's afraid. I feel his spirit reaching out to me."

"But you sense he's alive?" Sage asked surprised to feel a little tingle of hope. He didn't believe in psychics but apparently, at this point, he was willing to latch onto any favorable information, regardless of its source.

She nodded.

"You have no idea where he is?"

She shook her head. "No, I can only feel him. I can't see him or where he is."

Sage got to his feet, "Well, I better get out there looking. If you hear from him or get any ideas about where he might be, please let Ollie at the firehouse know. I'll be checking in with him."

She stood and trailed him to the door. Once in the hallway he turned to look down into her woebegone face. "We'll find him," he promised.

"Andy's my baby's only uncle. I need him," she said.

"Good Lord, surely you're not that desperate!" Mae's voice came from behind his shoulder.

Sage glanced down at the newspaper on the kitchen table. The headlines were big and bold—"Burdah Bernique, Know Thy Future, Clairvoyant Extraordinare!" and "Sir Francis Drake, the World's Greatest Living Psychic."

"Not yet, but I'm getting there," he answered. "Just wondered if there's something to it."

"What's sent your thoughts galloping in that direction?"

Sage folded the newspaper and gestured at the chair across from him. After checking that Mozart's kitchen was running smoothly, she plopped down. "Still no luck in finding Andy?" she asked.

"No, Fong's people have looked everywhere. There's no sign of him."

"So you are thinking of consulting a seer?"

"Not hardly. It's just that Andy's sister seems to think she's somehow connected to him that way. She says he's alive but hurt."

"Could be something to it."

"Really? You believe in that hocus pocus stuff?"

Mae shrugged. "Our family's had a seer or two. Not like that," she gestured to the folded newspaper, "Nothing public or money-making. In fact, we didn't talk about it to outsiders. But, if one of us wanted to know the future or find something we lost, we'd go to Aunt Moira and she'd haul out her crystal ball."

Sage snorted derisively and said, "That must have been exciting. Did she channel the dead?"

"You scoff but that Conan Doyle fellow believes in psychics."

"His character, Sherlock Holmes, uses logic."

"From what I've read, he also uses cocaine. But Doyle uses psychics in real life."

"I don't know," Sage said, shaking his head.

"That right. You don't. None of us do. So, you might as well believe the sister and get to cracking. You've still got a life to save." She stood, grabbed a stack of clean plates and headed for Mozart's dining room.

Sage didn't move because he couldn't think where to go. Then Matthew, Ida's nephew came through the kitchen door. The lanky redhead looked strong and seemed to have recovered from the horrors he'd experienced the year before. Not every sixteen year old could survive seeing the brutal murder of his brother and a jail stint as an accused murderer.

"Matthew, how was school today?" Sage asked by way of greeting.

"Pretty keen, Mr. Adair. We're reading H.G. Well's *War of the Worlds*. It's enough to scare the pants off a fellow."

"You still carrying messages for folks on that bike of yours'?"

"Yah, sure. Business is slow because of the rain and all."

"Do you think you could find out whether any of your fellow messengers carried a note yesterday to a firefighter by the name of Andy Hosier? He was at the Station 1 firehouse."

Matthew nodded and turned around, heading for the back door. Slapping on his tight cap he asked, "Same deal as always? You'll pay for their information and time?"

"You bet," Sage replied with a grin.

After Matthew departed, Sage sat puzzling over his next step. When a knock sounded on the back door, he was still staring into space, oblivious to the bustle around him.

FIFTEEN

They met in Stone's office. The head of the Fire Underwriter's board was pale and he'd aged in the few short hours since Sage had last seen him.

"Did Mr. Roberts make it?" Sage asked, dreading the answer.

"They hit him too hard." Stone's voice was muted.

"Cripes, I'm sorry," was all Sage could think to say.

"At least his wife got to the hospital in time to say goodbye. That wouldn't have happened if you hadn't found him, sent for help and come to tell me." Stone lapsed into silence. Then he drew a shaky breath, straightened in his chair and leaned forward over his desk. This time his voice was insistent. "What we need to know now, Mr. Miner, is exactly why you were looking for Andy Hosier and how you came to be in that burned out factory." Stone raised a finger and added, "And, how you knew to come to me. These are not idle questions, sir."

"Just who is this 'we'?" Sage asked.

Frustration lowered Stone's brows and Sage spoke to forestall an outburst. "Look, I suspect that you and I are on the same side. So, I will tell you this: Andy Hosier is a friend and his safety matters to me. Additionally, I find these arson fires suspicious, so much so that I have been doing my own investigating. I sure the hell don't believe any young black kid started them. Just like I knew Andy didn't start them when he was accused."

Those points yielded nods from Stone who relaxed in his chair. "You're right, we are on the same side. Roberts didn't believe the Cooper kid is an arsonist, either. Especially since there's still a firebug on the loose, even though he's using a different method. That's why Roberts was at the umbrella factory. He was looking for evidence."

"Who is responsible for the fires?" Sage asked.

"Unfortunately, all we have now is speculation." Stone's compressed lips signaled that would be the extent of his answer.

"Okay, then, who is the "we" you keep referencing?"

Stone's sidewise glance out his office window told Sage that the full answer to this question wouldn't be forthcoming. "Why, the Underwriters Board of course," Stone finally said.

"Who else? Is it someone Andy was working with? Someone who sent him a message that made him drop what he was doing and leave the firehouse? It had to be from someone he knew, someone he trusted. Did you send him a message like that?"

Stone shook his head. "I've never met Andy Hosier. Nor have I ever sent him any messages."

"Then who? Who else is working with you that might have sent a message to Andy?"

Stone blew out a gust of frustrated air. "As I said, I am not at liberty to say who else is involved."

It was clearly useless to keep asking so Sage remained silent, wondering why Stone had summoned him. He found that out when Stone switched topics.

"What exactly is it that you do for a living, Mr. Miner?"

"Odd jobs. Sometimes I work in the woods."

"I take it that you don't have a job right now?"

Sage shook his head, wondering what was coming next.

"How about you do some work for the Board?"

"I guess that would depend on the kind of work."

"I heard that you've been assisting with Station 1's fire engine. Would you be willing to work as an extraman, doing the same thing? Pay's not great but it's something. The Board will add a little extra for your trouble."

Sage's brow wrinkled as he pondered how the manager of the Underwriters' Board could offer him a job working for the city's fire department.

Stone misinterpreted Sage's hesitation and rushed to reassure. "We know you haven't been trained to fight fires but apparently you're good at shoveling coal. That's all you'd be doing." Stone paused to study Sage a moment before continuing, "Except for one more thing. We need you to observe and report on the spectators who show up at the fires. See if the same fellow keeps popping up." Stone hesitated a second before adding one more task, "And, tell me if anything unusual seems to be happening around the firehouse."

Awareness pushed Sage back in his chair. He studied the man who radiated grief and worry. "That's what you had Andy doing, isn't it?" Sage said quietly.

Stone looked down at his clenched hands and slowly relaxed them. "Yes, that's exactly what Andy was doing," he said.

Sage studied the Cooper's home. Something wasn't right. Then he saw it. Boards covered the front window and one side of the tidy, one-story cottage was blotchy, as if someone had thrown paint at it.

"Far's I'm concerned, them folks got exactly what they deserved," said a woman's voice behind him. He turned to see a tall, gaunt woman standing at her gate, her upper lip twisted by a sneer.

Sage took a moment to study her. Food stains dotted the woman's bib apron. It covered a faded dress with an uneven, raggedy hem. "What you mean?" he asked.

"Their boy's the one who's been setting those fires. That's what comes of letting them mingle with decent folk. My husband says Oregon law don't let 'em live here if we don't want them. I say they better move out. Go live with their own kind somewhere else." She crossed her arms over her flat chest and stared a challenge at him.

Sage rose to the bait. "Actually, the civil war changed all that. Those Oregon laws violate the U.S. Constitution and aren't enforced. Everybody's supposed to be treated equal."

"That don't matter. Folks shouldn't stay where they're not wanted. Putting on airs and all that."

"Edna Hoge! For shame!" scolded a voice from the yard next door. A round woman of middle age laid down her rake, opened her gate and stalked toward them up the sidewalk, anger scrunching her eyebrows together.

Reaching them, she stepped right up to the taller woman to shake a finger at her. "I cannot believe what I hear coming out of your mouth. How can you talk about Frances that way? When you were so sick with pneumonia, she brought you soup. When your husband broke his leg, she sent that boy of hers over here to mow your lawn. This is how you repay her? Shame on you!"

Although the woman was irate, Sage was not inclined to calm her tirade.

Hoge was briefly taken aback but then blustered. "Now, Molly. I ain't saying Frances Cooper's a bad colored but look at the trouble that family's brought to folks around here. All them fires cost good people their homes."

Molly's chin jutted forward aggressively. "That was none of their making, I guarantee you that. Young James is a fine boy. He studies hard and helps his folks. Neither one of us has a son as decent as him. If he set anything on fire, I'll eat that pile of leaves I just raked up."

She turned on Sage. "You better not be here to cause the Coopers more trouble. If you are, I'll fetch my husband to teach you a thing or two."

Sage backed away and held up his hands. "No, ma'am. I won't be making any trouble for them. What happened to their house?"

"Some fool threw a brick through their front window and painted nasty stuff on the wall last night. Poor Frances was home by herself. Cowards! Soon's we heard the glass break, I sent Elbert right over. He's the one who boarded up the windows and covered up the nasty words."

Sage noticed that Edna was retreating up the walkway to her house. "I got to go check on the cake I'm baking," she told them before turning tail and scuttling inside.

"Humph," the woman called Molly said, "Probably was her boy that done it. He's a lazy, no-good idiot just like his pa." With that, the little fireball turned and left. A smile twitched his lips. His mother would definitely like Miz Molly.

Left alone on the sidewalk, Sage crossed the street and mounted the two steps onto the Cooper's porch. Before he reached the front door, a figure jumped up from a low chair and blocked his way. It was a black man of middle age whose stance said he was tensely resolute.

"Pardon me, sir. May I know your business here?" he asked.

"Name's John Miner. I'm here to see Mrs. Cooper. I'm a friend of Angus Solomon's."

At that name, the man relaxed and, without another word, he stepped forward to knock a code on the front door. Another black man opened it. After mentioning Solomon's name, Sage was ushered into the house.

Through a wide archway he saw that the boarded up windows made the front room dim and that, indeed, glass was missing from one of them. A small woman sat in a rocking chair next to a Franklin stove. She stood when he entered the room.

"Mrs. Cooper? My name is John Miner," he said.

"Yes, I am Frances Cooper. I know that you are Mr. Solomon's friend. He told me that you might come. You are welcome. I apologize for making you run the gauntlet. Our friends, Mr. Tanner here and Mr. Randolph out on the porch, have decided they need to stand guard. We had some trouble last night and I am alone here because my . . ." She gave herself a little shake and said, "But of course you know. Please, Mr. Miner, take a seat. May I offer you some coffee?" Her words were soft-spoken and educated.

Sage sat, noting as he did, the respectable tidiness of the room. She was the same with well-dressed with hair carefully styled around a delicate face the color of wild honey. Jealousy was probably why the bitter woman across the street resented her.

"No ma'am, I don't need any coffee. I apologize for my intrusion but I'm helping your lawyer, Mr. Gray, with your son's case. I stopped by his office and he asked me to inform you that, unfortunately, the judge refused bail for your husband and son."

She looked stricken but recovered quickly, giving a dignified nod and saying, "I expected as much but hoped otherwise. Does Mr. Gray know what the police are doing? Whether they are investigating anyone else?"

Sage wasn't happy with the answer he had to give. "Gray said that your husband has confessed. They are keeping your son because he's the one the witness identified and because your husband's confession does not ring true. He couldn't identify the buildings burned nor the method used to set them afire. He claims that's because he was drunk every time. They don't believe him."

She pressed her lips together to stop their trembling, looked down at the floor and then up at Sage, her large, dark eyes earnest. "Neither my husband nor my son started those fires."

Sage nodded but said nothing.

After a beat she said, "My husband has a strong character. Despite being born to poor Louisiana sharecroppers, he obtained an education. He's an award-winning newspaper editor. He can take care of himself. But James is just a boy. He's been raised gentle. Tell me, are they letting him stay with his father?"

"I am afraid not, though Mr. Cooper's cell is nearby. I stopped at the police station to talk to the sergeant. He said he's keeping James separate from the other prisoners. So, your son is uncomfortable but safe."

She nodded grimly but remained silent—doubtless picturing both son and husband in the city's dank lockup.

Sage pressed on to the real reason he'd come. "Mrs. Cooper, does James have any enemies? Anyone who might try to frame him for the arsons?"

She hesitated and then said, "My husband and I discussed that after James was arrested. We suspect a young white man named Edward Orpin. He was in school with James but then dropped out. James is friends with a white girl that Orpin fancies. Unfortunately, for him, the girl does not like Orpin in return. They fought a few days ago and that's when James was first arrested."

"What do you know about Orpin?"

"Just that he lives with his grandmother and works as a plumber's helper now and again. They live one street over in a yellow house. He likes to drink and run with the ladies according to Edna. She's the lady who lives across the street."

"I believe I've met Edna. Bit of a busybody isn't she?"

Mrs. Cooper scowled fleetingly but she merely said, "Edna doesn't have it easy."

"What does this Orpin fellow look like?"

"He's about seventeen. Around five feet eight inches tall, slender with dark brown hair. He's got a weak chin, small mouth, long nose and buggy eyes with pouches underneath them." She raised her shoulders and let them drop. "To be frank, I don't know how he gets ladies interested in him. I doubt he has any money. Certainly his grandmother has very little."

Sage stood. "Thank you very much for your time, Mrs. Cooper. This has been helpful."

She also stood and reached out a slim hand to shake. "Thank you for your help, Mr. Miner. Mr. Solomon told me that you are a good man. My family appreciates your assistance."

Sage headed for the door but then paused. "You won't be staying here by yourself will you?"

She sighed but said, "No, not right away anyway. Our friends are pretty insistent about performing guard duty. And Molly and her husband—they live across the street—are keeping an eye out for me."

"Good. But, if that changes, please send word to Mr. Gray."

She looked puzzled but nodded and said, "Okay, I'll do that."

Once outside, Sage headed for the next street over. It was supper time and already dark. Still, he'd like to at least get a look at the Orpin fellow.

Darkness had brought a wind to slant the fitful raindrops. There was no place to shelter. So he stood a few steps down a basement stairwell and studied Orpin's home. Given the grandmother, that the trashy front yard and peeling paint had to be Orpin's neglected responsibility. Standing there, he breathed deep. The wind was pushing the neighborhood's smoke before it, leaving the air smelling clean—an aspect of the Pacific Northwest he liked best.

Passersby gave him curious looks but didn't pause. Everyone was eager to reach someplace warm and dry. When the lowering clouds let loose a pounding deluge he gave up. Either Orpin was already inside and unlikely to leave or, he was out on the town and unlikely to return home soon.

"My heavens, look at what the cat drug in," exclaimed Ollie when Sage arrived sopping wet. "Come on, let's get you some coffee and dry clothes," he urged and turned toward the stairs.

"Wait. Ollie, can we talk down here first?"

The other man paused and looked anxiously at Sage. "It's not Andy is it? The kid's not dead is he?"

"No, I haven't heard that he is." Sage glanced around. They seemed to be alone except for the horses. Still. Sage moved closer. "Ollie, I need to trust you. Can I do that?

The other man's eyes widened but he said, "If it will help you find Andy, I'll keep my lips buttoned tighter than a church lady's bodice."

Sage handed over the piece of paper Stone had given him.

Ollie looked at it and then up at Sage. "Looks like Campbell's assigned you to me as an extraman. Does that mean he doesn't think Andy's coming back?" Anger flushed the engineer's wrinkled neck.

"No! We're still searching everywhere for Andy. When he returns, he'll take over the same job. But, Ollie, Andy was more than an extraman."

Despite them being alone, Sage lowered his voice. "Ollie, Andy was gathering information about the arson fires. With your help, I'm going to be doing the same thing."

Ollie stared at him for a moment. "That black kid isn't the firebug," he stated flatly.

Sage shook his head. "No, someone else is behind the arsons."

After another long moment of staring, Ollie nodded thoughtfully and said, "Okay then. Guess I better introduce the guys to my new extraman. But I gotta let 'em know that you're just temporary. The fellows really like Andy." He turned and headed up the stairs.

SIXTEEN

Worry and the firefighters' snoring and snorting kept Sage sleepless and staring at cracked ceiling plaster that looked ready to fall. He was tense and knew it came from knowing that this lull was short-lived. At any moment the firehouse bell's shrill ring would send the sleeping men out to confront a danger everyone else was running from.

The sleepers' noise didn't help. Living here was like being back in a logging camp, he mused, except there was no firehouse cook. Instead, the firefighters were the cooks, performing the traditionally feminine task with the easy self-confidence of men whose courage was unquestioned.

After dinner, while he and Ollie washed the dishes, Sage had asked, "Why do you firefighters do it? It sure can't be your measly pay."

Ollie chuckled and answered readily, "Partly to help folks. Partly the excitement. It's like being in a war. But for us the enemy is fire, which means we don't have to kill anyone. And, if we're lucky, victory means that we've saved people's lives, livelihoods, and possessions. That feels damn good."

He glanced over his shoulder at the men playing cards or reading on their cots. Turning back to Sage he said, "And, it's the fellowship too. We trust each other with our lives. You don't get that tight a bond in very many jobs."

Fellowship is a powerful feeling, Sage now mused as he lay in the dark. It soothes and lightens the soul. He knew that because he shared a similar fellowship with Fong, Solomon, Gray, Hanke, his mother, and a few others. They also had an enemy to overcome. For them, victory meant economic and social justice. It was a war with victims too—victims like Wally Roberts. Grief for that loss slid in like fog as he recalled Roberts stooping to pet the stray dog and handing a coin to the beggar. Sage let that grief fill his heart, honoring the man he'd never met. Then he let it slip away. It was too late to save Roberts, but damn it, he was going to save Andy. That certitude overcame the worry and he finally slept.

Deep in the night, the city bell boomed and the station's bell shrilled. Around him, men were leaping from their cots, jumping into their gear and running for the pole while he was still surfacing from sleep. He hurried to follow, his boots hitting the ground floor while he was still only half awake.

The stall gates swung open with the movement of a single lever and the horses trotted out to take their place between vehicle shafts. The overhead harnesses dropped onto their backs and seconds later, the big doors flew open and the horses charged out with Sadie running beside the lead horse, her ears flapping and her bark sounding the alert. As their procession rumbled down the street, the huge city bell kept tolling, summoning more firefighters, extramen and volunteers.

The combination of cold night air and surging excitement drove away the last vestiges of sleep. The crew was heading north, away from downtown. "Where's the fire?" he shouted at Ollie over dog bark, bell clang, wagon wheel rumble and horseshoe clatter.

"Central dispatch signaled it's a three-alarm on the eastern edge of Nob Hill. Three-alarm's a big one!" Ollie shouted back.

Sure enough, from blocks away they saw huge embers shooting skyward and falling down, still burning. Another firehouse crew was on the scene, their fire engine huffing steam, their hoses shooting water. They'd cleared the street for incoming crews by moving their own vehicles far away. Neighborhood boys had already unhitched the first fire horses and were walking them in an open field a block away.

Sage's crew quickly jumped to their assigned tasks, moving with precision midst a pandemonium of billowing smoke, roaring flames, shouting firefighters, hissing steam engine and clamoring spectators. Hoses were uncoiled and joined to nearby hydrants, the firebox was lit and Sage began stoking coal. Ollie connected hydrant and fire hoses to the engine before turning to his gauges and valves. Only after the steam engine achieved pumping pressure did Sage pause to survey the conflagration. It was a furniture shop, which meant there'd be wood, fabric and glue for fuel. Worse, other buildings pressed close on every side, including a wood-frame boarding house. The first crew was wetting down its roof and walls.

"It's a hot one," Ollie remarked as he came to stand beside Sage and pointed. "See that fellow over there wetting the wall?"

At Sage's nod he continued, "That's Jimmy Baldwin, Andy's brother-in-law. He's a great firefighter," Ollie said with admiration.

"Why's he got that tied around his upper arm?" queried Sage.

Ollie chuckled. "Oh, the fellows have been teasing him over that. It's a purple ribbon. He took to wearing it after Violet got pregnant. Says it reminds him of his wife and gives him good luck. Ties it on before every fire."

The young firefighter, along with others, began positioning a long ladder against the two-story building. Baldwin snatched up a hose and was soon at the top of the ladder. From there, he sprayed water onto the nearby roofs and the burning furniture shop.

Sage shoveled in more coal, closed the firebox door and went back to watching the firefighters work. Over the tumult, he heard a shout and saw the figures at the bottom of Jimmy Baldwin's ladder gesturing and shaking their heads. When Sage looked up, he saw that Baldwin's hose no longer pumped water and, instead, was shut off and looped over a ladder rung. Baldwin, however, was climbing higher with the clear intent of mounting the roof.

"Oh, cripes," Ollie moaned.

"What, what?" Sage demanded.

"That young fool's going to climb onto the roof."

"What's wrong with that? It's not on fire."

Ollie turned to him, obviously worried. "Jimmy's been pouring water onto that flat roof. It'll be one big puddle. Look at all them wires strung over the top of it."

Sage got it. "You mean he could be electrocuted?"

Ollie nodded grimly, "We have to call so many electric companies to shut off the power. Until we get the word, we got to figure there's still a live wire up there—and we ain't got that word yet."

"Why's he doing it?"

Ollie shouted to the firefighters clustered around the ladder's foot. "Why's he climbing up there?"

One of them shouted a single word back, "Cat!"

Ollie turned to Sage. "He's trying rescue a cat."

Sage stood like the others, watching as Baldwin reached the ladder's top rung and reached out a hand to steady himself as he stepped off the ladder and onto the roof.

As Ollie feared, disaster struck. Horrified, Sage saw Baldwin grab the roof's tin-sheathed parapet, only to immediately stiffen and fall backward. An instant later, the wooden boardwalk partially collapsed under his falling body. The firefighter had landed flat on his back.

As Sage reached him, Baldwin opened his eyes and gasped out one word, "Ouch," before his eyes shut once again. His crewmates shoved Sage roughly aside, loaded Baldwin onto to a stretcher and ran to load him into a waiting hose wagon. The horse galloped away toward the nearby hospital.

Back at the engine, Sage told Ollie, "He opened his eyes," hoping that was a good sign.

The engineer shook his head glumly and started checking gauges. The routine back in place, Sage again stoked the firebox.

During pauses in his shoveling, Sage studied the crowd, trying to memorize each face. Stone had told him that firebugs often returned to wallow in the excitement. No one looked familiar. But then, he'd paid no attention to the spectators at the previous fires.

Dawn was a bright knife edge in the eastern sky as Sage fought to stay awake on the ride back to the firehouse. Only the horses remained frisky. The firefighters themselves were subdued. They'd extinguished the fire and saved the neighboring buildings but one of their own was severely injured. At least, that was the first word coming back from the hospital.

At the station, better news awaited them. Although Baldwin would remain hospitalized, the doctors thought he'd pull through. He had broken ribs but they said the fall had jolted his electrocuted heart back to life.

"Thank God for small favors,'" said Ollie with a grin.

Sage, however, was thinking of the very pregnant Violet. She'd said they had no relatives in town. Her apartment was far from the hospital—too far for her to walk. She'd be all alone with her fears.

He wearily climbed the stairs with the other fellows and removed his gear. Unlike them, however, he did not collapse onto the cot. Instead, he grabbed his coat and headed back down the stairs.

He found Mae in Mozart's kitchen polishing silverware, a cup of coffee at her elbow.

"Good grief," she exclaimed. "You look like you've been hauled through a knothole backwards."

He dropped into the chair across from her. "Hard night. I've got to get some sleep but first, I need your help with something," he said.

She stopped polishing and looked at him closely. "Tell me."

So, he told her about the fire and Jimmy Baldwin's attempted cat rescue. "So, like I told you, his wife is about to give birth. There's no one to take care of her, plus she's going to want to see Jimmy but they live far from the hospital. And, their apartment is too small for her to put up a guest."

Mae stood, untied her apron strings and lifted the bib from around her neck. "I'll go straight to her now. Then, I'll find us a bigger place to stay near the hospital. There's lots of boarding houses around it. Don't worry about Violet Baldwin. And, don't worry about Mozart's. Mr. Fong and Horace can cover for us. You go back to the firehouse and get some sleep so you can get busy finding her brother and catching the varmints behind all this upset."

Sage's head felt full of molasses. Why was he shaking? Ollie. Ollie trying to wake him.

"What, what is it?" Sage mumbled.

"There's a Chinese fellow downstairs, says he needs to speak to you. He wouldn't come inside."

Shafts of light streaming through the east-facing windows meant it was still morning. Sage rolled off his cot, donned his pants and stumbled downstairs. Outside, sunlight chased the fog wisps rising from the cobbles. Fong stood nearby, his shoulders hunched against the cold.

"What is it, what's happened?" Sage asked.

"Cousin watching Cooper house say rough men pay too much attention to house. Cousin worried. Maybe you should come," Fong said.

"Two men were standing guard. Are they gone?"

Fong shook his head, thought a moment then said. "Rough men are white. Guards black. They fight, black men get blame. Also, five white men, two black men."

Sage ran back inside the firehouse, told Ollie he had to leave and was soon trotting down the opposite side of the street from Fong. They seldom went anywhere together for fear of attracting attention. So, while their rapid pace might get noticed, it would be far less noticeable than if they were running side by side.

They arrived at the Coopers just as five roughly dressed men began crowding into the tiny front yard. The Coopers' two friends stood at the top of the porch stairs, hands at their sides. Although outnumbered, they clearly intended to make a stand. A door slammed across the street and a white man hurried up. He brushed past Sage, Fong and the hostile thugs, mounted the steps and turned. Sage was willing to bet this was Elbert, husband to the diminutive leaf raker, Molly.

"You men are bothering our neighbors and you need to leave right now," Elbert told them. Elbert was nearly as small as his wife but determination had his shoulders squared.

A growl rumbled through the ruffians. "What? You think a puny runt like you can take us on?" shouted a burly fellow to the delight of his companions.

Sage put a staying hand on Fong's forearm before pushing forward himself. Better not to insert a Chinese element into the conflict. In this city, white racism toward Asians was as strong as that toward blacks. Better that Fong jump in only if his help was needed.

Sage moved to the bottom of the steps and also turned to confront the aggressors but he said nothing. The Cooper's friends were in charge.

"You might whup us, but you'll get hurt too," called Mr. Tanner, the Cooper friend Sage had met the day before. Tanner spoke calmly with no hint of fear.

"You shut your mouth," yelled a cretin standing at the back. "It's five against three and one-half—them's damn good odds."

His shout acted as a rallying cry, sending the attackers surging forward, fists raised. Those on the porch didn't hesitate, quickly moving down the steps. Just before he stepped forward, Sage caught himself hoping that Fong would have no cause to criticize his student's performance.

SEVENTEEN

Elbert was first to leap into the fray, zooming past Sage to head-butt the big fellow in the forefront of the horde. His action surprised the other, sending him staggering backward. A "You go Elbert!" cry sounded from a distance. Sure enough Molly stood at her fence, cheering on her hero. Her jubilation was short lived The thug darted forward to give Elbert a powerful gut punch that knocked the small man back onto the steps.

A quick glance at the other two defenders showed they were holding their own. That left two unchallenged attackers. Time to grab a little advantage Sage thought. Silently apologizing to Mrs. Cooper for wrecking her flowerbed, he snatched two plant stakes free of foliage, each nearly three feet long. Fong had recently begun teaching him the "weaving" art. He figured he might as well attempt some of its simpler moves.

Legs separated, front and back, sticks resting on his shoulders, Sage shuffled toward the nearest man whose eyes widened at the strange movements. Then his yell brought the second man to his side. Now, Sage had two opponents.

Good, Sage told himself grimly. He snapped the sticks off his shoulder and, keeping them parallel, swung them to the right and then back, hitting the shoulder of the man on the right. Just as quickly, he swung the sticks in the opposite direction, hitting the shoulder of the second man. Both men yelped and clutched their shoulders. Sage knew from experience that the hands at the end of the hit arms were numb—incapable of striking a blow.

Before either attacker recovered, Sage stepped forward, this time swinging the stakes low, one at a time, aiming for their guts. He nailed one, but the other managed to get close enough to deliver a feeble thump to the side of Sage's head. Sage lunged toward him, swung low and walloped the man's knee. That was enough. The fellow dropped to the ground, clutched his knee and yowled.

The first man stopped clutching his stomach, straightened and advanced, blood-red with rage. This time though, he was more cautious, staying out of the sticks' range. After squinting at Sage, he grabbed a stick himself and parried Sage's next swing. To counter that defense, Sage shifted his weight onto his back foot and flashed out a high kick to the fellow's chin. The kick was powerful enough to knock the man down and nearly out.

That left just the other one who lurched to his feet and limped forward like an injured bear, his arms spread wide. Sage paused, raised an eyebrow and said, "Really?" Since the fellow kept coming, Sage dropped his sticks, grabbed one of the grasping arms, swiveled and sent the man flying past him to slam into one of the steps. He crumpled and didn't move. Sage jumped to his side, felt the man's neck pulse and let out his breath. He was still alive and his neck looked normal.

Turning to check, he saw that both Tanner and Randolph had their attackers down on the ground. Elbert was clinging to the back of the biggest attacker like an agitated monkey. Rearing backward, the small man used momentum to topple the fellow over, even as he jumped clear. Before the guy could raise his head, Elbert was astride his chest. Hauling back a fist, he let the fellow have it on the side of his jaw. That fist struck hard, fast and accurate, snapping the man's head to the side. It was a knockout punch.

Elbert got to his feet, shaking the pain from his hand. At Sage's inquiring look, he said, "Used to fight some when I was younger. Bantam weight."

Tanner and Randolph hauled their opponents upright and escorted them out of the yard. Randolph's lip was bleeding but otherwise the Coopers' three friends were fine. Sage helped drag the rest of the five attackers to the street where they revived enough to stagger toward the North End, cursing as they went.

The four defenders grinned at each other. Randolph was the first to speak, "Why thank you, Mr. Miner. That was some mighty interesting fighting. Care to teach us a few of those moves?"

"I'm still a student," Sage said and, looking around noticed that Fong was nowhere in sight. "But Mr. Solomon might be able to hook you up with my teacher."

After mutual congratulations and handshakes, Sage left. Initially he planned to head toward the firehouse. Then he remembered that the scene of last night's fire was nearby. He turned east and headed for furniture shop instead.

As he walked, he relived the fight. Except for that one feeble jab to his ear, he hadn't been touched. Recalling that blow, Sage groaned. Fong was sure to have seen it. He could imagine what Fong was going to say. Even worse were the thumps Sage would get at his next lesson since Fong sometimes used a little pain to emphasize his points.

Overhead, heavy clouds had rolled in from the west. Sheets of rain began bouncing off the wooden walkways and overflowing the dirt street's wheel ruts. Sage picked up his pace. As he walked, he eyed the mansions sitting atop a series of miniature hillocks. Most displayed Victorian architectural excess in the form of gingerbread, balconies, turrets, gables, and towers. It was not surprising that, in order to be close to their wealthiest patrons, the St. Vincent and Good Samaritan hospitals, the University of Oregon's medical school and the most exclusive boys' school, Bishop Scott Academy, had all erected ornate structures in this neighborhood. Named after the richest area in San Francisco, Portland's Nob Hill was doing its best to live up to its namesake.

Reaching the charred rubble that was once a furniture business, Sage saw that there was a small coffee shop with a good view of the burned out building. Entering, he shook the rain off his hat and noticed the owner giving him a disapproving look. Obviously, the man preferred to serve a classier clientele.

Fortunately the waitress smiled warmly, as if welcoming a friend. After ordering, Sage studied the fire scene and was still doing so when the young woman returned with his breakfast.

"We had us a fire over there last night," she told him, gesturing across the street.

"Yes, I know. I helped fight it," Sage told her, somewhat surprised at the pride in his words.

Impressed, she rushed to say, "My goodness that must have been exciting. I didn't get to see it, 'cause I live with my aunt down near the river, but folks say it was a hot one. I heard a fireman got hurt real bad. How is he? Did he die? I sure hope not, that would be a real shame what with him trying to save all the buildings and that cat. Why even this place might have burned down if it weren't for you firemen. Are you a real fireman or a volunteer?"

She finally had to pause for breath so Sage answered. "I'm a part time firefighter. And no, he didn't die but he is in the hospital."

"My lordy, that fire must have been something to see. I know a girl who lives in the boarding house across the street. She works in the laundry just two streets away. That was her cat up on the roof. Folks say the fireman was trying to save it. Ain't that something? He risked his life for a cat. Though, it is a nice cat. Sometimes, I give him milk our customers don't finish but Mr. Brackett, he doesn't like me doing that."

Sage remembered the cat. "Did your friend's cat survive?"

"Oh sure, he was here first thing this morning looking for some milk. 'Cause of all he went through, I figured he deserved some kind of treat so I gave him milk straight from the bottle but don't tell Mr. Brackett. He'd probably fire me."

Sage pantomimed sewing his lips shut with his finger and eyed the cooling scrambled eggs. Still, this was an opportunity to learn something. He began peppering the gal with a few questions of his own. "Who owns the furniture store? Has anyone said how the fire started? Have you seen anyone over there, looking around this morning?"

Glancing over her shoulder at her boss, she relaxed at seeing him conversing with the only other customer in the place. "Well," she began after taking a deep breath, "Mr. Whipple owns that furniture shop. He comes in here sometimes but I don't much like him. He's grumpy and never leaves a tip. I guess it's because he's been trying to sell the place seeing's how he doesn't have much business. Mr. Brackett says Mr. Whipple wants to go back East to live near his daughter but needs money to do it. I think he's wanting to leave because he isn't that good of a furniture builder, leastways that's what two of our rich lady customers said."

She seemed to have forgotten his other questions so he prodded her along. "Did anyone say how the fire started?"

"Well, not straight out though some were speculatin' this morning. He had that 'For Sale' sign in his window a pretty long time and there weren't no takers, apparently. Leastways it was still there yesterday, before the fire."

"They think he set it himself?"

She shook her head. "No, 'cause he was out in Hillsboro last night, visiting a cousin. That's what he told folks this morning. I speculate it must be true because it's so easy to check, you know?"

"You see anyone poking around over there this morning?"

"I sure did. Two men picked around in the smoking bits. Fact is, when it started raining, they came right over here to dry out and get some coffee. I know, 'cause I served them. Can't say as I liked them either. Sure is getting to be a lot of grumpy people hereabouts."

She leaned closer to confide in a quieter voice, "It were a fireman and a fellow in a suit. I couldn't help myself, I was ferret-curious about that fire so my ears were a'flappin' like an African elephant's. I think the man in the suit was an insurance man."

Sage had to smile. When the Lord passed out guile, this gal must have been bending over tying her shoe because she had none. "And what did those elephant ears overhear?"

"Now, that's the funny thing. I couldn't make no sense of it," she said.

Sage felt a spurt of excitement race through him. "What do you mean?"

"Well, I only heard a few words, you know?"

"Yes," Sage prompted again, aware he was holding his breath.

"That suit man said to the fireman, 'You sure nobody's figured it out?'"

"Maybe he meant figured out whether it was arson or not?"

She twisted her lips, considered his suggestion and then shook her head, dismissing it. "Nope. That weren't it. It sounded like he didn't want something figured out. Like he was afraid it'd be figured out."

"Okay, so what did the fireman say?"

"He just said, 'Don't worry.' Then he said, 'We still have that other problem. Not sure what to do about that.'"

"Did he say what the problem was?"

"Nope."

"What'd this fireman fellow look like?"

"He was kinda skinny with a mug that was long and narrow, sorta like a ferret's."

"Do you like ferrets?"

"Nah, don't like them at all. My brother had one when I was little and it bit me. Plus they're always getting into stuff."

"Daisy! Quit bothering our customer. You have dishes to wash!" The owner's admonition sent the girl hustling away.

"Long and narrow." That sounded like the station chief he'd seen at the house fire where Joey the Cockatoo died. Thoughtfully, Sage picked up his fork to find that, sure enough, his eggs were cold.

❀ ❀ ❀

"Boy Howdy, you are a popular fellow today," Ollie greeted him when Sage squished into the firehouse's living quarters. He was soaked through. Fall in Portland alternated between sunny glory and drenching wet. Lately it had been mostly the latter. But then, November was always a wet month.

"What, someone else came to see me?" Fear added an extra shiver as he stood toasting his back before the wood stove. Had something bad happened? Was his mother okay? Did Jimmy Baldwin die? Had someone found Andy's body?"

Ollie pulled a note from his pocket. "A red-haired boy on a bicycle asked for me when he learned you weren't here. He said to give you this. I didn't read it."

Matthew. Sage unfolded the paper and read, "I rented a place for me and Violet to stay near the hospital. She's holding up. You were right to send me. Her husband is awake and the doctors are hopeful. M."

Sage grinned at Ollie. "Read it yourself. It's good news."

Ollie read and smiled before looking inquiringly at Sage who said, "I sent a friend to keep Jimmy's wife company. She's going to have that baby any day now. I didn't want her to be alone. And, we moved her nearer the hospital to make it easier for her to visit Jimmy."

Ollie said nothing, only blinked rapidly, like he was peeling onions. After giving Sage a stout cuff on the shoulder, he turned away.

EIGHTEEN

"Where'd you disappear to?" Sage asked Fong when the other man entered the bedroom. Sage was grabbing clean clothes since he'd be bunking at the firehouse and helping Ollie until Andy was back on the job.

"I follow attackers back to nest."

"Where'd they go? Did you learn anything helpful?"

"Maybe. First they go lick wounds in saloon. On way, I figure out who is leader."

Sage sent Fong an inquiring glance. He wasn't sure why knowing who led a bunch of nasty toughs was all that helpful.

Fong sighed patiently and explained, "Outside saloon, leader man, he gives money to other men."

Sage pondered that bit of information—then Fong's point hit him. "If they were just a bunch of drunken louts, wanting excitement at the Cooper's expense, no one would be paying them."

Fong's eyes gleamed with satisfaction. "That it exactly," was all he said.

Sage changed his plans. Instead of heading back to the firehouse, he dressed in his fashionable John Adair duds and headed for the Portland Hotel. As he walked, he considered the meaning of Fong's discovery. Why would someone hire thugs to make trouble for the Coopers? Probably they thought it would reinforce the idea that James was the culprit. His gut was telling him that whoever was behind it had to be the same person who'd fingered Andy and then, James Cooper for the arsons.

Solomon took one look at Sage and quickly led him to the table behind the tired palm. "What has happened, John?" Solomon asked.

"Someone paid five white goons to attack the Cooper's house. We beat them back but I think it's urgent we clear the Coopers of arson."

Solomon scowled. "Who is doing this and why? B.J. is conciliatory toward the white community. Most of his paper's advertising comes from white establishments. Why would they be attacking his family?"

Sage could only shake his head before getting to the point of his visit, "Look Angus, I would like to talk to people who know B.J.—people who might know if someone has a grudge against him. His son got into a fist fight with a kid, but this situation is far too complicated to be the work of a kid."

Solomon nodded thoughtfully, a worry crease between his brows, and Sage continued, "My problem is that Fong's men are busy searching for a missing firefighter named Andy Hosier. He was the first one falsely accused of the arsons and now he's missing. Fong's posted a man to watch the Cooper's house. But he can't jump in to fight if the toughs return. It would draw unwanted attention. The most he can do is raise the alarm. That's what happened this morning. Bottom line, Mrs. Cooper needs more protection. Her two friends and the one neighbor just aren't enough."

Solomon blew out between pursed lips as he considered Sage's points. Then he said, "I have an idea. Let me go talk to one of my staff." With that, he returned to his podium and ushered two waiting customers to a table. That task concluded, he spoke to an older waiter and the two men entered the kitchen. Soon, they both returned to the dining room—the waiter to his serving duties, Solomon to Sage.

"If you are available later this evening, we'll call an emergency meeting at the Larrabee Avenue Masonic Lodge across the river. We'll get as many men there as possible."

"I've seen the Lodge. What time?"

"Nine thirty."

The afternoon rain had finally stopped, leaving a full moon to duck in and out of racing clouds. Once across the Steel Bridge, Sage turned north and soon reached the Lodge. It was a two story clapboard building with a sign proclaiming, "Enterprise Lodge of Masons, No. 47." Lights shone from the ground floor windows. Solomon was waiting just inside the entrance.

"We met a little earlier to discuss the situation among ourselves. I hope you don't mind. I thought it would save time," Solomon said while ushering Sage inside.

About twenty-five men waited. These Masons were some of the most prominent and well-respected men in Portland's black community. Accordingly, Sage had worn his best John Miner suit.

It was an elegant room with its mahogany refreshment bar, pressed-tin ceiling and decorative mouldings. Long wooden benches, similar to church pews, were arranged in a semi-circle. Once Sage took a seat, a man of about forty stood to address him. "We welcome you to our lodge. My name is Mr. Jonathan Bishop. Because it is late, we will dispense with further introductions and get right down to business. Mr. Solomon has advised us that you believe more men need to guard B.J. Cooper's home. That is Mr. Tanner and Mr. Randolph's opinion as well."

Sage nodded, relieved that he didn't have to explain.

"We have determined that rotating squads of four men each will be adequate. Is that not correct?" he asked the group. There was a murmur of assent, after which he continued, speaking directly to Sage, "Men will sleep at the Coopers during the night, with two awake and on duty at all times. In the morning, they will be replaced by a second crew, and then by a third crew in the afternoon. In this way, we will ensure Mrs. Cooper is protected around the clock."

Sage cleared his throat. "Sounds good. Also, a Chinese lookout has been posted by a friend of Mr. Solomon's. He'll alert those in the house should he see a threat. Then he'll run for more help. That's what he did this morning and it worked." The men around him nodded their approval.

"That problem solved, we now come to the question of who could be engineering these attacks against the Coopers," said Bishop. "Frankly, we are puzzled. He is a member of this lodge, so he is familiar to all of us. In fact, his money helped construct this very building And, while Mr. Cooper can be gruff at times, he is respected and has harmed no one." Again, there were nods all around.

Bishop's glance at the others signaled that he was about to say something controversial. "Mr. Solomon will have told you that some of us who work at the Portland Hotel are launching a newspaper, *The Advocate*. It will compete with Mr. Cooper's newspaper for readers and advertisers. We are doing so, not out of dislike for him personally, but because we disagree with certain of his positions."

Although Solomon had explained that difference in opinion, Sage used an inquiring look to spur Bishop into further explanation. "We believe that Booker T. Washington's meek approach is outdated and ineffective. The white race, present company excepted, must come to realize that the black man has a moral, intellectual, economic and constitutional claim to full equality. As Mr. Du Bois argues, we must speak that truth loudly and without apology. Mr. Cooper, however, persists in promulgating Mr. Washington's approach. That difference of opinion is the only conflict between some of us and Mr. Cooper. But it is, most assuredly, not the cause of the Cooper's current problem." This declaration elicited vigorous nods from everyone.

Bishop moved on to his next point. "Moreover, Mr. Cooper has good relations with the white community, so we are convinced that something other than racism is behind this attack on him. He may be a convenient scapegoat but we cannot conceive of anyone targeting his family out of hatred or revenge." Again, there appeared to be unanimous agreement among the men.

Bishop's next words held real regret, "In this regard, we are sorry we cannot identify any potential culprit. If we hear of anything to the contrary, no matter how seemingly insignificant, we will alert Mr. Solomon. In the meantime, we appreciate that you are trying to help our friend."

Sage stood, shook hands with Bishop and nodded at the others. Taking a step toward the door, he paused. "What about the Cooper's son, James? Do you know why anyone would accuse him like they have?"

They all shook their heads and Bishop said, "James is a fine young man. He's going make something of himself and certainly did not start those fires. The idea is ridiculous. To our knowledge, he has no enemies except for that one boy and Solomon says you already know about him."

Though relieved that Mrs. Cooper's safety was assured, Sage felt discouraged as he crawled under his blankets at the firehouse. Everyone else was asleep. He admired how these men could drop off the minute things calmed down. He wished he could. Instead, he lay thinking about Andy Hosier. He forced himself to envision the young man captive and alive. But where?

The sun had risen halfway to noon when he awoke, having slept soundly once he'd finally fallen asleep. Apparently the arsonist had taken the night off because the city bell hadn't rung. Lying there, Sage suddenly realized he still didn't know if the furniture shop fire had been declared an arson.

Quickly he rolled out of bed, drawing pants and shirt on over his long johns before jamming his feet into his work boots. Not seeing Ollie, he headed downstairs. Sure enough, the engineer was polishing his equipment. Ollie looked up to greet him with a smile. "You were snoozing so hard, the other fellows agreed to tippy toe around. I hope you don't mind. I told them you were out searching for Andy last night." Ollie looked a little anxious when making that confession.

"It's okay that you told them that," Sage assured him. "I was wondering, though. Did anyone determine whether someone deliberately set that furniture shop fire?"

"Wahl, that's a good question. When the fire marshal went there yesterday afternoon he didn't find evidence of it like he found at them other fires. Still, he says it was arson because there were burn patterns all over the back of the building. Accidental fires usually start in just one place. So, even though he didn't find anything, he's still calling it arson. He's thinking maybe we have us a different firebug."

"Hmm, maybe," Sage said as his thoughts rushed ahead. "You say the fire marshal looked yesterday afternoon?"

"Yup, kinda late. He said he waited until the rain stopped."

So there'd been plenty of time for someone to remove evidence, like a cap or straw. Daisy's words drifted into his head. "They was picking around the smoking bits," the waitress had said about the two men she'd seen first thing yesterday morning.

"Picking around or picking up?" he muttered softly to himself. Ollie sent him a curious look but asked no questions.

NINETEEN

"Philander, I need to speak to B.J. Cooper. Can you get me in to see him?" Sage asked his question of the lawyer's bent head when he entered Gray's office without knocking. The outer office had been empty, no doubt because it was noontime.

The startled lawyer jumped, his dropped pen sending a splatter of ink across his paper. "Criminey, Adair, didn't anyone teach you to knock?" he grumbled, as he wadded up the paper and tossed it into his wastebasket.

"Ah, jeez, I'm sorry. Between no sleep, trying to find Andy, trying to clear the Coopers, trying to protect Mrs. Cooper and playing firefighter, I'm going a little crazy."

"And you're telling me that's something new? I don't think I've ever seen you when you're not juggling at least three plates at a time. But, sure, I'll get you in to talk to Cooper."

"I hope he's got some useful information. So far, every damn lead I follow ends in a brick wall. I need something to grab onto."

Gray merely nodded, donned his coat and soon the two men were climbing the stairs into the police station. A few minutes and, a couple of dollars in the jailer's hand later, Sage stood before Cooper's cell. Gray introduced him to Cooper as his investigator on the case. Then Gray went to check on the younger Cooper in his cell around the corner.

Curiosity drew the dignified black man close to the bars. Sage spoke quickly, his voice low and urgent, "Mr. Cooper, I'm trying to discover who set the fires and why someone targeted your son to take the blame. My friend, Andy Hosier, was their first target and now he's missing. I'm sure that there's a connection. Can you think of anyone who could want to cause you or your son harm?"

"I've never heard of Andy Hosier. Who is he?" asked Cooper.

"He's a part time firefighter working out of Fire Station 1."

The other man shook his head and then said in a soft voice, "I'm afraid I don't know him. And, I have spent hours trying to determine who I might have offended. The only conflict in my life right now is with men who are starting a rival newspaper. But I know each of them well and not a one of them would stoop this low."

"I have to agree with you. In fact, they say exactly the same thing. And, they've pledged to do everything they can to help you and Mrs. Cooper."

Cooper nodded as if this was expected. Sage had to admire the man's composure. Four days, he'd been locked up in this dank basement. The heavy rain seeping through the concrete walls was sending rivulets across the floor and into Cooper's cell. And, the jail's use as a homeless dormitory meant noisy, smelly, bug infested, sleepless nights.

Sage had no choice but to speak the words that would shatter the man's calm. "Someone paid thugs to attack your house."

"Frances?" Fear crackled Cooper's voice, his composure gone.

"She's fine," Sage hurried to reassure. "Some of your friends, including your newspaper rivals, have set up a 24-hour guard. I think she's safe for now. But, we must discover who's behind this. I believe you when you say it's not anyone from the black community. I think the malefactors are white. The attackers certainly were. Are you sure you can't think of any white person you've offended? You're an influential man in this town. Influential men tend to create powerful enemies."

An ironic twinkle flashed in the other man's eyes as he answered, "My mere existence offends some white people." Before Sage could clarify, Cooper showed he understood Sage's original question, "But no, to my knowledge, I have not offended any specific white man to such a degree that he'd frame my son for arson and hire thugs to attack my home. Oh, some men are peeved that I've stopped supporting the Republican party and am now urging my people to vote for the best candidate regardless of party affiliation. Since we have over nine hundred Negro voters in this city, their votes can turn an election," he added with pride.

Sage raised his eyebrows. It was a stretch to think the current problem had anything to do with Cooper's political stance. Cooper caught this unspoken comment because he hurried to say, "No, I don't think that could be it either. Of course, I don't like the editor of *The Gazette*, and he doesn't like me. We trade newsprint barbs every now and then. But, he can harm me more with his paper than he can employing some arson scheme."

"What about your son? Does he have any enemies capable of carrying out such an elaborate frame up?"

"Good heavens no! Edward Orpin is the only person with whom James has had a conflict. But, Orpin's just a few years older than James. From what I hear, he's a rather stupid boy. I'm certain he's incapable of engineering the mayhem you describe."

For the second time that afternoon, Sage charged into an office without knocking. This time, he was trailed by the clerk who futilely tried to grasp his coat sleeve while squeaking, "Sir, sir . . . ."

Stone was in the midst of talking with two men sitting across the desk from him. Both had notebooks in their laps and pens between their fingers. Sage's abrupt entrance halted Stone in mid-sentence. He calmly studied Sage for a moment then said to the two men, "Gentlemen, if you could wait outside? We will continue our review once I have addressed the reason for this interruption."

Without a word, the men rose and returned to the reception area. "Roger, please close the door." Once they were alone, Stone said, "What is so urgent that you had to steamroll over Roger?"

"I need to know," Sage began in a raised voice. Stone glanced at the door and snapped, "Keep your voice down, Miner. These walls are thin. The others will hear."

Sage sucked in a deep breath, then said quietly, "As I was saying, I need to know exactly what you think is going on with these arson fires. I have a woman whose house is under siege by a bunch of thugs, two innocent people in jail, one of them just a kid, and Andy Hosier is still missing. I am certain it's all related and I want to know how."

Stone put his elbows on his desk and his head in his hands. When he looked up, he looked determined. "As I've told you, I can't tell you who I'm working with. I also can't tell you at this time who we suspect. We're still trying to put the pieces together. I will tell you that we think the arson attacks are for the purpose of defrauding our member insurance companies. We don't know for certain whether anyone from the fire department is involved and we don't know which insurance agents, if any, might be involved. We certainly don't know who is setting the fires. That's why we need you to observe the spectators at the scene. As I told you two days ago, firebugs like to watch the fires they set."

Sage took a seat across from Stone. "How do you plan on finding out who is involved and how long will it take?"

"Our problem is that, if a local insurance agent is involved, we won't get accurate information about the burned building from that agent. We've had to write the national offices of all the various insurers to see if they've paid out on the same addresses. It takes time. Roger out there has been working his fingers to the bone getting those letters typed and mailed. And, some of our biggest companies are proving awfully slow to respond."

Sage silently considered Stone's information. The pieces softly clicking into place was almost a physical sensation in his head. "Thank you," he said.

"Did Jimmy Baldwin die? Is Violet alright?" Sage demanded when he saw his mother in Mozart's kitchen. She sat at the table with their cook, Ida, who quickly rose and went over to the sink. She was used to the strange relationship between the restaurant owner and Mae, always sensing when they'd want privacy.

"My goodness, what's got your knickers in a twist? Everybody is just fine. Violet is sitting with Jimmy. He's recovering. She seems to be doing alright, though she's getting big as a house."

"I'm sorry about being pushy. I'm jumpy and frustrated because this mess keeps getting more and more complicated. It feels like someone's handing me a jigsaw puzzle one piece at a time."

Mae's eyes softened but she only said, "Well, I'm afraid I can't make things any easier. Fong was just here. He said to tell you that his men have scoured the North End and other places. They can't find a single clue as to where Andy might be. The only thing I can add is that Violet insists he is still alive but suffering."

Minutes later, a discouraged Sage climbed the stairs into the attic. He intended to try a Fong technique to find answers. More than once, Fong had told him, "Snake and crane good for solving problem. Thoughts slide through mind. Some pass quick. Some stick longer. Once exercise over, pay attention to thoughts that stick longer."

So, Sage assumed the beginning stance as the fall afternoon sky began to dim, making the shellacked fir floor look dull and dispirited. Still, he heard Fong's voice in his head say softly, "Raise hands."

Half an hour later dusk had darkened the attic. Still, Sage sat quietly contemplating the thoughts that had stuck longest in his mind as he performed the snake and crane.

The first thought was that Fong's men had always been successful in the past. They had ways of finding people above and below ground. "So, what did that mean?" Sage asked himself. "It means that Andy is being held somewhere very private. A place Fong's men cannot access," he concluded.

The second sticking thought was that Stone had confirmed Sage's growing conviction that their problems were the result of a conspiracy involving a number of people. Something about that fact niggled at the back of his brain. He was considering whether to do another snake and crane exercise in order to tease out that illusive thought when the fire bell's call rang out over the city.

"Cripes," he yelled in frustration even as he leapt to his feet and raced toward the stairs. "At this rate, I'll never figure anything out!"

Once again he reached the firehouse just as the doors flew open, letting Sadie and the horses charge out. Seeing him, Ollie pulled on the reins, slowing his horse enough that Sage could leap onto the engine. "Hey Miner. Glad you made it. Your turnout bag is under the seat," Ollie told him as the horse broke into a trot that jerked the fire engine forward. This time, Ollie said it was a barrel-making factory on fire, downriver from the North End in the semi-rural area near Guilds Lake.

Sage quickly donned his gear. Minutes later, they were at the scene with hoses run, ladders raised and firefighters stepping lively as they shouted to each other. Comfortable now with his role as engine stoker, he was better able to observe. Fire Chief Campbell was there, which made Sage wonder why the fire chief had become so conscientious. Maybe it was the rash of arsons. Or, maybe Campbell was part of the conspiracy and wanted to make sure the fires went off without a hitch. Sage studied the man confidently issuing commands.

Campbell seemed to sense Sage's interest, because he turned his head to stare at Sage, his face mask-like in the flickering firelight. Dread sank through Sage though he couldn't tell if it was because he sensed, or because he feared, that Campbell might be involved. He concluded it was the latter—fear. He didn't want his good opinion of the man proven wrong.

Ollie's hollering broke through his musing, "Hey, Miner, you gonna let my fire go out?"

Sage got busy and when next he paused, he studied the spectators. Some showed fright. He figured those were the ones who owned buildings nearby or had empathy for the harm being caused to others. But some were hop-footed with excitement. Those were the ones he studied more carefully.

Then he noticed a figure standing across the road deep beneath a big evergreen. The person's stance was tense, angled forward like a hunting dog nosing a scent. Suddenly there was an explosion and in its flaring Sage saw more of the skulking figure. It was a young man, his nose long and sharp above a receding chin in a bloodless face, like a character out of Bram Stoker's vampire book, *Dracula*. A vague recollection stirred in Sage's mind but vanished in the next second when a second explosion split the night, jerking Sage's attention back toward the fire. Hundreds of tiny yellow suns shot into the sky before raining down onto the vacant fields that surrounded the burning factory. Campbell shouted over the noise and a firefighter dashed toward a nearby alarm box to signal for reinforcements.

TWENTY

He couldn't remember when he'd been so tired. Every muscle and bone in his body ached with fatigue. The only part of Sage that didn't hurt was his brain. That organ still revved fast as a motor with a snapped belt thanks to the sagging cot springs—painful reminders that he lay in Andy's place. Whether it was guilt or the assessing looks cast in his direction, he worried he wasn't doing enough to find the missing firefighter. But what to do?

At last sleep began overtaking his thoughts only to stall momentarily as he came half awake, tugged there by the forgotten thought that had niggled his brain during the exercise and what he'd later seen at the fire. It wasn't much, but it was something. This time the sleep he fell into was deep and untroubled by indecision because he now had a direction to go.

Early morning found him once again standing in the concrete stairwell across from Orpin's house. The yellow house looked abandoned beneath a solid gray sky. Should he boldly walk up to the door, hoping Orpin would open it? And, if he was the spooky kid from the fire, what then?

Sage decided against alerting the fellow just yet. Instead, he studied the house. It was small, one story, but looked to have a brick foundation.

So there could be a basement. Or, if they'd dug out beneath it, there might be a dirt cellar. Either one would make a good prison. Sage crept out of the stairwell, walked up the block and made his way to the next street over. Once there, he crept between the houses to a point where he could see the rear and sides of Orpin's house. There were no openings into the foundation. It was solid brick. So, there must be a cellar or basement because crawl spaces always had an outside opening in case the plumbing needed repair.

He returned to his stairwell post but the house remained lifeless. Presumably Orpin's grandmother was elderly. If that was the case, then someone had to be fetching her groceries. Logic dictated that would be the grandson who lived with her. But, after a couple hours of watching, he never saw Orpin. Maybe Orpin had a job and had left for work before Sage arrived. Disgusted, he gave up and left to find Fong.

As Sage walked, he pondered how to get inside Orpin's house. Soon he reached the western edge of the North End. Here, the streets were quiet with few people about because most were either working or warming up after spending a cold night outdoors. Uneasiness crept across his shoulders. He whirled around but saw no one. He resumed walking but couldn't shake the unease. He began to turn once again when a sharp report echoed between the buildings just as he felt a fiery blow to his right arm.

He jumped sideways into a doorway. There he waited, heart thumping wildly in his chest. Quietly, he tried the doorknob at his back. Locked. If the man with the gun came after him, he'd be trapped. A faint scrape sounded in the empty street as footsteps cautiously approached. With a silent apology to the shop owner, Sage whirled and snap kicked the door. It flew open and he burst into what appeared to be a storage space. As he charged down a narrow corridor between stacked barrels and crates, his eyes searched for a weapon, something sharp he could throw. He saw nothing. His only hope was that there was a rear window or door he could escape through.

A painful throbbing started in his upper arm. Glancing down he saw blood darkening his coat sleeve.

Boots pounded across the wood floor behind him. Ahead was a solid door. He reached it, slid back the bolt, opened the door outward and charged through, finding himself in an alley. Near to hand was a large wooden crate. Sage slammed the door shut and pulled the empty crate across to block it.

He was half a block away when he heard the door hit the crate and shove it across the cobbles. Shouting sounded over the rooftops from the building's front. Someone had discovered the break-in. "Hope the bastard gets caught," he thought as his feet pounded down the wooden sidewalk. Then he regretted his wish. His attacker was, after all, armed. He was fairly certain the angry shopkeeper wouldn't be.

Four blocks later and with no sign of pursuit, Sage finally slowed to a walk and allowed himself to feel the pain. It was as if someone had slammed a sledgehammer down on his upper arm. He felt weak though he couldn't tell whether it was from loss of blood, pain, exhaustion or a combination of all three.

Salvation appeared around the next corner in the form of Solomon's New Elijah hotel. He made his way around to the kitchen door and stumbled inside where the startled kitchen help turned toward him. "Miz Esther" was all he could mumble before his knees buckled and he was out.

A soft female voice in the far distance said, "Drink this," and he felt a glass vial against his lips. A bitter liquid burned his tongue and he swallowed. Laudanum's bite stung his throat even as it tumbled him further into the mist as someone gently eased his injured arm from his coat. After that came the metallic snip of scissors cutting the sleeves off his shirt and long johns. The opiate dulled the pain, keeping it at the edges. "Ah the sweet surcease of opium," he mused before drifting off.

Awakening later, the first thing he saw was Solomon sitting in the chair beside him. Sage gazed around the familiar room dreamily admiring the ornate walnut buffet, graceful silver candelabra, thick Persian carpet and the long wall of leather-bound books. "I've always liked this room," he mumbled.

Solomon laughed and said with a broad smile, "John, it looks like you'll live. I think Esther's painkiller had more impact than the bullet. It's just a flesh wound. No permanent damage."

Sage groaned as he struggled into a sitting position and swung his feet to the floor. "I was lucky and turned just in time. Otherwise he'd have shot me square in the back."

"Tell me, did this have anything to do with you trying to clear the Coopers of that ridiculous arson charge?" Solomon looked guilty as he asked the question.

"Lord, I hope so. I have certainly managed to alarm someone with my snooping. Unless there's a gun-toting madman running amok."

"I wanted your help John, but not if it's going to get you killed," Solomon told him in a voice that said he meant it.

"Do me a favor, Angus?" Sage said.

"Sure, anything."

"Instead of 'John,' please call me 'Sage' when no one else is around. That's the name I prefer my friends use."

Solomon's head reared back in surprise at the request before he grinned. "Okay, 'Sage' it is. But, I still don't want to see you killed. I enjoy our little escapades too much."

They were in Sage's room where his mother made him remove his coat so she could examine Miz Esther's handiwork. She nodded, reassured, "Couldn't have done a better job myself," she told him and Fong.

Before leaving the New Elijah, he'd thanked Esther, the older woman whose nursing skills, according to Angus, rivaled Florence Nightingale's. Sage was a believer having watched her nurse his friend, Stuart Franklin, back to health after a near-fatal beating. As Sage left the hotel, she'd sternly ordered him not to tangle with any more bullets although there'd been nothing except kindness and concern in her eyes.

After he related what happened, Fong spoke first, "This is good sign. How far from house before you feel someone following?"

"About six blocks."

"Anyone follow you to stairwell where you hide?"

"No. I am sure they didn't. I worried that someone might have noticed me searching the crowd at last night's fire. So, I left the firehouse just as it was starting to get light. The streets were practically empty. No one followed me. I would have noticed," Sage said.

Fong was nodding. "Okay, then. Only explanation is they pick you up outside Orpin house. Next question—why they there? How they know to go there?"

Silence settled in until Mae cleared her throat to speak. The two men looked at her. "Violet told me this morning that Andy is failing. She says he's dying."

Sage thought about that. "What if whoever has him is not feeding him or giving him water? How long can a human go without food or water?"

Fong answered, "Food not a problem. Water is problem. Only one week at most. Probably more like three or four days."

A sinking feeling in his gut, Sage said, "It's been four days already."

"Well, I think Violet does sense her brother. She's told me some of the things she's rightly sensed in the past, so I believe her. We've run out of time. He must be found," Mae said.

The three of them exchanged a silent look.

"We need to act today," Sage said matter-of-factly. The other two nodded. "That means searching Orpin's house and cellar any way we can." They both nodded again.

Half an hour later, they had their assault on Orpin' s house planned from beginning to end. "You going to take gun?" Fong asked.

"I wouldn't want to use it," Sage said, "But, I better carry one."

When Mae left to get ready Sage trailed her into her room. "This could be dangerous. Maybe Orpin's the one who shot me."

She put a hand on his shoulder. "Sage, it's risky just crossing the street. Besides you and Fong will be right beside me. You know I've done more dangerous things than what we're planning." Excitement shone in her eyes as she turned away to change her clothes.

After leaving her room, he realized that this was the first time he didn't try to discourage her from taking part in a dangerous action—which likely explained that affectionate squeeze of his shoulder she gave him before leaving.

TWENTY ONE

Wind-driven rain hindered sight and sound in November's early dusk. For once, it was welcome. They met a block from Orpin's house, beneath the arched doorway of a church. Mae was dressed simply in black cloak, hat and boots. Sage wore his John Miner clothes and had the Dalmatian on a leash.

"Nice dog," Mae said and bent down to pet Sadie who accepted the attention with great dignity. "Is she here for a reason or did you just adopt her?"

"She's pretty much Andy's dog. I figured maybe she can help us find him."

Fong arrived a few minutes later accompanied by two of his cousins. They'd brought a handcart with a canvas tarp lashed down to keep its bed dry and its cargo hidden.

"Mr. Fong, in this instance, with so much at stake, I think it would be better if you took charge of Orpin. I'll step in to assist if needed," Sage said, knowing that was very unlikely.

Fong cocked an eyebrow but nodded his assent. Both men looked at Mae. She raised her chin and said, "I am perfectly ready. I know what to do." With that, she set off down the street, the two men and dog trailing behind. Fong's helpers stayed put. They wouldn't move the cart until they got the signal.

Reaching the Orpin house, Mae waited on the sidewalk while Fong, Sage and Sadie silently climbed the two porch steps and took positions on either side of the front door, their backs pressed against the wall. After carefully looking up and down the street, Mae pulled hair loose from her bun and settled her hat so it sat lop-sided. Then she opened her mouth and hollered, "Help!"

Sage had to admire her volume control. She was loud enough to be heard inside the house but not so loud as to be heard by Orpin's neighbors. One more cry and she was stumbling up the steps, her feet thudding across the porch floor. Reaching the front door, she cried out again and pounded frantically.

From his side view, Sage saw a hand twitch the door curtain aside. Seconds later the door opened and a querulous male voice asked, "What do you want? What's all the racket?"

Mae stepped back, put a trembling hand up to her hat and pointed down the street with her other hand. "See that man over there? He just attacked me and stole my purse. Look! He's still hanging about. What should I do?"

Sage had to admit she was convincing. So much so, that Orpin did what every other man would do—he stepped out onto the porch to look where she was pointing.

Instantly, before Orpin even registered his presence, Fong was yanking the man's arm up behind his back. Seconds later, Sage was through the front door gun in hand, Sadie trotting beside him. He scanned the room before nodding for Fong to hustle his captive inside. Mae followed, quietly closing the door behind them.

"Wha . . . Orpin's words were cut off when Fong's "shh" in his ear was accompanied by a painful twist of his arm.

Sage studied their surroundings. Sputtering gas in dirty mantles provided weak light. The layout was simple. A small living room at the front with a closed door to one side. Probably a bedroom. Behind that was a kitchen. And, in its far wall, another closed door.

He turned back and for the first time, got a good look at Orpin. Bits of recognition crashed together in Sage's mind. This was the man who'd pointed a finger at Andy in the police station lobby. He was also the fellow who'd been lurking under the fir tree at the recent cooperage warehouse fire. "Where's your grandmother?" Sage hissed.

Orpin's eyes widened. "You!"

"Yah, you missed yesterday. Not a very good shot are you?"

It had been a guess but an accurate one. "I wouldn't have missed the second time," he snarled.

"Where's your grandmother?" Sage repeated.

"Sleeping in the back room." Orpin's voice was sullen.

"And the gun?"

Orpin clamped his lips shut but Mae hadn't missed his glance toward the door off the front room. She went to the door, opened it and stepped through. They heard drawers being opened and shut. Soon she was back, revolver in hand. She sniffed the barrel. "It's been fired recently," she told them and tucked it into her coat pocket.

Sage studied the strangely pale face, the long nose and receding chin. "You find watching fires exciting, do you?"

Orpin stared up at the ceiling.

Sage stepped closer. "Where's Andy Hosier?"

That snapped Orpin's eyes down but all he said was, "Andy who?"

"Now, now. Didn't your grandmother teach you not to lie? I saw you in the police station lobby the other day. You remember, the day you pointed at Andy Hosier and said you'd seen him at that house fire?"

Orpin's eyes widened but he clamped his lips shut.

Sage glanced around the room and then turned back to Orpin. "You got a cellar under this house?" he asked.

"Nah," Orpin responded.

Sage studied him a moment then switched his gaze to Fong. "How about you two guard him while I search?

Fong's answer was to wrench Orpin's arm a little higher, sending the man up onto his toes. Mae took Sage's gun and pointed it at Orpin.

Sage and Sadie moved toward the back of the house. Sage couldn't find a cellar door. When he looked into the back room he heard soft snores issuing from a hump under the bedcovers. The room had only the one door. Sadie turned away before he did.

They returned to the kitchen and Sage looked around. He was about to give up when he noticed Sadie. She was staring at a small rug in the middle of the kitchen floor. Her tail stood straight out and her head was cocked to one side with a faint whimpering coming from her throat.

Sage looked at the rug. People didn't put rugs in the kitchen unless it was in front of the sink. This rug was near the room's middle. He stepped over and flipped the rug back. Beneath it was the outline of a trap door with a lift ring. It was bolted shut. Sadie gave a yip and scooted forward until her black nose was touching the crack between door and floor. Her backend wiggled vigorously. She looked up at Sage, appeal in her dark eyes.

He hesitated. If Andy wasn't below, they'd reached a dead end. Sure, they could question Orpin about his role and his partners in the insurance fraud conspiracy but Andy would still be missing. And, according to Violet, dying. Sadie ended his hesitation by scratching at the trap door and excitedly yipping.

Taking a deep breath he drew the bolt, lifted the trap door and laid it on the floor. Peering into the opening he saw a wooden ladder stretching down to inky dark.

Mae was watching him from the living room, her gun still trained on Orpin. Sage gestured that he was going to descend into the cellar.

The climb was short, only five rungs down. Reaching the dirt floor he peered around. The ceiling was so low, he had to stoop to see. At first he saw nothing but a pile of rags in one corner. Then the rags moved. Sage quickly crouch-walked across the dirt floor and knelt. The man was filthy and unrecognizable in the gloom but Sage was confident they'd found Andy. A weak voice rasped. When Sage bent closer he heard, "Water."

Sage jumped up and raced to the ladder. Above him, Sadie was leaning down into the opening, bare inches from tumbling down. "We found him girl. I'll bring him up in a minute," he told her as he climbed up and headed to the sink pump. He flashed a grin at his mother who was watching from the living room.

Seconds later he was again beside Orpin's captive, holding a glass to his lips. "Slow now and not too much or you'll throw it up."

Sage raised the man and half carried him into the pool of light at the bottom of the ladder where he confirmed that they had, indeed, found Andy Hosier. Sage slung him over his shoulder in a firefighter carry and began climbing, hoping the rungs would hold their combined weight. Reaching the kitchen, Sage gently lowered Andy onto the floor. Instantly, Sadie was atop the weak man and joyfully licking his cheeks, chin, hands and every other bare patch of skin she could reach.

Sage went into the living room. "Will you go take care of him?" he asked Mae.

She handed him his gun and soon he heard her softly reassuring the young man.

Sage glared at Orpin, wanting to clout the firebug upside his head with the gun barrel. Only Fong's steady, sympathetic gaze from behind Orpin's shoulder stopped him.

Fong spoke, "We tie him now? Get him ready for trip?"

Once Orpin was bound, gagged and lying on the floor, Fong slipped out. Minutes later he returned with his two helpers. Through the open front door Sage saw that they'd backed the cart snug against the porch steps. Rain drummed loudly on the canvas tarp. One cousin stepped off the porch, looked up and down the street and gestured wildly. Fong, Sage and the third man lifted Orpin, carried him out of the house and slid him beneath the tarp that was soon snugged down. Fong and his two friends headed off, pushing the cart away down the street. Sage glanced around. No one was in sight.

After closing the front door, Sage returned to the kitchen. Andy sat on the floor, his back against a cabinet, his arms around the dog. "Thank you," he said to Sage.

"You going to be alright?" Sage asked, even as he looked at Mae for the answer. Andy said "Yes" while she grinned in agreement.

"I just need more water and some food. I ain't had either since they took me." Andy's voice was weak and raspy.

"We can take you to the hospital or to your sister. Which do you want?"

"Violet, I need to see Violet. She'll take care of me. She's been so worried."

"You know that?" Sage asked.

Andy nodded. "We have this way of knowing about each other," he said.

Sage and Mae exchanged a look, with Mae's lips curving in an I-told-you-so smirk.

"I'll go find us a cab. There's no way he can walk the distance. Will you be alright holding the fort until I get back?" Sage asked Mae.

"Shouldn't be too hard," she told him.

Sage left the three of them in the kitchen and shortly returned in a cab. While it waited on the street, he went in to retrieve his passengers. Stepping into the kitchen he was surprised to find his mother seated on the floor next to Andy who had his arms wrapped around Sadie. Mae held Orpin's gun in her hand, aimed more or less at an unconscious, gray-haired woman who lay on the floor, a baseball bat beside her.

"What the hell happened?" Sage demanded. "Did you shoot her?"

"She came out swinging that baseball bat," Mae said pointing to the bat with her gun barrel. "Fortunately, I heard her stirring and Andy had already told me she was in on it. So, I waited behind the door. When she charged at Andy with the bat raised, I clunked her a good one with the gun butt."

They left Orpin's grandmother on the floor, breathing but still out cold.

The four of them crowded into the cab, Sadie stretched across Sage and Andy's laps. Every once and awhile the dog gently licked Andy's hand.

Mae sighed. "Well, leastways I don't have to worry about who'll be taking care of the poor old lady. She sure didn't act like no invalid and she smelled like a gin mill."

Between them, they managed to get Andy up the stairs to Violet's second floor room. When Violet opened the door she was already grinning and crying joyful tears. "I knew the minute you were rescued," she told her brother as she did her best to enfold him in her arms. It wasn't easy. In the short time since Sage last saw her, she'd become way more pregnant.

They stayed only a few minutes, after getting Andy's promise he'd remain indoors and out of sight. Sage emphasized the need for Andy to stay hidden. "Capturing Orpin is just the first step. There are others involved and we don't know who they are. They could come for you again. You can't even go see Jimmy in the hospital," Sage told him.

"Jimmy's in the hospital?" Andy said with alarm.

Violet rushed to reassure him. "He's going to be fine, Andy. Silly fool fell and broke a few ribs trying to rescue a cat from a roof."

"Did the cat make it?" Andy asked.

Sage rolled his eyes. Typical firefighter.

Sadie dug her paws in and refused to leave Andy's side so they decided to leave her with him for awhile. Mae carried her belongings when they left. "No need to stay with Violet now that she's got her brother to watch after her. He's young. He'll be right as rain in a day or two."

Sage helped her into a cab and minutes later the cabbie dropped him at the firehouse while she continued on to Mozart's. All was quiet inside the firehouse except for the sleepy snuffles coming from the horse stalls. The men were upstairs. Except one, Sage realized when he heard a soft clink of metal on metal. Sure enough, Ollie stood at his workbench fiddling with some engine part.

He whirled at Sage's approach. Sage decided Ollie had worried long enough and grinned.

"He's been found?" Ollie asked, his voice tremulous with hope.

Sage nodded. "And he will recover. But you must keep it strictly secret. He's still not out of danger. And, we suspect someone in this firehouse is involved. They can't know he's alive. Promise me you'll say nothing to no one."

"Oh boy, I promise that with every single bone in my body. Can I see him?"

"Yes. I'll tell you where he is but you have to make sure you're not followed."

"I promise. Boy, do I promise," Ollie said, joy chasing years off his face. "Let's go upstairs and secretly celebrate," Ollie said, throwing an arm across Sage's shoulders.

"I'd like to, Ollie. But, this isn't over. I have more things I have to do. I'm heading out. I may not hear the city fire bell if it sounds. Can you handle the engine by yourself?"

"Yah, sure. One of the other fellas will help." Ollie grabbed Sage's hand and shook it so vigorously Sage thought it might detach from his wrist. "Thank you, thank you," Ollie said before dropping his hand and turning away, his Adam's apple bobbing as he swallowed for control. When the engineer turned back to Sage, his voice was shaking. "Andy's a good fella. I've grown awful fond of him. It's a big relief to know he's okay," he said, adding, "The wife and I never had children, you know. And now that she's gone . . . "

Sage left the garage, feeling alert despite the long day. "Now comes the fun part," he murmured to himself. "I'm actually going to enjoy this."

TWENTY TWO

Although another downpour was bouncing raindrops across the cobbles, Sage walked with a spring in his step to where Fong waited in the entryway just inside the New Elijah's kitchen door.

"Any problems?" Sage asked, his voice low. Beyond the little entryway, kitchen workers were cheerfully bantering as they washed up. The supper hour was over.

"No problem. Orpin down there. Nobody saw," Fong assured him in a whisper.

Sage understood Fong to mean Orpin was imprisoned below them and that no one had seen them taking him down.

Fong opened the cellar door, lit a lantern and headed down the stairs. Following, Sage felt a familiar twinge of unreasoning fear but firmly suppressed it. During the prior shanghaiing escapade, the one involving Matthew, Sage had learned how to conquer his fear of the musty dark—a fear born in the coal mine.

Like most businesses situated above Portland's underground, the New Elijah's storage room was walled off. A locked door opened into the bigger basement which, in turn, connected with all basements beneath the block. Brick tunnels ran under the streets, connecting these block-sized basements. It was this arrangement that created an underground stretching west from the river to Eighteenth Street and north and south even farther.

Originally, the underground provided dry transport for goods to and from the riverfront. Once the streets were paved the goods were transported by wagon and the underground was put to less desirable uses. This was where kidnapped men were imprisoned before being sold to ship captains. Opium and gambling dens occupied its remotest corners.

Fong's cousins were master navigators of its dark expanse. Restricted housing forced some Chinese to live in walled-off basement rooms. And, it was also where they nursed some of their sick and dying out of fear that whites would use the illness as an excuse to drive them all out of the city.

Sage had mixed feelings about the cell where Orpin waited. A building owner had constructed it to aid the shanghaiers. Portland's merchants encouraged shanghaiing—even blocked legislation to curtail it. For economic reasons, they wanted men to be kidnapped and sold to ship captains because sailors tended to jump ship on America's west coast and sailing ships required a minimum number of crewmen. Without that minimum, the ship got stranded in port. A port with a high incidence of stranded ships drove up shipping rates. Shanghaiing was how the monied men kept those rates low. Their greed kept the deadly practice alive.

At first, Sage planned to destroy the cell but Fong resisted. Subsequent events proved Fong right. So far, it had persuaded more than one criminal to speak the truth. Hopefully, tonight, it would do so again.

Fong's raised lantern lit their way. Rodent squeals and Sage shuffling through the bone dry dust were near sounds heard against a backdrop of the distant human sounds filtering down through the floorboards overhead.

Reaching the cell, Fong lifted the lantern so that its light hit Orpin's fish-belly white face, causing him to squint.

Sage stepped forward. "Okay, Orpin. You are now going to tell us exactly what you've been doing," he said menacingly.

"I ain't been doing nothing," came the surly reply.

"You tell us what we want to know or one of two things will happen. We'll treat you just like you treated Andy Hosier and leave you here to die of hunger and thirst. Or, maybe we'll just sell you to the captain of a whaling hell ship. How'd you like to swim in the Bering Sea? I hear tell that's a right quick death.

Orpin swallowed hard. "I set the fires," he mumbled.

"How did you pick which fires to set?"

"He told me."

"Who told you?"

"Don't know his name."

"Oh, come on. You risked going to prison for someone you didn't even know?" Sage didn't rein in his sarcasm.

Orpin just shrugged.

"How'd you meet this man who told you where to set the fires?"

Orpin stared into the dark before taking a deep breath and saying, "I tried to rob him with a knife. He pulled a gun and made me tell him my name and address. We worked out a deal."

"What deal was that?"

"He sends a note to my house with the address of the place I'm supposed to torch. Afterwards, he sends me money."

"You never saw him again?"

Orpin's headshake was adamant. "Nope, never. Truth be told, it was kinda dark that night. I don't know if I would recognize him if I saw him again. But, his voice was gnarly. I'd recognize that."

"You ever set fires before you met this gnarly-voiced man?"

This time, Orpin's voice dropped as he said, "Just small ones, here and there. Sheds and stuff like that. Never big buildings. Like lately."

Sage exchanged a steady look with Fong before saying to Orpin, "How'd you end up shooting at me?"

Orpin shuffled his feet. "Same thing. I got a note saying that a fellow was snooping. Said you'd taken over Hosier's job on the fire engine at Station 1. So, I stuck around at the one of the fires and saw you. Plus, my neighbor said some man had been watching my house. So, I hid out and watched. Sure enough, there you were. Soon as you left, I followed." There was a pause before he added with heat, "Too bad I didn't aim better."

"Where'd you get the gun?"

"Messenger brought it at the same time as the note saying you were snooping."

"Where's the note?"

"I burnt it in the cookstove. I always burn the notes. That's what he said to do."

Sage watched Orpin closely as he asked his next question. "Why'd you hit Wally Roberts on the head?"

Puzzlement appeared to wrinkle Orpin's brow. "Who is Wally Roberts? Why would I hit him on the head?"

"You didn't go to the umbrella warehouse after you burned it, find a man, hit him on the head and then hide his body under rubble?"

Orpin's watery blue eyes widened. "No, I didn't! I don't know nothin' about it. Anyone says I do, is a damned liar!"

The firebug's outrage felt genuine. Deciding Orpin was probably innocent of Robert's murder, Sage moved on to the next issue. "About Andy Hosier. How'd he end up in your cellar?"

Orpin turned evasive, his eyes flicking to one side.

Sage's tone sharpened, "Don't think of lying, Orpin. You're already in swamp water up to your ears. Don't step out any deeper."

Orpin sighed. "Got another note. This one said they'd be bringing him and I should find some place to keep him quiet. Luckily, we had the root cellar."

"Not so lucky for him," Sage snapped and got a shrug from Orpin in return. "Who brought him to your house?"

"Couple of rough looking fellows came after dark. He was out cold. They just carried him in, dropped him down the hole and went away. They never said nothing. Didn't leave me no money for his food or his keep. Never seen 'em since."

"You the one who told the police Andy was the arsonist?"

"Yah, the fellow sent a note saying to do it but to give the cops a phony name. That's what I done."

"What about the Cooper boy. You write that note?"

For the first time Orpin scowled and he said, "He ain't got no business making eyes at a white girl."

"You set him up to go to prison for years because he talked to a white girl?" Sage didn't bother to suppress his disgust.

"They hang 'em for less than that down South. Why, one of them got lynched not that long ago right here in Marshfield, Oregon."

Sage stared at Orpin, shook his head and moved out of the light in an effort to bring a spurt of sudden anger under control. He wanted to smack the idiot.

When he returned he spoke to Fong, not Orpin. "You ready to go?" he asked.

At Fong's nod, Sage stepped away into the dark, followed by Fong and his lantern.

Orpin shouted after them. "What about me?"

"You're going to get to experience what you put Andy Hosier through," Sage called back.

"But there ain't no water or a pee bucket or anything in this cell."

"Exactly," Sage said and kept walking.

Only after they'd passed under a street and were beneath the neighboring block did Sage speak, saying with disgust, "I didn't want to give that cretin even one more minute of light."

"How long you plan he have no water?"

"I hope he thinks it's forever. But we'll be back early in the morning with Sergeant Hanke. He needs to hear the whole story."

"Hanke will fuss you get him in new mess."

Sage chuckled. "Yah, he'll fuss but he'll go along. He always does."

As they headed toward the New Elijah, Sage said, "So, we have the Coopers cleared and Andy rescued but the men behind the arson scheme are still running free. They're also responsible for Wally Roberts death—I'm sure of it."

"Maybe we find messenger who bring notes to Orpin. See if he knows who sent them."

"Good idea. Matthew will help with that, since he's friends with most of them," Sage said. "But, I bet you all we'll hear is that a stranger just stopped them in the street and paid them in advance to deliver the notes."

"Best we think how to catch whole gang," Fong said.

Sage had to agree. The most important task was catching those behind the fires. He smiled to himself and said, "Since Orpin's locked up, there might not be any more arson fires. It'll give us time to think." He was also anticipating an uninterrupted night's sleep at the firehouse. But first, he had to stop at Mozart's.

"Do you think Matthew's still up?" Sage asked Mae when he found her in her room. She was sitting in her rocking chair, feet on a small stool, mending in her lap.

"I just heard him clomp up the stairs. You might be able to rouse him without waking Ida and Knute." She voiced an important consideration. Ida rose at four a.m. and so did Knute—she to make pies, Knute to head off to the shingle factory. Sage could never think of Knute without seeing those whirling saw blades, mere inches from his hands. The Swede definitely needed to be well-rested.

Matthew immediately snatched the door open at Sage's light tap. The auburn-haired young man held a book with his finger marking his place. Seeing Sage, he stepped out in the hallway, softly closing the door behind him.

As expected, the boy jumped at the chance to help out. He'd done so reliably in the past, once he'd learned to follow directions. His initial failure to do so is what had gotten him shanghaied. It had been a hard but, effective, lesson.

"I don't want you missing any school," Sage told him.

Matthew nodded eagerly. "Don't worry, I only meet the other messengers at the public market after school. There's an overhang out of the rain where we get together.

Sage handed him a slip of paper. "See if you can find anyone who took messages to this address. It's on the eastern edge of Nob Hill. I'm hoping someone will remember who paid them to carry it."

Matthew took the piece of paper, asking, "Is there money in it for the messenger, if I find him?" he asked.

"For him and for you," Sage answered.

That response triggered an adamant headshake from Matthew. "For him yes, but not for me. You already do enough for me, Mr. Adair," he said.

"Now Matthew," Sage began.

Matthew's chin rose, "My books, my tuition, even my bicycle, Blue Beauty. You've done enough."

"We'll talk about it later," Sage said. "Just do your best to find someone who's carried notes to that address."

Matthew straightened like a soldier at attention. "Yes, Sir," he said.

As he turned away, Sage said, "And, be careful. Don't get yourself into trouble."

Matthew didn't turn around. He merely nodded and slipped soundlessly back inside his aunt and uncle's apartment.

Sage stood on the stair landing, thinking that Matthew's lessons with Fong were making him less the clumsy colt. Next he thought of his comfortable bed on the floor above. Sighing, he slapped on his floppy John Miner hat and headed downstairs. It was the lumpy iron cot for him.

TWENTY THREE

Despite the late hour, Ollie lay in wait, sitting alone at his workbench. Sadie's head rested on his knee, her eyes slits of pleasure as the engineer scratched around her ears. The air was ripe with the smell of horses but also warm from their body heat, giving the garage a cozy feel. The minute Ollie saw him, he was on his feet and so was the dog, her rear end wagging an enthusiastic greeting. Ollie was grinning from ear to ear.

"I went and saw our friend after you left. Truth be told, I couldn't wait until morning. And, I fetched Sadie here. The horses missed her." He leaned forward and continued in a lower voice. "Andy says he's already feeling better. I took them some groceries, I figured Violet has enough trouble getting up the stairs without having to haul their vittles too."

"You are probably right, Ollie. How'd he look?"

"Well, a bit peaked to be honest, but I didn't tell him that. I'm taking Sadie over there tomorrow 'cause she didn't want to leave him. She's missed him something terrible."

Sage knew from experience that it would take Andy awhile to recover. Hopefully, watching over Violet would take his mind off what had happened to him. "Any word about Jimmy, her husband?"

"He's coming along good too. The doctors think he might go home in a few days with his ribs taped. He's chomping at the bit. Wants to get back to firefighting."

"You went to see him?"

"Yes, Violet asked me to. Soon's I saw Andy was safe I took off over there. She didn't want to leave Andy by himself. She asked me to go tell Jimmy the good news." Ollie held up a forestalling hand, "Yah, yah, I know that you said I had to keep it secret but Jimmy's family and Violet said he's been worrying about Andy something awful. It's probably why he got injured. His mind was elsewhere."

Sage smiled, "It's fine that you told Jimmy. He knows not to say anything, right?"

Ollie's nod was vigorous. "I whispered the news into his ear. He raised his hand to promise he'd keep quiet, even though it hurt him to move."

The firehouse doors rattled in a sudden gust of wind.

"Sure hope no fire bell rings tonight. That's a powerful wind out there," Ollie said. "When it comes to fires, I'll take rain over wind any day. Let's hope it dies down soon."

Ollie's hopes went unfulfilled. At three in the morning, the Station 1 bell had them rolling off their cots and sliding down the fire pole. But this time it was just a small, one alarm fire. A chimney, choked with creosote, had set a house roof on fire. Fortunately, an inebriated passerby spotted the flames and was sober enough to alert the holder of the fire box key. That fellow wasted no time in raising the alarm.

Between the fast alert and the misting rain, the fire was out within minutes of their arrival—despite the gusting wind. As a shivering Sage helped roll and stow the hoses, he felt eyes on his back. Turning toward the spectators, he saw that they'd all returned to their warm beds. No one like Orpin lurked in the shadows.

Still, he couldn't shake that sensation of being watched. It had to be either someone hidden in one of the houses or one of the firefighters. Riding back to the firehouse, he tried to puzzle it out. He quickly dismissed the thought that someone had been hiding in one of the houses. The fire had been spontaneous. No one could have anticipated it.

He considered the firefighters who'd been at the scene. Because it was a small fire, only Station 1 had responded so there'd only been a crew of eight and the fire station chief. Even Fire Chief Campbell had stayed home.

Sage climbed down from the fire engine to help stable the horses. As he lifted off a neck collar, he gazed into the horse's intelligent brown eyes. These had to be the smartest, best trained horses in the whole city. Someone said they'd come unbroken from Eastern Oregon. He chuckled to himself. If he didn't watch it, he'd forget about buying a motor car and stick with horses and buggies. Sage smiled, thinking how Andy would love tinkering with a motor car's engine.

Thought of Andy triggered an idea that made him want to kick himself. He'd been so worried about the young man, so intent on getting him safely hidden that he'd forgot to ask a very important question: "Who had lured him away from the firehouse and how?" He need to ask that question and soon.

Stepping into the living quarters he saw rain drops pinging into metal pots. Sadie, having trailed him up the stairs, curled onto her stove-side pile of blankets with a huffing sigh. He followed her example and soon added his own noise to what remained of the night.

Early morning sunlight reflected off the street's wet cobbles, sending fog wisps swirling across the ground. This late in November, the leafy trees were bare, leaving the evergreens to loom like hulking sentinels. Smoke from stove and furnace fires hung heavy in the air. Still, sunny fall days like this lured people outdoors in an almost celebratory mood. Sage smiled. Oregonians talked about weather more than any other group he'd lived among. If it didn't rain for a few days, it was discussed. If the sun hid for too long, it was discussed. He'd finally concluded that they were addicted to changing weather or, at least, to discussing it. So long as it varied most every day, they were happy.

His ruminating ceased when he reached Violet's boarding house. His mother surprised him by answering his knock. Anticipating his reaction, she quickly reassured, "Everybody's fine. I stopped by to bring Violet some of Ida's soup and bread. And, her last fresh apple pie of the season."

"Oh, Philander won't like that," Sage said. "I'll be sure and tell him what you've done when I see him later." She shook her head in feigned disgust and opened the door wider.

For the first time he took stock of the new apartment. It was larger than the one room place Violet lived in when he'd first met her. This one had two rooms which meant that, once Jimmy came home, he and Violet could have privacy in the back room.

Andy lay stretched out on a divan in the front room which also housed a kitchen area complete with dining table. Ollie was right. The young firefighter did look a little "peaked". When Sage entered, Andy quickly sat up and swung his feet to the floor. From the way he clutched the side of the divan, it was evident he was still weak and dizzy from his ordeal.

His spirits were high though, as he reached out to shake Sage's hand. "Mr. Miner, thank you for sending Ollie to see me. Between him and Mrs. Clemens, we have enough food to feed an army." He looked toward the other room and said softly. "Violet is having a bit of a rest. She just got back from visiting Jimmy. She gets tired pretty quick what with the baby due any day now. I've tried to help out but I'm like a fiddle missing a couple strings. I can get up for a bit but then I've got to lay back down."

Sage chuckled. "I know just what you mean, Andy. I've been like that a few times myself. It takes a while to recover from what you went through. Don't rush it. I know Mrs. Clemens is happy to help." A glance showed her nodding in agreement. Sage continued, "The most important thing is for you to get strong and for Violet to take very good care of herself."

He grabbed a nearby chair, slung it around and sat. Leaning toward Andy, Sage said, "You weren't in any condition last evening to answer questions. Are you up for it today?"

"Why sure," Andy said.

"What was in that note you received? The one that made you run off from the firehouse?"

"It said someone wanted to meet with me about something I was doing for them."

"Who? Who were you to meet? What were you doing?"

Andy heaved a sigh. "I can't tell you that. I promised on my mother's name I'd hold all that secret."

"I understand. Mr. Stone of the Fire Underwriters said you were gathering information in the firehouse and noting the spectators at fire scenes for him. Stone asked me to do the same. That's one reason we were able to find you."

Andy perked up. "That's how you figured it was Orpin who had me?"

"It's one of the ways. I noticed him lurking around an arson fire and thought that he looked familiar. So, once he opened his front door and I got a look at him, I knew we were on the right track. Of course, Sadie gets the credit for finding the trap door."

Mae set a cup of coffee on the table beside Sage before moving the other chair so she could also sit facing Andy.

Sage decided that he had to get the answer Andy had promised not to give. The only way he could think to do that was by trickery. Glancing at Mae, he saw her give a tiny nod. "Andy, I think Chief Campbell is part of a gang that is trying to defraud the insurance companies."

Instantly Andy protested, "No, Sir! Chief Campbell is not one of the bad guys. I know that for a fact." His tone was fiercely adamant but his eyes shot toward the ceiling before switching to the pale blue sky outside. When his gaze returned to them, his lips twisted up on one side in a grimace. He knew he'd been tricked.

Sage slapped both hands on his thighs and rose. "Well, I better get going. I have to check in with Mrs. Cooper and then set things in motion to release father and son.

Andy's puzzled look reminded Sage that the young firefighter didn't know about Orpin framing James Cooper. He shot a look at his mother.

"I'll tell him all about it. You go ahead on," she said.

As he exited the boarding house, Sage's spirits were again high. Andy's vehement denial suggested that Chief David Campbell was one of the good guys.

Mrs. Cooper had spent a peaceful night. No doubt because the presence of so many able defenders prevented another attack. Joy sparked in her eyes when he told her that her husband and son would both be home by evening though, all she said was, "I guess I better put the roast in the oven."

As he was leaving the Cooper's, the city fire bell rang out sending him at a run to the nearest firehouse. There he learned that the call was for a minor eastside fire, Station 1 was not being called up. Glad of that, he headed to the police station where he found Sergeant Hanke filling in reports. Hanke stood to shake hands when Sage entered his office. There was just a hint of reserve in his welcome.

"Sergeant, you are going to be pleased with me. And your police chief, in turn, is going to be very pleased with you."

Hanke's cheek twitched. The big policeman lay down his pen and lumbered over to shut his office door. "A shudder just galloped up my backbone. What shenanigans are you up to this time?" he asked.

Sage grinned, "Now Sergeant, don't be so suspicious. As it turns out, we've caught the real arsonist."

Hanke grunted. "By we, I assume that means Mr. Fong and yourself?" He followed up by lifting both hands questioningly. "So, where is he? Downstairs?"

"Well, not exactly," Sage began.

"Oh, Christ. Don't tell me he's stashed away in the underground? Really, Mr. Adair, you have to stop running your own interrogation jail. It forces me to dream up all sorts of unlikely explanations for how I capture the bad guys." Despite the sergeant's words, Sage sensed that Hanke was feeling a mix of exasperated, intrigued and excited. He'd been roped in by Sage's schemes before. And, each time, the outcome had increased his stature within the police department.

"So, you up for getting your boots dusty?" Sage asked. "And, I need to use your telephone to get Philander Gray down here so the three of us can meet up with Fong and Solomon," Sage checked his pocket watch, "in half an hour."

Sighing heavily, Hanke pointed to the candlestick telephone on the corner of his desk. Then he dropped down in his chair and started closing his open files.

Sage allowed himself a smug smile as he lifted the earpiece. As predicted, the sergeant was on board.

TWENTY FOUR

The New Elijah's kitchen was unusually silent when Sage, Hanke and Gray crowded into the small entryway. Poking his head around the door frame, Sage met Fong's eyes. Fong and Angus Solomon sat at the kitchen table, drinking coffee. Solomon, seeing Fong come alert, turned in his chair. Spying Sage, he grinned and said, "Ah, our hero and his friends have arrived. Everyone, please enter. My head waiter is holding a staff meeting in the dining room. No one's here to see you."

They were soon drinking coffee and letting the kitchen's warmth dry clothes made sodden by the walk from the police station.

On the way, Sage had explained the situation to Hanke and Gray. Fong, in turn, had explained the same to Solomon.

"The tricky part will be getting Orpin to repeat what he told me and Mr. Fong yesterday," Sage said. "He just might say it again, provided he thinks he is just repeating it to the two of us. If he sees the three of you, especially you Hanke, he might change his tune—thinking you'd never leave him to rot in an underground cell."

"If I was Orpin, I wouldn't be too sure of that," Hanke said but he, Gray and Solomon agreed to remain out of sight.

Soon, the four of them were trailing Fong's lantern across dusty basements and through seeping tunnels. As he walked, Sage pictured Orpin first perceiving the dim light as a trick of his eyes. As the light strengthened, he'd grasp that someone approached. Then fear would mingle with hope. Fear it would be shanghaiers—hope that the light meant rescue.

Once they arrived, Hanke, Gray and Solomon waited behind the cell's brick wall leaving Sage and Fong to approach the barred door alone. Setting the lantern on the dirt floor, Fong faded into the shadows.

Orpin was already upright though the dust on his clothes said he'd spent the night lying on the dirt floor. His hands gripped the iron bars like a drowning man's. He licked his lips. "Did you bring me water? I need water," he whined.

"Did Andy Hosier beg you for water?" Sage asked.

"He . . ." Orpin started to say, then fell silent.

"Lucky for you, we're decent men," Sage said as he removed a glass water jar from his pocket and unscrewed and filled its lid with water. Orpin watched his every move.

"You don't deserve this," Sage told him as he passed the lid between the bars. Orpin carefully took the lid and drained the water. He handed it back to Sage, expecting a refill.

Sage screwed the lid back on, taking his time. Only after he'd stowed the jar back in his jacket pocket did he look at Orpin.

"So, Orpin, did you consider what you've done and what we want to know?"

Orpin, staring at the pocket holding the water jar, answered dully, "I told you everything I know and all that I done."

"Maybe, you should tell me it all over again. I tend to have a faulty memory."

So, with some prodding, Orpin repeated how he'd set the fires at the behest of a stranger. That he'd met the stranger when he tried to rob him. That both the instructions and payment were sent to his house by messenger. That he'd first tried to frame Andy and later, imprisoned him—all at the stranger's behest And that, once Andy was cleared of arson, Orpin tried to frame James Cooper as a personal vendetta. He also admitted that he'd shot Sage. Finally, he again vehemently denied have clubbed Wally Roberts.

"And you still don't know who that stranger was, the one asking you to set all those fires?"

"I don't. If I did, I'd tell you in a minute. He's the one that got me in all this trouble."

Sage shook his head, amazed as always by the human ability for self-deception. "You were already heading that way, Orpin. You met him trying to rob him and he wasn't the first, either. Was he?

Orpin shook his head.

Sage, aware of those listening, prodded Orpin. "What did you say? Was the stranger the first person you robbed?"

Orpin cleared his throat, "No, he wasn't."

"How many others?"

Orpin squinted in thought. "Maybe seven or eight or maybe more. I can't remember exactly." That answered Mrs. Cooper's question about how Orpin managed to get "ladies" interested in him. Between his arson payoffs and his robberies, he had plenty of ill-gotten gains to spend on them.

"And you were already setting fires in sheds and outbuildings before you met the stranger, isn't that true?"

Again Orpin silently nodded.

Sage again pulled the water jar from his pocket, "I'm sorry, I didn't hear your answer," he said.

"Yes, yes. I told you already. I've been setting little fires for awhile."

Sage unscrewed the lid, filled it and passed it over. As he did so, soft footsteps sounded behind him. The sergeant's brass buttons gleamed on his broad chest as he moved into the light, up close to the bars. "Hello there, Mr. Orpin," he said.

Orpin cried out with relief, "Oh, thank god you're here. This man broke into my house and kidnapped me. He's kept me down here without food or water. Arrest him!"

For a long moment Hanke stared at Orpin, then he said, "I guess he must of thought you deserved a bit of your own medicine. Isn't that what Andy Hosier might say?"

Orpin stepped back, his mouth going slack with realization. "You were listening, just now?" His question squeaked with incredulity.

Hanke motioned for Sage to unlock the cell door. As Orpin dumbly stepped from the cell, Hanke turned him around and snapped handcuffs onto his wrists. "Edward Orpin, I am arresting you for bearing false witness, multiple arsons, multiple armed robberies, kidnapping Andy Hosier and the attempted murders of Andy Hosier and John Miner. And, if any more charges come to mind while I'm escorting you to jail, I'll add those."

Soon the six of them were heading back through the underground and up the New Elijah's cellar steps. Sage would have been grinning the whole way but he didn't want to eat the dust their feet stirred up. He and Hanke kept firm holds on the prisoner's arms, after taking the precaution of blindfolding and twirling Orpin around before they'd set out. That way Orpin couldn't find the cell nor identify the New Elijah, Gray or Solomon.

Once they were aboveground, Gray headed for the jail eager to tell the Coopers that freedom was imminent. A few minutes later, Hanke and Sage followed, escorting Orpin through a drizzling rain that soaked the coatless firebug. Sage felt no pity. Andy's near-fatal treatment, Jimmy Baldwin's injury at Orpin's arson fire and even the death of that innocent bird, Joey Cockatoo, killed any sympathy he might have ordinarily felt. As did the painful twinge in his injured arm.

The minute Sage entered the Underwriters' office the clerk jumped up and hustled over to Stone's door. He knocked once, opened the door and said in a shaky voice, "That Mr. Miner is back. This time, he's brought a policeman." Stone murmured a response and the clerk opened the door wider, gesturing Sage and Hanke inside.

Stepping forward, Sage said, "Mr. Stone, this is Sergeant Hanke with the Portland Police Bureau. He's been working on the arsons as well as on the murder of Mr. Roberts,"

Stone rose and shook Hanke's hand. He said, "Please gentlemen, take a seat." To the clerk he said, "Roger, kindly close my door."

Once seated and the door shut, Sage said, "Mr. Stone, we found Andy Hosier and he's safe. We also caught the real arsonist. It is not the Cooper boy nor his father. But of course, you already suspected that."

Stone said nothing, just compressed his lips as if preventing words from inadvertently escaping.

Sage continued, "The arsonist, a fellow named Orpin, has confessed. He says a man has been paying him to set fires and frame Hosier. He doesn't know who that man is. He's admitted he accused the Cooper boy on his own initiative."

Stone licked his lips, "Did he kill Wally?" he asked, his eyes fierce.

"He says not. He claims he knows nothing about the attack on Mr. Roberts. We think he's telling the truth about that."

Hanke decided to intervene. "Mr. Stone, it appears that you have been withholding information about the arson fires. Now someone's been murdered. I fully intend to charge you with obstruction of a police inquiry unless you tell us everything you know about these fires. That includes telling us who is working with you."

Hanke spoke in a seldom-used stern voice that was usually effective. Stone, however, seemed only mildly troubled by the threat. He thought for a moment and then said, "Someone else needs to be at this meeting. Let me get him here." Before they could disagree, Stone stood and left his office, shutting the door behind himself. Through the door they heard the low murmur of voices before Stone returned to take his seat again.

"It will be about ten minutes. I've had Roger call."

The door opened and the clerk entered with a coffee tray, its porcelain cups rattling as he set it down on Stone's desk and departed. Without asking, Stone filled three cups, placing one before Sage and another before Hanke before taking one himself. After a long swallow, he said, "If you have no objection, I'd like to give you a little background while we're waiting."

At their nods, he continued, "The purpose of fire insurance is to spread the cost of harm. The more people who are insured with a particular company, the lower their premium rates."

"Insurance companies get themselves into serious trouble when they start competing by lowering their premiums in order to snag new customers. If there's a major fire or other disaster, they won't have enough premium money in reserve to cover all their customers' losses. That's what happened in the 1871 Chicago fire. That's exactly what will happen in San Francisco unless the insurance companies heed our reports finding that the city's a firetrap and raise their rates accordingly."

He paused to look at them, making sure they understood. Getting their nods of agreement, he continued, "And that situation is what gave birth to my organization, the National Board of Fire Insurance Underwriters. Our member insurance companies pay us to determine risk so that they never lower premiums to inadequate levels. But that's not all we do. In the U.S., the annual cost of fires keeps rising. It exceeded $153 million in 1899 which is why the Board recently decided it had to get into the fire prevention business."

Stone paused to sip his coffee, then continued, "Consequent to that decision, we created our National Board of Fire Engineers. They are inspection teams assigned to different cities. Each team member specializes in some aspect related to firefighting and prevention—water supplies, alarm systems, firefighter training, firefighting equipment, building codes, building conditions, and even fire equipment access."

He studied his hands before looking up and continuing, "Wally Roberts was my electrical inspector. He'd survey buildings and determine whether the wiring was safe or whether it posed a fire hazard."

Stone fell silent. His gaze turned inward as he swallowed hard and grief sagged his entire body. Sage and Hanke waited, busying themselves with their coffee. Stone cleared his throat and said, "Wally's was a relatively new position. It came about because, in the last decade, there's been a huge uptick in fires. Eventually, we determined the cause was electricity. Even today, every man jack and his brother is stringing wire, with no understanding of the fire or safety risks involved. That's exactly why Jimmy Baldwin got electrocuted the other night. Live wires were all over that roof. It was a death trap every time it rained."

Stone gave a rueful smile before continuing, "That's the reason we developed a national electrical code and why we are arm-twisting cities into adopting it. And, we successfully 'encouraged' your Common Council to enact the current fire prevention regulations for buildings in what we call the conflagration zones. Your Council calls them "fire limit areas" . . . zones where buildings sit close together like those here in the central business district. New or remodeled buildings have to install sprinkler systems, enclosed stairwells and brick-lined elevator shafts."

Sage interrupted. "What if they don't agree to adopt the Board's recommendations? What if a city tells you to go to hell?"

Stone's smile was sardonic. "Well, then, we simply tell them we will raise the premium rates in that city. Between the threat to their own pocketbooks and the potential outcry from their constituents, they usually see the light."

Now it was Hanke's turn to ask a question. "Didn't I read something about the Powell and Milwaukee roads and the Board?"

Stone dipped his head in acknowledgment. "That's a perfect example of what I'm saying. Our access inspector found that both those roads turn so boggy when it rains that the fire equipment can't reach the fires. We told your Council to either gravel or plank those roads or else our members will refuse to insure the structures in that area."

"That's a hell of a threat," Sage observed.

Stone spread his hands wide. "What else could we do? Houses were burning to the ground that could have been saved. And our insurers were taking a beating which forced them to raise the premiums of everyone else in the city." Stone's tone became confiding as he leaned forward over his desk to say, "It's a secret right now, but we've about convinced the Council that they better buy a fireboat and soon. Those wooden pilings and warehouses along the waterfront are fire-traps. Look at what happened to the Victoria dock just a few days ago.

Without water access, there is no way to stop a major waterfront con-flagration—especially here on the west side where the warehouses and docks are wooden with no firewalls in between."

Sage thought back to his first day as a firefighter. Stone was right. Fire totally destroyed the Victoria warehouse and dock partly because the hose water couldn't reach the dockside.

The three men sat in silence until Sage broke it. "This is all very interesting but what does it have to do with the arson fires Orpin has been setting?"

Stone's answer came in angry, clipped words, "Arson for profit is a problem. It always has been. But it's getting worse. And, not just because someone torches their own building to collect the insurance. Here in Portland, someone has expanded that ploy into an on-going scheme involving a number of buildings. This endangers the whole city be-cause these arson fires can run wild and destroy countless structures."

Stone stopped talking, slapped his palms on the desk and stood at the sound of someone entering the outer office. "Good," Stone said. "Perfect timing."

TWENTY FIVE

The clerk ushered Portland's fire chief into Stone's office and Sage felt relief. Campbell paused briefly, looking efficient in a plain uniform that sported neither the gold braid nor the shiny medals worn by other cities' fire chiefs. Campbell thanked the clerk who nodded, exited and closed the door behind him as he went.

Hanke stood to shake Campbell's hand. Both men were big: Hanke as solid and substantial as a tree trunk, Campbell looked equally strong but more sculpted, with the well-developed shoulders and crooked nose of the bare-knuckle fighter he'd once been. When Sage also stood, Campbell greeted him with an easy smile and firm handshake.

Once all were seated, Stone said to Campbell. "David, you'll be glad to know that Andy Hosier is safe and Sergeant Hanke arrested the real firebug this morning. He's gotten us a legitimate confession."

As Stone spoke, Sage watched Campbell's reaction and saw relief wash through the fire chief's body.

"Andy's safe? That's great news! In fact, that's really great news." He sounded like a man shedding a wagonload of guilt. Jumping up, he vigorously shook Hanke's hand as he declared, "And, by God, I thought we'd never find the real arsonist. Are you sure it's really the firebug? Did the arsonist kill Wally Roberts? It's not a false confession like the last time is it? Is there someone else behind the fires?"

"David," Stone interrupted before Hanke could respond. "Other people are involved in the arson scheme. Unfortunately the firebug, whose name is Edward Orpin, claims he doesn't know who they are. And, Hanke believes Orpin had nothing to do with Wally Robert's murder. All of which means, we still have to find those behind the scheme. Then we have to figure out how to put every one of them behind bars."

Campbell's excitement dimmed but he was still smiling as he turned toward Sage and said, "I'm sorry, Mr. Miner. I should be shaking your hand too. Stone told me that you've been helping us. I thank you for that. I'll bet you also had something to do with catching this Orpin fellow."

Sage shrugged even as Hanke said, "Miner's the one who found Andy and caught Orpin. I just did the arresting."

Sage shot a squelching look at Hanke and said to both Stone and Campbell, "No one can know about my involvement. I am secretly helping and it has to stay that way."

The two men exchanged puzzled looks but both nodded their agreement.

Sage turned to Campbell, "Mr. Stone was just starting to tell us about the arson scheme you two think is underway here in Portland. Would one of you explain exactly what's going on?"

Campbell sat down and cleared his throat. "Insurance companies don't track which company is insuring which property. That means a bad guy or, a conspiracy of bad guys, can insure the same building with multiple insurance companies, burn it down and receive duplicate payments. For this to work though, the scheme requires crooked insurance agents, crooked fire officials and an arsonist.

"Sounds like an easy way to make a lot of money. Though I suppose the insured has to pay them for their services," Sage said.

Stone nodded grimly and joined in. "It gets worse. A crooked agent can insure the building for far more than it's worth and, under state law, we have to pay the amount of the policy, regardless of a structure's actual worth."

At Stone's pass-off gesture Campbell continued, "And, a crooked fire official can sign off on papers attesting that the damage is much worse than it actually is. For example, affirming that the building is a total loss when, in fact, it can be repaired at very little cost."

"Don't the insurance companies track those kind of duplications and patterns?" asked Hanke.

Campbell looked at Stone who answered, "The Board has been trying to get the insurance companies' agreement to set up a clearing house to catch duplications and suspicious claim patterns. So far, the companies are resisting. They don't want to share their sales or their insured's information. We're confident that will change because arson is increasing which means premiums are rising. Eventually, the companies' fear of insufficient reserves and their customers balking at sky high premiums will force their cooperation."

Campbell cleared his throat. "Meanwhile, we've got to put a stop to the current scheme. Until we do, the city's at risk. They'll find another firebug to take this Orpin fellow's place. There's too many hungry men roaming the streets."

Stone jumped in to add, "What's frustrating is that there is no way to tell from this end what fraudulent claims are being submitted. No crooked insurance agent is going to show us those claims."

"Won't the insurance companies provide you with a list of claims coming out of Portland?" Sage asked.

It was Stone who answered, "There are nearly fifty insurance companies issuing fire insurance policies here in Portland. Like I told you earlier, Roger has been typing his fingers to the bone, sending out letters asking for that information. But, there's been a tremendous delay in getting a response from many of those companies. In the meantime, the city's in grave danger. Some of the arson fires have destroyed adjacent homes and businesses that were underinsured or uninsured. People's lives and commerce have been devastated. We've got to stop them, now. We can't wait any longer."

"When did this scheme first get underway?" Sage asked.

Campbell sighed. "It crept up on us. A little over a year ago, we noticed the fire rate was rising but we thought it would taper off as prevention measures were adopted. But then," he paused and looked toward Stone, cleared his throat and went on. "Actually, it was Wally Roberts who first got suspicious. He thought that, once the city adopted the fire limit zones and building codes, the fire rate would decrease. He took it personal when the rate continued to rise. So, even though he was an electrical inspector, on his own time he started snooping around fire scenes. When he did, he found signs of arson and witnessed what he believed was suspicious activity after those fires. When he told me what he was finding, I talked to Stone who temporarily assigned him to investigating."

"What do you mean, 'suspicious activity'?" Hanke asked.

This time it was Stone who answered and his tone was bitter, "More than one man in a suit turned up with a fire station chief at the same fire scene."

This time it was Hanke and Sage who exchanged looks. "And, exactly what does that mean?" Hanke asked.

"It suggests that crooked agents and crooked fire officials were visiting the scene to sign-off on the claim reports sent to the insurance companies. If only one agent turned up at the scene, that would make sense. But, Wally kept seeing multiple agents and fire officials at the same scene. He thought that suggested duplicate claims and other fraudulent shenanigans."

Sage remembered. There'd been that boarding house fire where the firehouse chief, Faden, had met with two men in suits, one after another. That recollection triggered another memory. Ollie had said that Faden had left for the scene of the Joey Cockatoo fire. But, there'd been a different fire station chief at that scene. Not Faden. Two fire station chiefs at the same scene made no sense . . . unless.

"Did Roberts discover the names of the fire station chiefs he saw?" Sage asked.

Campbell hesitated, rubbed his chin and looked at the floor.

"Oh, damn," Sage said before Campbell could reply, "One of them's Ray Faden, the Station 1 chief isn't it?"

Campbell nodded. "Roberts identified a couple others as well. He was just starting to identify the crooked insurance agents when he was murdered. We think that's why he was murdered."

For a beat, no one spoke and the silence felt heavy with thoughts of the dead inspector. Sage knew what they were all thinking. Roberts, eager to expose the malefactors, had likely been discovered and died because of it.

"That's why Andy Hosier got assigned to Station 1, isn't it?" Sage asked, though he already knew the answer.

"He's a bright fellow. Honest as the day is long," Campbell said. "Somehow, they must have figured out that Andy was helping us. I personally owe you a huge debt of gratitude for rescuing him, Mr. Miner. I assigned him to that task and I've not been able to sleep thinking I'd gotten him murdered."

"He's safe but in hiding. Until we clean this mess up, he's in danger. Funny thing is, he doesn't know why they snatched him. According to him, he never saw anything helpful," Sage said, adding, "Does he know you suspect the Station 1 chief?"

"No, we decided it was better that he not know. Because he is such an honest fellow, we were afraid he might give himself away. As far as Andy knew, he was only watching for the firebug and reporting on whatever happened at the fire scenes. I asked him about happenings at the firehouse but tried to sound casual so he wouldn't catch on to my suspicions about Faden."

Recalling Andy's earnestness, Sage thought Campbell had made the right decision. He looked at the fire chief and said thoughtfully, "Maybe he saw something but didn't realize its importance. Since I have him hidden away, do you mind if I tell him about your suspicions regarding Faden? It could jog his memory."

"You might as well. As it stands now, we're dead in the water. The only thing we can hope is that the bad guys are also stalled until they locate another arsonist," Campbell said and again received Stone's agreement. Clearly the two men were a close-knit team. No way either of them was cahooting with the wrongdoers.

"Whatever Andy Hosier might have seen," Hanke said, "You still have the problem of getting enough evidence to arrest and convict the men behind the scheme."

"Yes, and that's the nut we've been unable to crack. Once we identify the insurance agents in the gang, we can find out which companies they're defrauding. Eventually, we'll get the documentary evidence necessary to convict. So, worrying about a conviction is less important than having grounds to arrest them in the first place. Our urgent problem is that we need arrests now to end their scheme and keep this city safe," said Stone.

They all fell silent as each tried to figure out how to identify the conspirators and gather enough evidence to arrest them. Sage was the first to speak. "How many insurance agents are there in the city?"

Stone opened his desk drawer and removed a piece of paper. After running a finger down it, he said "About thirty on our member list. There are more who aren't members of the Board. But, they're small companies. The ones on this list sell the bulk of fire insurance in Portland."

"Do you think some of the crooked insurance agents are on that list?"

This brought a twist of disgust to Stone's expression. "Most, if not all, I'm afraid," he said. It's the mid-size and big companies that belong to the Underwriters' association. The little companies don't want to pay the membership fee. But, it's those little fellows who'd notice right away if there was a surge in Portland claims. So, I'm afraid it's our bigger, member companies that are taking the brunt of the scheme."

"So, we're looking at about thirty agents. Are there any agents that you are certain can't be involved?" Sage asked.

Stone looked uncomfortable so Campbell stepped in to answer for him. "Here's the problem, Mr. Miner. I completely trusted Ray Faden. Heck, Charlotte and I have even had Ray and his wife over for dinner. So, I seriously misjudged his character. That's been a damn bitter pill to swallow. But, it's taught us that we have to distrust everyone until they prove themselves."

Sage knew exactly what Campbell meant. Betrayal was a thread woven into his own family's lineage. When he was an infant, his own father had betrayed his grandfather and uncle to the mine owner's thugs. That act caused their death and permanently tore the family apart—Sage had never known his own father. "Okay," he said. "It might take some time to set up but I think I know what we can do."

Simultaneously, both Stone and Campbell leaned forward and said, "What?"

Sage shook his head. "Before I lay it out, I need to see if she's willing to do it."

"She?" Hanke said sharply. "I hope you're not planning to put her in danger."

Sage laughed. "As if the threat of danger would stop her. You know how she is. Besides, she's the only one who can pull this off."

TWENTY SIX

As expected, Mae's eyes lit up when he explained his idea though her tone was thoughtful when she said, "That's some plan. We'd have to get our ducks in order. And, it's still rough around the edges," she added thoughtfully. "First off, we better look for a house. It' be hard to do from a hotel."

"And Fong," he said.

She looked puzzled. "I don't think it'll work if we make him my husband."

Sage chuckled. "Now that would cause some excitement. The whole town would gab about it. No, he'll be your servant."

"Good lord, you're not telling me I have to act the la-de-da lady, are you?" Her nose wrinkled in disgust.

"Nope, I was thinking of a sudden inheritance that comes complete with Chinese cook and servant. An inheritance you are eager to cash out in the biggest way possible."

"I do believe it just might work," she said and grinned.

It had been awhile since he'd seen her this excited. Maybe when they were packing to move up here to Portland. They'd been leaving New Orleans following a successful general strike by twenty thousand workers. Mae and he deserved some credit for that success which garnered wage increases. Sage had helped unite forty-two unions behind the strike. And, Mae had led the women workers and workmen's wives into the fight as equal partners. That battle won, though, they'd been happy to relocate to the cool, rainy Pacific Northwest.

"I'm thinking it'd work best if you said you're from New Orleans," he said. "Since we stayed there, you can mention familiar places if you get quizzed."

"Anyways, what else do we need to get done if we're going to make this work?" Mae wondered aloud.

"Well, now that you're on board, I need to get Stone, Campbell and Hanke's agreement and assistance. It'll only work if everybody dips in an oar."

Lowering clouds muted the mid-afternoon sun. "How many interviews do you think you can conduct in a day?" Sage asked her.

"Probably, no more than eight or ten. We don't want them tripping over each other on the front stoop," Mae said.

"Think you'll have any trouble playing the scheming, money-hungry woman come from afar?" His question was half teasing, half serious.

For a few beats, only the horse's clop and the axle's squeak disturbed the quiet. Then she took a deep breath and answered, "Well, I can lie with the best of them. But, I've never needed to keep it going for so long a stretch. Usually, it meant looking at the mine owner's gun thugs straight on and saying, sweet as molasses, "'Why no, Mister. I don't rightly know where my daddy is.'"

Sage laughed, picturing that deceptively sweet, clever young girl. "Chief Campbell found us a decent house. That'll make it easier. They'll tend to believe you in that setting," Sage said to encourage her. Her hesitation was a little worrying.

"We better hope the neighbors don't spill the beans," she said.

"Campbell had the owner tell the neighbors that his cousin and her servant would be staying there in his absence. Then he warned them that she was one of those women who'd never stop talking if you gave her an opening. He figured that since his neighbors weren't particularly friendly, that tidbit of information would keep them away."

Their buggy wheels jostled into and out of a pothole. Mae clutched at both seat and hat. "I don't see why we need go to all the trouble of having me ride the train in from Vancouver."

Sage reined the horse to stand behind a line of other vehicles. He turned toward her and said, "Because these aren't stupid men. They might check to see if you arrived by train. So, when you get to the Portland station do something memorable."

Minutes later, with a whistle and churn of backwash, the ferry nudged against the dock. Once its passengers and vehicles off loaded, their line boarded. Soon they were in the middle of the Columbia, the crisp breeze more than a little chill. "At least the train will be warmer," Sage observed.

"I don't know why you think it is so darn necessary to come across the river with me. I could get from the ferry dock to the train station on my own," Mae said.

"Hey, you're about to put yourself in danger. It's made more so by the fact that the crooks are, somehow, always one step ahead of us. To keep you safe, I'll have to stay clear from now on. So, this ride's my last chance to see you for awhile. Besides, someone has to make sure you get on the right train," he added with a grin.

Her gloved fist punched his shoulder. But, she was grinning back at him.

Once he saw Mae and her luggage aboard the inbound train from Chicago, Sage didn't hang around.

Less than hour later, the Chicago train pulled into Portland's Union Station. Passengers surged through the platform doors, heading for the street. The cacophony of noise ricocheted off the marble floor and walls until silenced by a woman's shriek. She'd entered in the midst of a particularly dense throng of arriving passengers. As people turned to look, she shouted. "My land sakes what kind of barbarian place is this? Some scoundrel just pinched my nether region and another scamp tried to snatch my handbag." She held aloft a small leather purse.

Her declaration sent a policeman hustling in her direction. "Excuse me ma'am," he said politely. "Were you just assaulted?"

"I certainly was if that means getting pinched where no lady should," she declared in a loud, shrill voice. "Just what do you intend to do about it?"

It took some time but ultimately the lady, who said her name was "Mabel Davis," settled down and the policeman learned she hadn't seen who'd pinched her or who'd tried to grab her purse. Since they were now nearly alone in the cavernous hall, her identification no longer mattered. Any potential suspect had long since departed.

Eventually, after a few more minutes of loud berating, she huffily accepted his apologies and his offer to obtain a hansom cab for herself and her luggage. She smiled at how relieved he looked when her cab began rolling away.

Forty minutes later, Mae descended from that same cab on the eastside, just a few blocks south of the Sunnyside business district. The minute her boots hit the dirt street she started talking non-stop in a strident, carrying voice. "Are you sure this is the right address? Driver, put my luggage on the porch, I have a man who'll take it in. Is it always this wet? How do you keep warm in this infernal rain?" Her braying voice continued on and on until the neighbors' curtains twitched aside.

The house before her was a one-story, well-maintained, miniature Victorian, complete with sharp gables, tiny bay window and scalloped shingles. Not her favorite style. She preferred the newer design—simple, unadorned boxes with big front porches. Still, it was pretty. Sage had told her that a brother-in-law to Campbell's sister owned the house. A bachelor salesman, the fellow frequently left town to drum up business for his employer. Since he'd already planned a trip, he'd willingly lent his home for Campbell's mysterious purpose.

Before the cab rolled away, a black-clad Chinese man appeared, though later, none of the neighbors could say whether he came from the cab, the house or from around the corner. Within minutes the cab was gone, the luggage carried inside and the woman's jabber finally cut off by a closed door.

Inside, Mae dropped into a parlor chair. "My gracious, I don't think I've ever talked such a blue streak in my life. My mouth is dry as grit."

"I bring hot tea, one minute," Fong said.

While she waited, she surveyed her surroundings. It was a tidy home. The furniture was well-kept and sturdy, with snow white doilies on every chair back to protect against greasy hair pomades. Only a few knickknacks sat on end tables that were bare rather than draped with the heavy Victorian brocades she disliked. Her spirits lifted. She'd been right. This home would make her role believable—better than if she was in a hotel.

"Here tea," Fong said, setting down a tray holding a pot and two cups. He poured for them before taking the chair across from her.

After a sip, he said, "I think better I speak no English. That way, they not worry if I stay close."

"That's a good idea. I'll figure out a way to let them know. Though, I think Sage is overdoing it. I do not need you to stay within five feet of me at all times."

Fong laughed. "Sometimes, he fall overboard."

"With a big splash," she agreed. "Anyways, I'm fairly certain you could cover twenty feet in an eye blink."

"Maybe I stay just outside this room. It look less funny."

"Was a telephone instrument installed?"

"Yes. Mr. Sage had installed yesterday."

She was quiet for a moment then she said. "I've never talked through one of them contraptions. "

"No worry," Fong assured her with a toothy grin. "After two weeks, we both be expert."

Silence fell and as the sky darkened, they quietly sipped their tea until Mae said, "He gets us into the darndest messes."

Fong smiled. "Yes, much fun."

Mae snorted, "See if you still think that after days of playing the mute servant."

"Yes, you get best part," he said blandly.

"Why, you devil!" she exclaimed. "As if it will be easy to act like a greedy, conniving woman."

She expected a playful verbal jab from him in response but got a somber look and thoughtful nod instead. "For you, it will be hard," he said.

Her eyes prickled at the unexpected compliment but she only said, "Land's sakes, we're sitting here in the dark. What will the neighbors think?"

Later that evening, after Mozart's nine o'clock closing, Matthew was standing in the doorway of Sage's room, shifting from foot to foot. Sage had shed his hosting suit and was pulling on long johns. His turnout coat hung over the chair back, his helmet sat on the seat and his boots stood before it on the floor. That way, he wouldn't waste time getting to the station if the city fire bell sounded. Though, with the downpour outside and the firebug in jail, a middle of the night summons is unlikely, he assured himself.

He gestured the boy into a chair, saying, "Since you seem a tad antsy, I conclude that you are eager to tell me that you succeeded in your mission."

"I got them letters delivered," Matthew began.

"You mean you delivered the letters," Sage corrected.

For a moment Matthew looked puzzled, then light dawned and his face reddened beneath its smattering of freckles. "Yes, sir. I delivered the letters."

"All thirty?"

"Yes, sir. Put each one in a human hand, just like you said."

"What else? As Mrs. Clemens would say, you wouldn't be 'fidgeting like a hoppy toad on a hot stove', if there isn't something else you want to tell me."

Matthew took a deep breath. "I found a messenger who look a note to that Nob Hill address you gave me. He usually hangs out on the same corner downtown because he has regular customers in the near-by office buildings."

Sage straightened in his chair. "Really? Did he know who gave him the note?"

That question brought a vigorous shake of the head from Matthew, "No, sir. He said it was a stranger who came up to him."

"Could he describe the stranger?"

Another head shake. "It was near dark and raining. The fellow had a long coat, big hat and an umbrella."

"Where did this happen?"

"Down around Sixth and Alder." Matthew looked at Sage, "But, he told me there was one thing peculiar about the fellow."

"What's that?" So far, Matthew's report contained nothing helpful. That street corner sat in the heart of the business district and saw a lot of foot traffic. Meaning the stranger could have been anyone.

"He said the fellow sounded funny."

"You mean, he had an accent?" That was a bit promising unless it was a common one like British, German or Missourian.

"Nah, he said the fellow talked like he had a frog caught in this throat that he couldn't get clear of. He said that's why he remembered him from before."

"Before?" Sage prodded.

Matthew nodded. "Yup, he says it's the same man who had him deliver a note to that Andy fellow at the firehouse."

The "new fangled" telephone instrument started jangling promptly at nine a.m. After about ten calls, Mae no longer stared into the ear

piece as if she expected an insect to crawl out before she said "hello." Her side of the conversations remained the same with little variation,

"Yes, this is Mrs. Davis speaking."

"Why, certainly. Let me check my calendar."

"Why yes, it looks like I can meet with you on that date and time."

"Yes, that's the address. The same as on the letter I sent you."

By evening, it became harder to find openings in her schedule. Finally, she lifted the ear piece, laid it on the table and covered it with a pillow.

A tinny noise erupted from the beneath the pillow. Fong, on his way into the kitchen, paused to stare at the pillow and raise an inquiring eyebrow.

"It's the operator. I figure she'll get tired of telling me to hang up and will just unplug the dang thing. One more ring and I swear I'll throw it halfway to China. I'm going to bed. The first appointment is at nine a.m.. You better get some sleep too."

TWENTY SEVEN

ANDY OPENED THE DOOR TO Sage's knock. "Come in, come in," he exclaimed. "Did you catch them? Can I go back to the firehouse? Violet's fed me up to the gills and then some. All I do is eat."

Sage eyed the young firefighter who did, indeed, look fully recovered from his ordeal. But he had to shake his head. "We haven't caught them yet but we've got a plan in the works. I know you want to get back to the engine and Ollie but you're still in danger."

He glanced around, didn't see Violet and the bedroom door was closed. Noticing Sage's look Andy said, "Violet's having a lay down. She does that a lot because it's her last weeks and she has trouble sleeping. Let's sit at the table and drink some coffee. That Mrs. Clemens sent us a whole bunch of groceries, including lots of coffee. I keep the pot hot."

Mae hadn't told Sage of her gift, but it didn't surprise him. She was the toughest woman he knew but she was also the most kind-hearted and generous—like so many people raised poor.

Once seated, Sage said. "What I am about to tell you must stay completely secret. You can't tell Violet or Ollie or your brother-in-law Jimmy or anyone else."

When Andy nodded eagerly and leaned forward, Sage continued, "First, I know about Chief Campbell. I met with him and Jasper Stone two days ago."

Andy breathed a sigh of relief. "That's good. It's bothered me something awful not to tell you I was helping him, especially after you rescued me. But I promised."

"That's why I'm going to trust you. You're a man who keeps his word," Sage said and saw the young firefighter's spine straighten. "Campbell told me that all you were supposed to do was observe at fire scenes, study the spectators and make a report."

"That's exactly right. Other than the one time in Mr. Stone's office, I've been meeting Chief Campbell at his friend's house, down in Lair Hill. And, I only meet him once a week to give my report."

"Is that where you were going when you were grabbed?"

Andy shook his head. "No. I got a special message from Chief Campbell. It was the first time he sent me one. It said it was urgent and I should meet him behind a shop up near Nob Hill. When I got there, these fellows jumped out and knocked me down. Next thing I knew, my hands were tied behind my back, a gag was in my mouth and a flour sack was over my head. They kept me somewhere close until it got dark, then hauled me in a wagon and dropped me into that cellar where you found me."

"Did you see the men who attacked you?"

Again, another head shake. "It happened so quick that all I saw was the dirt they pushed my nose into."

"Did they say anything?"

"One told me to cooperate or I'd get a pig-sticker in the ribs. I believed him because he was pricking me in the neck with it." Andy's eyes darkened with remembered fear.

"Andy, can you recall anything you said or did that might have drawn their attention to you?"

This question brought a vehement shake of the head. "I know I didn't do anything. Chief Campbell told me over and over that I shouldn't do nothing but observe and report. I wasn't to go following people or snooping or saying nothing to nobody. And, I didn't."

"Somehow they've figured out that I'm helping you, that I'm not just a stranger you picked up somewhere. Did you say anything about that to anyone?"

Andy's mouth fell open before he said, "My Lord, no! I kept it totally secret. Just told the fellows I met you at a café. Said I didn't know you but since you thought maybe you'd like to be an extraman, I was showing you the ropes."

Sage believed him. Andy was a black and white kind of guy. Not the type to stretch clearly set guidelines to encompass the gray. Sage pondered the situation. Someone had figured out Andy was working for Campbell. And, they'd figured out that Sage was helping him and Campbell. But how?

"Andy, did anyone follow you to your meetings with Chief Campbell?"

"They sure didn't. He made me take a trolley across the Burnside Bridge. Then I had to walk down the eastside, on neighborhood streets until I could take a trolley back across the Morrison Bridge. The whole time I was supposed to study everyone I saw just to make sure no one was following. I did just like he said, every single time."

Campbell had been just as adamant that Andy wasn't followed. He'd watched the young firefighter arrive from a block away and never once saw a follower. So how did the wrongdoers discover Andy's participation in Campbell's secret investigation?

Sage took a deep breath. "Okay Andy, what I'm about to tell you must remain strictly secret. Don't even casually ask Ollie anything about it. If you do, you could put him in serious danger."

For the first time, Andy paled. "Ollie? He's in danger?"

Sage gave a sharp shake of the head. "No, no, not so far as I know. And, I've told him to be extremely careful that he's not followed when he visits you. But you can't tell him anything I'm about to tell you because he might give himself away. It's better he doesn't know."

"Yah, he told me that he's being real careful. Except for bringing Sadie one time the other day, he usually visits Jimmy first thing in the morning. Then he sneaks out a hospital side door to see me. He's certain no one sees him come here. It works out good, 'cause he visits Jimmy in the morning, Violet says she feels she can sleep in. She sits with Jimmy in the afternoon."

"How is Jimmy?" Sage asked, feeling guilty that he hadn't already asked after the cat-rescuing firefighter.

"Oh, he's all taped up but he's doing great. We expect him home tomorrow or the next day. Doctor says falling off the ladder probably saved his life even if it did break his ribs. Says hitting the ground started his heart a 'going after it got electrocuted."

Sage paused to ponder that medical fact. He once crashed into a man clutching a live wire, slamming them both to the ground. Maybe that was why the man had lived.

Sage gave himself a mental shake and returned to the present. "Okay Andy, like I was saying, what I'm about to tell you has to be kept strictly secret. You can't tell Ollie or Jimmy or Violet. Do you promise me that?"

Andy turned somber. "I've learned the hard way that these folks mean business. I don't want to put anybody in that kind of danger." He smiled ruefully and added, "or myself. You have my solemn promise."

So, Sage quickly outlined the insurance fraud scheme they believed was underway in the city. He saved the most startling news for last, "And, we're afraid that Ray Faden is up to his eyebrows in the scheme."

That statement sent Andy back in his chair as shock dropped his mouth open, dismay evident as he said, "Oh, no."

"Did you say or do anything around Faden that would have made him suspicious of you or me?"

That brought a moment of thought before Andy said, "I'm positive I didn't. I was so careful. Chief Campbell told me that a firefighter might be involved with the firebug so I was extra careful when I was at the firehouse and at the fire scenes. But, I sure never dreamt it might be our own station chief."

He fell silent again. "I guess that's why you don't want me going back to the firehouse. Faden could sic the bad guys on me again." Realization turned his mouth into a small "oh" before he added, "Or he might do something worse than cut loose my boot soles. Or order me to haul the hose under a burning sign."

"About those bad guys. Do you remember anything at all that might help us find them?"

"Well, the one that took me down was bigger than me. Taller and heavier. I could tell he was taller because his voice came from above my ear and, after he knocked me down, he jumped on my back. He felt like a ton of bricks." Andy brightened, "But you'll sure the heck know him when you find him."

Sage sat forward, hoping this would be the breakthrough. "How? How will we know him?"

"'Cause his voice is raspy—like how firefighters sound after they've swallowed too much smoke."

Sage trudged slowly back to the city center. Uneasiness—heavy as the overhead clouds—lay across his shoulders. The mid-November chill penetrated his canvas coat and the household smoke, pushed down by the moisture-filled air, was thick enough to taste. Sage noted these things but didn't dwell on them. He was worried. He'd been careful not to lead anyone to Andy's hiding place but his fear for the young man was sharper in the aftermath of his visit. Somehow, the crooks knew about him and Andy. Until he figured out how, both of them were in danger.

Inside the firehouse, Ollie was again babying his steam engine, quietly waxing its red paint to a high gloss.

After making sure no one else was about, Sage said softly, "Andy sends his regards."

Ollie smiled, "I'll be glad when it's safe for him to come back to work. I miss his jibber jabbering."

"Well, he for sure misses you as well. I've had a hard time convincing him to stay hidden."

Ollie nodded and looked worried. "I did something I hope was alright," he said hesitantly.

His words alarmed Sage, but he only said, "Tell me."

"You know that Chinese fellow who came to see you the other day?" At Sage's nod, Ollie continued talking. "He turned up here looking for you and it was raining dogs and cats outside, so I told him to wait for you over yon in the empty stall that belonged to that electrocuted horse. Sadie's keeping him company. She took to him right away."

Relief made Sage grin. "He's waited for me in worse places. Anybody see him?"

"Nope, I made certain to sneak him in. You two want to talk, I'll stand guard. Someone comes, I'll start talking to them real loud."

Sage patted the older man's shoulder and headed for the stall. Sure enough, Fong was there, lying on his back, his coat draped over the straw to dry, his hat over his eyes. Sadie lay curled in a tight ball against his side. Without moving, Fong said. "Straw soft, dog warm. Maybe I live here."

Sage opened the stall gate and sat down in the straw. Sadie lifted her head for the customary scratch between her ears. Scratch received, she sighed, closed her eyes and tucked her head back beneath her tail.

"Did something happen?" Sage asked softly.

Fong hesitated then replied in an equally soft voice. "Not sure. I see strange man lurking outside house."

"Then why the hell are you here?" Fear lent volume and snap to Sage's question.

Fong sat up, put a cautionary finger to his lips, before saying mildly, "Two reasons. Lady Mother want you to know about suspicious man and to stay away. Second reason, I escort her to Portland Hotel for late lunch. Angus say he watch over her until I come back."

A flush traveled up Sage's neck. "Damn, I'm sorry Mr. Fong. I should've known better. You're always more cautious than I am. As for the fellow you spotted, I'll bet the bad guys are watching her to make sure she's legitimate."

Fong accepted the apology with a shrug so Sage continued, "I just came from seeing Andy."

"He know anything to help?" Fong looked hopeful.

"Just that the man who snatched him is tall, heavy and has a gravelly voice."

Fong shook his head. "Not much," he observed.

"It does match the description the messenger gave. Anyway, I guess we'll know him when we hear him talk," Sage said. "I can't shake the feeling that someone's following me around—even though Orpin's locked up. So, don't worry. I'll stay well clear of the house. Has she met with any agents yet?"

"Three this morning. She taking break and will see three more this afternoon."

"How's she doing?"

Fong's teeth showed in a big grin, "Lady Mother lie pretty darn good."

"Lord, don't tell her that. She won't like hearing it."

Fong made a show of being offended. "Fong Kam Tong not stupid." he said, tapping his forehead for emphasis.

TWENTY EIGHT

"Land sakes! I do not know how you people stand this damp cold. It sinks right into the bones," were her first words to the insurance agent as Fong ushered him into the room. "I swear my teeth haven't stopped chattering since I stepped off the train." To Fong she ordered in a loud voice, "You, boy! Go fetch more fire wood!" while pointing at the potbellied stove. Then even louder she said, "First, tea!" Fong bowed himself out of sight.

"Please, sit yourself down," she said to the insurance agent. "That Chinaman doesn't speak a word of English. I don't know why those people don't learn to speak the language of the country they invade. And, to top it off, I don't think he's even Christian! I can't believe I've got to sleep under the same roof with that heathen."

Once the agent was settled, she continued, "Well, now. I do believe your name is Jasper Danvers, mine is Mrs. Mabel Davis. I'm from New Orleans. My great uncle died and left me this house in the middle of nowhere and now I have to figure what to do with it. He's also left me that heathen Chinaman. Uncle's will says I have to give the darn Chinaman $2,000 before I can collect my inheritance. Now, in my opinion, this house and its contents aren't worth much more than that. So, I've got to figure out a way to make this expensive trip worth my while." She paused, narrowing her eyes as she studied the man in the chair.

He took advantage of the pause. "Excuse me ma'am, Mrs. Davis" he said. "There must be a misunderstanding. I'm an insurance agent, not a real estate agent. If you want to sell the house, I can give you the names of . . . ."

Mrs. Davis looked offended, puffing out her chest and staring down her nose at Danvers. "Well, really. As if I wouldn't know the difference, Mister Insurance Man. I have to get this house insured. What if it burns down around my ears? There's fires burning in every room to chase out the chill. Fine howdy-do if all I get for traipsing across the country is a pile of ashes atop a piece of worthless ground. In the meantime, firewood's costing me a fortune."

"Well ma'am, I can certainly insure the . . . ."

She cut him off again, "I want to insure it for more than it's worth. That way, if it burns down, at least I'll get my trip paid for—and cover what I have to pay that heathen Chinaman."

"Well, my company doesn't insure structures for more than they're worth . . . ." he managed to get out.

"Well, then, tell me this. Does your company still pay if I've got more than one policy on the house? Maybe a second policy with someone else?"

The man reddened and switched from being genial to stern, his blue eyes turning frosty. He rose from his chair and donned his hat. "Madam," he said, repressively, "I do not like what you are insinuating. I will not issue a policy that duplicates another insurance company's policy. Furthermore, if and when I discover that has happened, I alert both companies."

"I'm sorry madam, but my company can do without your business. Thank you for your time and good day!" Danvers slapped his hat onto his head and walked rapidly to the front door, brushing past Fong who stood in the archway holding a tea tray. The front door opened and shut with a bang.

Fong's eyebrows rose above twinkling eyes. "Did not land that fish?" he asked.

She looked rueful but still smiled. "Nope. He's a good one, I'm thinking. That makes four in a row that have let me know, in no uncertain terms, that I'm a conniving criminal they want nothing to do with. Either I'm a bad actress or maybe we're on the wrong track."

"Twenty-six more to go. Not time to worry yet. Maybe next one."

Fong's optimism was justified. Because, when Mae's questions began hinting at fraud, her next appointment leaned forward, his eyes keen as he oozed sympathy. And his voice, according to Mae who later told the story, turned slug belly slimy. "You poor woman. You came all the way from New Orleans, you say? I am sure your uncle thought he was doing you a good turn. Too bad it's not working out that way."

Mae, figuring it was time to turn on the waterworks, pulled a handkerchief from her sleeve and began snuffling and dabbing at her eyes. "My son was supposed to come help me but he got delayed in Chicago and now I'm here, stranded in this miserable place all by myself except for that heathen Chinaman who can't speak English," she said, her voice quavering.

Reaching to pat her hand, the insurance man by the name of Hill said, "Oh, I am so sorry."

Mae straightened but kept her woebegone expression. "I'm not a poor woman by any means," she told him, "but I expected my uncle to leave me better off. I have a home and a son to take care of in New Orleans. And, now almost every penny I get from selling this house will go to pay off that heathen. I don't know what I am going to do."

"Surely, your uncle's lawyer can help you get out of paying the Chinese fellow," Hill prodded.

That brought forth another wail, "No. He's the problem. He says I have to pay and he won't budge an inch. My uncle supported that heathen Chinaman for ten years. I don't see why he should get any more of my money but the lawyer says my uncle called him a loyal friend and that's that." One dry eye stayed on Hill as she dabbed at her cheeks with a hanky. Sure enough, calculation washed across the insurance agent's face.

"Well, Mrs. Davis. You may have come to just the right man. Tell me, do you have any personal attachment to this house?"

She shook her head vigorously and said, "I've already shipped home my uncle's few valuable bits and pieces. I don't care what happens to the rest or this house as long as I get my money out of it." The look she sent him was her best effort at a mix of hopeful and determined.

"You do have money for more than one premium, don't you?" he asked.

She nodded eagerly, sorrowful pretense gone. "Yes, indeed, I can pay for quite a few premiums."

Hill rubbed his hands together, "Well, then. I believe I have a solution for you. Let me talk to some of my colleagues in the insurance business. I am sure that, between us, we'll be able get you what you deserve," he said and actually winked.

She sent him a trembling smile from below two very calculating dark blue eyes. "You are such an understanding man, Mr. Hill. I am so very grateful."

Gushing gratitude, she walked him to the door where he turned to her, saying, "Give me a today to set things in motion. In the meantime, it might be better if you stop interviewing other insurance agents. If you have more appointments scheduled, you'll need to cancel them. You promise?"

She nodded, her eagerness genuine.

He put a reassuring hand on her shoulder and squeezed. "I'll be back tomorrow with some of my colleagues to explain the details and have you sign some application forms. Be ready to pay the premiums then."

He donned his fedora, buttoned his overcoat and gave her a big smile. "You do as I suggest, dear lady, and I can guarantee you'll be heading back to sunny New Orleans sooner than you think."

Her profuse 'thank you's' trailed him down the sidewalk. Once he was gone, and the door closed, she turned to Fong. He'd been standing out of sight in the hallway behind a large grandfather clock. "Did you hear all that?" she asked. "Guess I'll spend this afternoon on that confangled machine canceling all those meetings. Thank the Lord."

"I think you land very big fish," he said, his grin mirroring hers.

"I suspect he's the big daddy whale of them all," she told him smugly.

"Your 'darn' Chinaman go make tea now so we can celebrate like heathens," he said.

Halfway up the airshaft, the kid clinging to his neck stops sobbing. Far above, a tiny patch of blue sky keeps him climbing. His legs tremble as he searches frantically for hand and foot holds. Then he abruptly halts, his shoulder snagged on a rock outcrop. No matter how hard he tries to wriggle away, it holds him fast. His hands and feet begin slipping. He, and the boy he's trying to save, are going to fall. He screams as his fingers tear loose.

"Sage. Sage, it is dream." Fong's soft voice abruptly ends his plummet into the coal mine's depths.

Heart pounding, Sage opened his eyes to see Fong, candle in hand, worry wrinkling his forehead. "Back in coal mine?" Fong asked.

Sage nodded. Fong knew all about the nightmares. Then panic hit him. "What time is it? Has something happened? Is she alright?" he said, flinging the covers aside.

Fong knew to answer the most important question first. "She is fine. It is two in morning. Sorry so late but Sunnyside house being watched near round the clock. Necessary I wait until watcher leave. Then slip out back door and over neighbor fence."

"What's happened?" Sage asked while pulling on his trousers.

"Plan working. Insurance agent take bait. Say he is going to bring others. Problem is, for sure house watched now. At least one man, sometimes two men."

"Great. I'll go get Hanke. Did she remember to mention her son?"

"Every time she talks to them," Fong reassured him.

Sage knocked softly until Hanke flung the door open, a striped robe wrapped around his big frame. Even though he had to have been asleep, the police sergeant looked wide awake. "Time for me to appear?" he guessed.

"Yup. Fong says there are men watching the house. He thinks she'd be safer if you are there when he has to leave."

Hanke nodded. "Okay, I'll send a patrolman over now to see what he can see and to make those watchers cautious. In the meantime, the morning train is due in around nine. I'll head over to Vancouver and be at the house before ten. Do you think that's early enough? Or should I just go straight there?"

"No, no. Arrive on the train. It doesn't look like they intend to do anything other than watch just yet. Probably too greedy to pass up the deal. I think that they're just being cautious. Besides, Fong's still there and he certainly can handle two of them without any trouble."

"Unless they have guns," Hanke said grimly.

As Sage headed back to Mozart's a drizzle drummed his hat brim. Feet cold and eyelids heavy, he was thinking only of his warm bed. Then the city fire bell began tolling its summons. Briefly, he considered ignoring it but then his mind's eye saw the firefighters rolling off their cots. And, he'd promised that he'd keep helping Ollie until Andy returned. If I don't, Sage thought, Andy will throw caution out the window and decide to help his friend.

With a sigh, he changed direction. At least, he wore his John Miner outfit and the firehouse was only a few blocks away.

As he reached Station 1, the doors crashed open and the ladder truck rumbled out, followed by the fire engine. Sadie was at the front, barking a warning as her eyes scanned ahead for any charging canine. Sage ran to the fire engine, grabbed Ollie's outstretched hand and was hauled aboard. Andy's turnout bag was stashed beneath the seat.

This time the fire was in a cooperage. Fire Chief Campbell was already on the scene. Glancing at Faden, Sage observed that the fire station chief's jaw was clenched. He'd been delegated to hauling hose with the rest of his men. Evidently, Campbell was taking no chances with the safety of the Station 1 crew.

The fire chief's eyes met Sage's and Sage gave him a slow nod. The other man's look of fleeting satisfaction was followed by one of regret. Then Campbell turned his attention back to the conflagration. Sage glanced in Faden's direction and caught the fire station chief staring at him, speculation narrowing his eyes. A cold finger ran down Sage's spine and it didn't come from the dribbling rain.

Gray dawn broke as they were rolling up the hoses. The fire was out and since the barrel-making factory sat far from any neighboring buildings, no other property suffered a loss. The successful outcome left the men easy in their movements and tiredly joking. Campbell remained on the scene, picking his way among the blackened timbers. His lips were a tight line in his tired, soot-covered face as he passed Sage. Under his breath, he said, "Arson," before climbing into his buggy.

What they had feared had happened. The conspirators had found Orpin's replacement and were back in business.

TWENTY NINE

THEY WATCHED AS A BIG, placid-looking man, carrying a suitcase, trudged up the walkway and mounted the stairs to the Sunnyside house. The door opened and the Davis woman brushed past her Chinese servant to throw her arms around the stranger. Had to be the son they'd said she was expecting.

"Sure don't envy him that mother," said one.

"Why's that?"

"Boss had me check the train station. She made a real scene there. Claimed someone tried to steal her purse. A real harridan, somebody said."

Both pulled their scarves up to cover their mouths, having nothing more to say. It was getting bitter cold and this was a boring job. So far, only the son and their boss had entered the house since the day before. She must have canceled all the appointments like she'd been told. She and the Chinese fellow had stayed indoors all night according to the man they'd relieved that morning. The only activity had been an alert patrolman strolling up the street a few times. The man they'd relieved said he'd ducked out of sight before the copper saw him.

Inside the house, Mr. Fong and Mae enthusiastically welcomed Sergeant Hanke. "Glad to see Mr. Adair got a hold of you," Mae said as she helped him shed his wet coat. Hanging it on the hall tree, she asked "You see our friends outside? Any news from Mr. Adair?"

Hanke nodded grimly. "I saw the two of them. As for Mr. Adair, he was on the train platform when I arrived. 'Course, he didn't look like himself. Instead, he was dressed as that Miner fellow. He told me there'd been another arson last night. It means the criminals are back at it. He said Campbell's plenty worried. The weather's turning bad. That will make it hard to fight fires."

"You arrived just in time. Hill called early this morning. He and his friends will be here around eleven with papers for me to sign. You'll have a front row seat when it comes to hearing about their shenanigans," Mae said. "Did Mr. Adair say what he planned to do next?"

"Mr. Adair said he plans to follow that insurance man, Hill. "

Hanke saw an exchange of worried looks between Mr. Fong and Mrs. Clemens. Fong nodded and quickly left the room. Seconds later, a distant door opened, sending a chilly draft scooted across the floor, before there was the sound of it closing.

"Where's Mr. Fong going?" Hanke asked.

"Over the backyard fence, I suspect," Mae answered drily. "He's gone to ask some of his friends to keep an eye on Mr. Adair. I just hope that happens before my boss gets himself into trouble."

Hanke nodded in agreement. "I know what you mean. I don't know how that head of his survives all the thumps."

Angus Solomon stood at the Portland Hotel's dining room podium, tallying the number of patrons they'd served for lunch. Usually, the dining room was empty in the lull between lunch and supper. Today the exception was a group of five businessmen who'd taken the large round table in the far corner. They'd only ordered coffee and cakes. He doubted they'd stay for supper.

Hearing a timid clearing of throat, he glanced up to see a messenger boy standing before him. "Excuse me, Sir," the boy said, "But I have message to deliver to a Mr. Solomon here in the dining room."

Solomon identified himself, took the message and gave the boy a coin. After unfolding the paper he read, "Can you meet me outside, by the hotel garbage bins? Sage."

Turning his duties over to a nearby waiter, Solomon donned his overcoat before stepping out the hotel's side door. Sure enough, Sage Adair leaned against the hotel's brick wall using the narrow window sill above his head as miniscule shelter from the rain.

"Thanks for coming, Angus. Sorry about the rain," Sage said.

"You'll catch your death out here," Solomon chided. "The temperature is plummeting and some guests said it's already snowing in the Columbia River Gorge.

"I can believe that. I'm hoping the man I'm following doesn't stay too long in your dining room. I spotted him coming out of his house but lost him when he got into a cab. I was trying to pick up his trail when I just happened to see him enter the hotel. If I stay out here much longer, I'll be stiff as a statue."

"He must be one of the men at the corner table," Solomon said. "They've been there about half an hour. I suspect they'll soon leave since they waved off more drinks. Which one is he?"

"Fellow by the name of Hill. He's an insurance agent."

Solomon was nodding. "Yes, I know him. He seems to be leading their little gathering. Looks to be some kind of celebration—lots of raising their glasses to each other."

"Any chance that you might know the names of the other men with Hill?"

Solomon thought for a moment. "I believe I do," he said.

"Could you write them down and send them to me at Mozart's? In case I get caught, I don't want the list on me."

"Caught, Sage?" Solomon's brow lowered. "Are you saying Hill and those other men might be part of that arson scheme you've uncovered?"

Sage shivered and shoved his bare hands deep into his pockets. "Good. Fong's told you about that. But, yes, it's beginning to look that way. We're slowly putting the pieces together and gathering evidence. Hanke's helping."

"And you intend to follow Hill when he leaves the hotel?"

"Yup, that's the plan.

"Didn't the rascals kill an Underwriters' man the other day?"

Solomon's question triggered yet another painful recollection of Wally Roberts before Sage answered, "Yes. A guy by the name of Wally Roberts. He was clobbered and left to die beneath a pile of rubble."

"So, where's Mr. Fong? I don't think you should be doing this on your own."

"We're laying a trap somewhere else. He's involved in that. He's amazing but not even he can be in two places at once."

When Solomon returned to the dining room he was both thoughtful and worried. Once there, he called his nephew, Nathan, to him. "You remember Mr. Adair? You took him a message a few days back."

At the young man's eager nod, Solomon continued, "He's out front, in the disguise of a poor workman—brown canvas coat and pants, flop-brimmed hat. He's going to be following one of the fellows at the corner table. I need you to follow along, but without letting either man see you. If something happens to Adair, if he's attacked or in danger, you run and fetch me or you fetch Mr. Cooper—whichever one of us is closest. If you go to Cooper, tell him to bring some men and be prepared to rescue Adair. You understand?"

His uncle's instructions widened Nathan's eyes but all he said was, "What if Mr. Adair goes inside a building? I won't be able to follow. How will I know if he's in danger?"

"Good question, Nathan. If Adair goes inside and he's in the same place as the man he's following and he doesn't come out, come get me or Mr. Cooper—whichever one of us is closest. If we're lucky, it'll be me. If you have to get Mr. Cooper, you must call Mr. Adair, "Mr. Miner." That is an alias he uses and the one Mr. Cooper knows him by. Can you remember to do that?"

Nathan looked perplexed at the instruction but he simply nodded and left the dining room. Soon he was wearing his outdoor gear, waiting in a side hallway from where he could watch the men sitting at the corner table. Ten minutes later, as the meeting adjourned and they began to rise, Nathan slipped out the side door.

By the time Hill exited the building, Sage was glad to get moving. His feet were blocks of ice. Hill walked at a fast clip, his head bent beneath an umbrella. A mix of rain and ice pelted down. Sage pulled his hat low though he wasn't worried about being seen. The weather was too nasty.

Twenty minutes later, Hill entered an office on the ground floor of a new Victorian house, a few blocks into the Nob Hill neighborhood. Fortunately, there was a small coffee shop a few steps away and Sage gratefully ducked inside.

The café was warm and fragrant with the mingled smells of coffee and baking. His stomach growled. After he ordered coffee and a sandwich, he took a stool at the front window's narrow counter. It was the perfect spot from which to observe Hill's office. Gradually, the heat of the nearby woodstove warmed his feet and hands. A man entered and went to the back counter. Sage was vaguely aware of a rumbly rasp as he placed an order. The man soon left carrying a paper wrapped parcel. Others entered and left with their orders.

Outside, a mix of ice pellets and raindrops was slanting sideways and freezing as it hit the ground. Such an early sleet meant, according to old timers, a harsh winter. Sage thought about what Campbell had said that morning in Stone's office. Once, Roger, the ever-helpful clerk had delivered coffee and departed, the fire chief shared his worries about the weather.

"The arson starting up again is bad enough but, if it ices up, we're going to have serious problems. Once the streets turn icy, it takes us longer to get to the scene, if we can get there at all. We've had horses fall and break their legs, and rigs tip over because they've lost traction. Below 32 degrees, we've got to chip ice off the hydrants and our hoses freeze. Leaky gaskets in the fire engine ice up and cut off the flow. Sprinkler systems inside the buildings burst, flood and then freeze underfoot which means the men fall. And, if the wind kicks up, the fire can quickly get out of hand. Those scoundrels have to know all that so I pray that they have enough decency not to start a fire tonight."

The fire hydrant beyond the window already wore a skim of ice and the breeze had turned into a blustery wind. If the weather worsened and the night brought another arson, Campbell's worst fear would be realized.

There was action across the street. Two men charged up the steps and disappeared into Hill's office. Sage hadn't caught sight of their features. "Crap," he muttered. As he stared at the closed front door, he saw someone enter the building by the side door. That meant there were now at least four men in Hill's office.

Sighing, he stood. He had to learn what was going on in that office. Given the deteriorating weather, Hill's visitors were unlikely to be customers—at least not honest ones.

Stepping outside, Sage raised his collar and shoved his hands into his coat pockets. Ice crystals pattered his hat and bounced off. Fortunately, the dirt street had turned into frozen mud which made tripping a danger but a slip less likely. Carefully, he stepped across, noting the absence of both foot and wagon traffic.

On the other side, he paused to listen but heard only the swish of falling sleet. Hopefully that meant nobody inside Hill's office would hear him moving alongside the building. Like most Victorian-style houses, the front door sat at the top of a long flight of stairs. That meant the side windows were at least two feet above his head. Standing underneath one of them, he could hear voices but not the words. Spotting an empty paint can, he grabbed it and carried it to a spot beneath a window. Quietly setting it down, he braced himself on the wall and stepped up. Sleet falling on his shoulders, can rocking underfoot, he strained to hear the words coming from inside the room.

"Yes, I know there's been a delay." The speaker, standing near the window, was using a soothing voice. "Couldn't be helped. We just lost a key player." That had to be Hill since he was trying to calm someone down. Sage hoped Hill wouldn't glance out the window because he couldn't miss seeing a man's hat just below the sill.

As for the other men, all Sage could hear was their rumbling voices.

Hill's tone changed, now impatient as he said, "Yes, yes. I know what we promised. I know you need the money. We'll do it tonight at midnight but the payout's still going to take time. We'll have to complete the paperwork afterward and submit the claims. You won't get your money in an instant."

"Rumble, rumble," sounded in return.

"I promise. We're set now. Like I just said, we have everything lined up for tonight."

Hill's comment spurred Sage to act. He had to see who else was in the room. He had to discover who it was that wanted their property torched during this ice storm. His fingers braced against the wall, he slowly rose up onto his toes. As his weight shifted, the paint can beneath his feet tilted and thumped against the wall. For a stunned moment Sage froze, then fear got him dismounted and turning toward the back of the house.

He saw a way clear. He'd run through the backyard, jump any fence he encountered and be gone before they could get out the front door.

It was a good plan except for one thing. As he sped alongside the house toward the rear, he heard the front door open and footsteps pound down the wooden steps. Looking back over his shoulder, he didn't look where he was running. That was his mistake. When he finally glanced forward, it was to see the figure of a big man filling the gap between the house and side fence. Sage could have bowled him over or knocked him out of the way with one of Fong's moves except for the cocked revolver the man had aimed at Sage's chest.

THIRTY

There was a moment as frozen as the falling sleet. Then Sage slowly raised his hands while hoping that the neighbors' close proximity would stop the thug from pulling the trigger.

Maybe it did because, as he walked forward, the man used the weapon to gesture Sage toward the glass-paned side door. Sage glanced over his shoulder and saw Hill advancing, two other men at his heels. Although the big man jabbed the gun barrel into his ribs, Sage couldn't move, transfixed as he was by the sight of Wesley Glicker, frequent Mozart's customer and, owner of warehouses fronting the river.

Glicker's presence stunned Sage into immobility. Glicker's operation abutted the business district. If his tightly packed warehouses caught fire tonight, the entire riverfront could go up in flames. And, given the wooden buildings, creosoted docks and lack of a fireboat, the wind-driven fire could take out most of central downtown Portland just like it had in 1873.

Sage quickly turned away. If Glicker recognized him as Sage Adair, then Glicker would know he'd been identified. On the other hand, if Glicker thought their captive was a stranger, maybe he'd feel safe. That difference could mean his life or death.

Then cold realization hit. It didn't matter whether Glicker recognized him or not. They could never let him go. He was a dead man because, whatever arson they planned, he could tie them to it.

Escape was his only choice. Neither Hill nor his friends held guns. Maybe the thug wouldn't shoot in his boss's direction. Close to hopeless but he had to try because, once they got him somewhere isolated, they would kill him.

His body must have telegraphed his intention because the big man finally spoke in a familiar raspy voice. It was the first fellow who'd bought a sandwich in the shop across the street. "Don't even twitch, Miner. This gun's cocked and my finger's on the trigger. Open that door and step inside."

The sound of his own name caused Sage to stumble crossing the threshold. They knew exactly who he was. They'd been expecting him. The gun barrel jabbed painfully into his ribs. Sage slowly opened the door while considering whether to grab the frame and kick backward. That idea died when the man planted a hand on Sage's back and shoved.

They stood on a stair landing. Steps led upward to the first floor while other stairs descended into the basement. The man rasped, "You go on down. If you make a fuss, I'll kick you down the stairs. It'd be my pleasure."

Sage glanced over his shoulder as the other three men crowded onto the landing. Escape was hopeless so he obediently went down the stairs while they climbed up. At the bottom, Sage paused. It was dim with barely any light filtering through the dirty casement windows. His fear of the earthy dark fluttered briefly but he ignored it as his eyes searched for an escape route. Other than the stairs and the two windows set high in the walls, there was nothing but concrete walls and a concrete floor.

"Over there," the man ordered, grabbing Sage's shoulder and shoving him toward a long crate sitting beside a wood pile meant for the nearby furnace. Sage's feet instantly braked. The raspy voiced man chuckled. "Looks just like a coffin, don't it? Lucky for you Hill's new grandfather clock came with a lot of packing so the box is fairly roomy."

His gun prodded Sage forward until they stood next to the crate. "Here's the thing," his captor rasped. "You either crawl in that box, like a good boy, or I shoot you right now. No neighbor's gonna hear a shot coming from down here."

When Sage hesitated, the man added, "Cooperate and you'll gain a few hours more. I ain't going to kill you now and I won't leave you in the box because Hill would have a conniption fit if I did. He's gonna want it to look accidental. I just need somewhere safe to hold you until I arrange things. Think of it as getting a little extra time to ponder your life."

Dreading the cramped space, Sage crawled into the box to lie on his back and watch as the lid dropped. Huffing, the man set something heavy on top and Sage swallowed the urge to cry out.

Time to use Fong's trick for controlling panic—breathe deep, study the surroundings. How is it different than a coal mine? The first thing he noticed was that light was leaking in between the boards above his head. That meant he wouldn't smother.

He heard his captor stumbling around, searching for something. Sure enough, when he came back, the man began nailing down the lid. For the next minutes, Sage's wooden prison shook under hammer blows. When that stopped, but while his ears still rang, the man spoke, "Be glad that wood burner keeps it from freezing down here. Yell all you want. Nobody will hear you."

Footsteps crossed the basement and mounted the stairs. The outside door opened and shut, leaving Sage with only the sound of his ragged breathing and the distant murmur of voices above.

B.J. Cooper's pen raced across the page. The *New Age's* copy had to be in the printer's hand by the end of day or it'd be late coming out. His stint in jail had proved beneficial in one regard. He'd been able to talk to and observe his fellow inmates. He learned what he'd expected—that at every step, a black man received worse treatment than a white man from the moment he was suspected of a crime.

Not him and James though. He'd overheard Sergeant Hanke's strict instructions about how they were to be treated. Briefly, he pondered Angus Solomon's mysterious influence over the sergeant. Still, that special treatment couldn't change the truth. His forthcoming editorial was blistering.

A loud thump sounded on the porch, followed by frantic pounds on the door. Christ, not again! Jumping to his feet, Cooper first instinct was to run for the back door. He wasn't ready to be arrested again. Frances appeared in the archway and her wide-eyed fear gave him courage. He strode to the door and flung it open. Nathan, Solomon's nephew, stood there anxious and shivering.

"Good Lord! Come in, boy. Frances, please hurry and get Nathan something hot to drink." He guided the boy into the armchair beside the parlor stove. After scooping more coal onto the grate, he adjusted the draft so it burned hotter.

Frances returned with hot cocoa that the boy accepted gratefully. After taking a sip, he said in a soft Carolina drawl, "My uncle said I should come to you for help if Mr. . . . if Mr. Miner was in trouble. He said Mr. Miner was following a man and I was to follow them both. My uncle told me that I should come get you and, tell you to bring help, if Mr. Miner went into a building where the other man went and didn't come out."

The young man's words came in a rush. Glancing at Frances, B.J, saw she looked as puzzled as he felt. Then her face cleared and, slapping her hands on her thighs, she rose, "I'll get my coat. Miz Molly told me that I could use her telephone whenever I needed to. I'll ring up Mr. Randolph and see if he and Mr. Tanner can come."

"Please do that," B.J. said before turning his attention back to the boy. "Now, Nathan, I want you to slowly tell me exactly what you saw. Can you do that?"

The young man gulped air and began again, "My uncle said that Mr. Miner was following a dangerous man. He was worried about Mr. Miner's safety. So, I went outside and followed Mr. Miner. We ended up about six blocks from here. The man Mr. Miner was following went into an office in a house. For a long time, Mr. Miner stayed in a café across the street from that house."

"You waited outside in this sleet?"

Nathan nodded, shivered but continued his story, "I was afraid they'd throw me out if I tried to go inside. Besides, my uncle said not to let Mr. Miner know I was following him. He's seen me before, a couple of times—Mr. Miner, I mean.

"Anyway, after awhile, two men also went into the same office Mr. Miner was watching. That's when he came out of the café real quick and crossed the street. I saw him go down alongside that building. Next, I saw three men run down the front steps and alongside the house."

The young man's eyes widened with remembered alarm. "Then nothing. I thought maybe they all just stayed outside, beside the house. So, I decided to walk by and take a look. When I did, nobody was there. Everybody had disappeared. That's when I saw that the house had a side door. I figured all of them must have gone inside that way—including Mr. Miner."

"What happened next, Nathan?" Cooper prodded.

After a big swallow of the cocoa, Nathan said. "I waited a couple houses down and watched. Pretty soon, two men came out the front door, got into a carriage and rolled away. Mr. Miner wasn't with them. Then another man came out. It was the man Mr. Miner followed. So, I kept waiting."

"Did anything else happen that made you worry about Mr. Miner's safety?"

That question triggered rapid nodding of Nathan's head. "I couldn't decide if I'd waited long enough before coming get you. So, I figured maybe I should check to see if Mr. Miner was lying in the backyard. So, I snuck back there but nobody was in sight and there was no way out of the backyard because the fence was real high.

"I figured that meant he had to be inside somewhere. Just as I stepped out from beside the house, a big man came out the front door. He saw me and hollered. I took off running but he kept up pretty good. I couldn't lead him here so I ran all over. Finally, he got tired and stopped chasing me. That's when I came here."

Cooper put a hand on Nathan's shoulder. "You did right," he said just as Frances returned.

"They're both coming. They'll be here within the half hour," Frances told them.

Nathan looked worried. "So, you're going to go help Mr. Miner?"

"We surely intend to try. He did our family a good deed. We'll be happy to return the favor." Cooper went over to the bureau, pulled out a pistol, slid bullets into the chambers and slapped it shut before pocketing it. He turned to his wife, "Frances, would you mind bothering Miz Molly again for the use of her telephone? Call Angus at the Portland Hotel and tell him briefly what has happened. Tell him we're all meeting here and, if he can get away, he should join us. Be careful what you say. Those telephone operators listen to every word."

Twenty minutes later, Randolph, Tanner, Nathan and the Coopers were joined by Angus Solomon. He was accompanied by a slight, middle-aged Chinese man that Solomon introduced as "Mr. Fong." Seeing Cooper's confusion, Solomon explained Fong's role in protecting Frances from the bullying thugs. Solomon also added that Fong had helped capture and question Orpin.

Minutes later, a thawed out Nathan led the six men to Hill's office. Four of them mounted the steps and knocked on the door. No one answered. Meanwhile Fong and Randolph slipped around the side of the house hoping to spot Miner through the windows.

When they all met again on the sidewalk, Randolph reported that he'd boosted Mr. Fong up to take a look though the office window. Since no one was inside, Fong had raised the sash and climbed in. He'd dashed through the office, second floor and basement but found the place empty.

Upon hearing that, Solomon sent each of them knocking on neighbors' doors with the explanation there was an urgent message for Mr. Hill. One of the searchers got lucky. The maid who answered his knock said that she'd been shaking out her dust mop when, only twenty minutes prior, she'd seen Mr. Hill climb into a closed van with two other men. And yes, one of the men wore a tan canvas coat. At the end of the block, the van had turned east. She said she'd noticed because she thought it peculiar that Mr. Hill got into the back of a van when he kept such a nice buggy in the neighborhood stable.

THIRTY ONE

"I wonder where Mr. Fong has got off to," Mae said as she and Hanke sat in the parlor of the Sunnyside house. "I expected him back long before this." It was full night outside, close to six thirty. Her tone was light but her nervous plucking at a pillow fringe said she was worried.

"Maybe it's taking him awhile to find Mr. Adair," Hanke offered.

She said nothing, just stared at the flames flickering behind the stove's mica window. Straightening in her chair, she asked, "Tell me, Sergeant Hanke, do we need to keep up this charade? You and I met this afternoon with Hill and his rascal friends. I signed the papers, paid the premiums and got their assurances that I'll get the payouts when this house burns. Hill even promised they'd burn it down two days from now. You heard them say all that. Surely, you're not going to let them set this house ablaze before arresting them, are you?"

Her worry about Adair seemed to have increased with each passing hour. There never was a more loyal employee he thought but said instead, "I think we are done. We've got five insurance agents to arrest, Orpin and at least three fire station chiefs. We'll be able to search the insurance agents' homes and offices because we now have enough evidence to justify warrants. We'll surely find something to incriminate them. Once they're jailed, one of them will spill the beans. One of them always does."

"Okay, then," she said and stood up. She left the parlor and he heard her clicking the handset hook to get the operator's attention. She came back into the room, her coat on and holding his hat and coat. "I've called for a cab. We might as well head to Mozart's. I haven't seen hide nor hair of those watching men the last five hours. Nobody's going to stay out in this sleet. Besides, if we don't cross the river now, we could get stuck here in Sunnyside for Lord knows how many days.

She stepped into the hall and donned her hat and gloves. When she spoke her tone made clear that she would tolerate no objection. "Anyways, we'll walk right in the front door of the restaurant like we're customers. Those two want to stand outside on Second Street and freeze their rear ends off, that's fine with me. I can't wait around here any longer. I need to see if anyone has heard from Mr. Fong or Mr. Adair."

He almost wished he was back in Hill's clock crate. Since he wasn't and hadn't been there for a number of hours, he focused on visualizing a burning stove sitting in his gut—in that place Fong called his dantien, just below his navel. Cold was nothing new. He'd been cold before like when he cracked his head on the wild sled ride into the Klondike and woke up with a broken leg. It had been a long crawl through deep snow before he'd found help.

He should have known they wouldn't keep him in that basement for long. At least he still had all his clothes on. He smiled grimly against the gag tied across his mouth. After that little ruckus in the van and his near escape, they'd stayed well clear of him. When the raspy voiced man had finally reined in the team, they'd tied him up tight as a Christmas goose. Raspy voice had done the tying, while Hill held the gun and informed him there was no one around to hear the shot. When they'd finally hauled him out of the van and into the sleeting dark, he saw that was true.

They'd thoughtfully explained their plan. He was to die of hypothermia in this hole. After which, they'd untie the ropes and leave his body on a street, in a gully or under a bridge. He'd be just another hobo victim of the freezing weather. Nothing new. By winter's end, there'd be scores of dead on Portland's streets.

Supposedly it wasn't the worst way to go. Leastways that's what he'd heard. A few hallucinations, a sensation of warmth and then sleep.

Sage started. He'd been drifting off. He thrashed around violently, pulling against the ropes binding his ankles, knees, arms and hands. At least he was out of that wind-driven sleet overhead. When they'd tossed him down here, he'd nearly landed in a pool of water. Ironically, it was water he'd probably helped put there. He'd managed to wriggle over to a dry spot. Still, being dry didn't mean he'd survive. The temperature was dropping and the sleet still fell. No one would think to look for him here. Only the factory owner could know about this small cellar and he, for certain sure, would say nothing..

It had to be nearing midnight which meant they'd soon be setting Glicker's warehouses and docks on fire. The wind he was hearing would quickly fan the flames, sending them roaring through the old, wooden and tightly packed warehouses and beyond.

He listened. The sleet that had been falling for hours now seemed to be lessening. The wind, however, had strengthened. They'd piled debris atop the heavy metal plate covering the cellar opening. The rattle of that debris was getting louder. From what Campbell said, the combination of ice and wind would be deadly. Someone had to warn Campbell and stop Hill's plan. He began frantically tugging at his bindings but stopped when he realized panic couldn't set him free.

He breathed deep and calmed himself, using his pause to search overhead for the opening to the outside. As he stared upward he thought of how he'd found Wally Roberts. They'd used rubble to bury him too. Only coincidence and dumb luck had led Sage to him. That wouldn't happen twice. He was on his own.

First things first. Get rid of the gag and then the ropes, he told himself. There must be something down here to snag the gag on. Breathing deeply through his nose and envisioning a hot stove in his dantien, Sage began to wriggle across the dirt floor.

They all felt discouraged as they sat in the New Elijah's empty dining room just before eleven o'clock that night. Solomon was there, having taken the evening off from his Portland Hotel duties. His nephew, Nathan, sat beside his uncle. Cooper, Randolph and Tanner were also there. And so was Fong who had intercepted Mae and Hanke just as they were leaving the Sunnyside house. He'd squeezed into their cab and the three them were also now at Solomon's hotel. Fong kept watch out the cab's rear window. No one had followed.

"I can't think of any other place to look," declared Hanke and was met with everyone's glum silence. For awhile, the only sound in the room was the distant clank of cutlery in the hotel's kitchen.

"Maybe we ask Chief Campbell," Fong suggested.

Hanke shrugged. "Might as well," he agreed getting to his feet. "The rest of you stay here. It's not that far to Campbell's house but it's turned even nastier outside. If Campbell has any good ideas, we'll come fetch you."

The others nodded wearily while Solomon rose to brew more coffee.

Hanke was right, the outside temperature had plummeted below freezing with the deepening of night. The wind was now a strong, steady blow. Ice coated everything. At least the sleet had stopped. In fact, the swiftly moving clouds were thinning, at times revealing a distant half moon. Still, between the stiff wind and the ice underfoot walking was treacherous.

An alert Campbell opened his front door. Evidently he'd been reading since he held a newspaper in one hand. "Come in, come in," he said, "I'll be up keeping an eye on the weather all night, so you're welcome company." As they clomped past him on frozen feet, he cast a questioning glance toward Hanke.

"Chief Campbell, I'd like you to meet Mr. Fong Kam Tong. He was a great help in catching Edward Orpin and getting Orpin to confess."

Fong sent a cautionary look at Hanke and the police sergeant didn't elaborate further. Instead, once they were in Campbell's parlor, Hanke refused Campbell's offer of a seat and said, "We can't stay. Since this afternoon Mr. Fong, myself and some others have been hunting for Mr. Miner. He went into the ringleader's office and never came out. When Mr. Fong searched the building, everyone was gone. Miner isn't at his home and he isn't at Station 1. We're certain that the crooks have Miner and mean to do him harm."

Campbell tossed the newspaper aside. "Those men are killers. Look what happened to Wally Roberts," he said and started pacing back and forth before his fireplace, running a hand through his tousled hair and throwing out suggestions of where to look. In every instance, Hanke had to tell him that they had thought of that idea and had searched there without success.

Fong had remained silent but now, for the first time, he spoke, "Chief Campbell, they attack Roberts in place of fire?"

"Yes, he was inspecting the scene and got surprised by someone."

"Please, where last arson fire?" Fong asked.

Campbell threw out, "A barrel factory, downriver."

Hanke caught Fong's idea before Campbell did because excitement raised his voice. "Was that barrel factory in the middle of a bunch of buildings or does it sit by itself?"

"It's at the edge of town, away from other structures. That's why we were able to get it under control without any other building catching fire."

By the end of his answer, Campbell had caught up. "Let me get my coat! We'll take my buggy! But, Sergeant, it will take the three of us forever to search those ruins. The building covers an entire block and it's dark. And there's all the ice to contend with. If they've buried him under debris . . ."

"No problem. What address, please? I go tell army," Fong said.

Campbell told him and Fong swiftly left the room. After the front door opened and closed, Campbell looked inquiringly at Hanke. "Army?" he asked.

Hanke smiled grimly. "You'll see. I can't explain it."

THIRTY TWO

HANKE RAN TO THE BACKYARD stable to harness up Campbell's horse and buggy while the fire chief raced around his house finding and filling kerosene lanterns. Once they set out, Campbell held the horse to a slow walk. "Jumper is skittish and with the ice I'm afraid to let him go any faster. We'll be of no help if we turnover or break Jumper's leg before we can get there," he told Hanke who twitched anxiously on the seat beside him.

Solomon's crew didn't have nearly as comfortable a ride. When Fong ran into the dining room with his news, Cooper jumped up, raced into the street and hailed a passing freight wagon. He paid a considerable sum to overcome the teamster's reluctance to continue driving on the ice. Within two minutes, all seven of them had piled into the open bed—Mae with an armful of blankets and Solomon with all his available kerosene lanterns.

After a chillingly slow journey, the wagon reached the burnt out barrel factory. As soon as they jumped down, the teamster snapped the reins and the wagon rattled off into the dark. They turned to look at the building.

It was a dismal place. The nearest business was dark and a block away. A strong wind rattled through the iced field grasses and stung their faces. A fleeting half moon lit a skeletonized building, open to the sky. Sooty tendrils streaked upward from the factory's broken windows. Indiscernible black mounds and fractured timbers filled the interior.

They were standing there, shivering and dismayed, when Campbell and Hanke rolled up. The fire chief quickly tied his horse to a curb ring and turned to them, hiding his surprise at the makeup of the "army"— five black men, a white middle-aged woman and Mr. Fong. Looking at the woman, he said, "I'm really not sure if this is a place for . . . " but stopped when his words were met with a steely-eyed stare chill as the wind.

"Okay, then," he started anew. "You are about to enter an extremely dangerous place. Once you're inside, find something you can use to poke the floor ahead before you step. Fire and water may have weakened the floorboards and I don't know if there is a basement or cellar under any part of it. Even if the structure sits on the ground, there'll still be a crawl space below. You can break a leg if you fall through. We don't want any broken legs because that will slow our search. Got it?" he asked, staring at each one in turn.

At their grim nods, he continued, "There's lots of fallen timbers, equipment and junk you won't even recognize. All of it can hurt you. So, be extra careful if you have to move something. Also, if you smell anything strange get far away and call me. There were chemicals in this factory and some of them are deadly."

Campbell took a deep breath, exchanged a look with Hanke and continued, "When they killed Wally Roberts, they piled debris on his body. That means if you see a pile of rubbish, big enough to hide a body under, you must very carefully lift it up to make sure Mr. Miner's isn't underneath." A whimper sounded. Campbell looked at the woman but decided it must have been the strengthening wind because her return look showed nothing but resolve.

He concluded his instructions by saying, "Finally, you must search in pairs. Only I will go alone. I'm going to be looking for a stairway or opening into a basement or cellar. But the rest of you must stay with your partner. That way, if you get hurt or if you need to lift something heavy, you'll have someone to help you. Everyone understand and accept my conditions?"

Hearing no objection, he directed the four teams to their respective search areas: Mae with Fong in the far northern section, Hanke with Cooper in the southern section, while Randolph with Tanner and Solomon with Nathan each took a middle section.

As the teams started searching, beginning along the front wall, Campbell went straight to the far back, quickly jabbing a stick into the charred floor ahead before taking a step, his lantern lifted high. The building's rear was where the fire had started and burned the hottest. It was where the floor would be the weakest. Despite his words of warning, he was taking no chances with his novice searchers. From behind him came the sound of things being lifted and dropped.

Sage stopped gnawing and strained to listen. Had he heard something besides creaking timbers and the strengthening wind? He shook his head violently. Probably it was just his ears hallucinating—he was so cold. Still, it could be worse, he again reminded himself. It was warmer down in this hole than up above. After a minute of hearing only wind, he went back to gnawing on the rope they'd wrapped tightly around his hands and wrists.

At least his mouth was free to gnaw. He'd found an upright support timber and, after much rubbing and painful splinters in his cheek, he'd dislodged the gag so that it now hung around his neck. After that came the seemingly endless shoulder wrenching to bring his tied hands under his feet and to his front. Now he was using his teeth to gnaw at the rope around those hands.

He'd made progress. A few gnaws more and he'd have his hands free. He stopped again, having heard a strange sound. No, he told himself, it was only the wind shifting debris.

He returned to gnawing, feeling like a wharf rat and wishing he had a wharf rat's long, sharp teeth. A spurt of fear that Hill and his hireling would soon return, sped up his gnawing. He tried for reassuring thoughts and found a few. They were probably off setting Glicker's warehouses ablaze. And besides, they had to know that it was too soon for him to have died. They'd want to be certain he was dead before they hoisted him out of this pit. Otherwise, they'd have a battle on their hands.

Momentary despair jabbed him but he shoved it away. He had to get out of this damn hole. For sure, there'd be no rescuers. His mother, Fong, Solomon and maybe others must be frantically searching for him. He didn't doubt that. But they'd never think to look for him here. And, even if they did come to this factory, they'd never find the cellar—Hill and old raspy voice had made sure of that. He wasn't even in a proper basement. This was just a tiny dirt cellar beneath a pile of debris in a huge, burnt out factory.

His teeth broke the last rope and he twisted his hands free. Burning blood flowed back into his fingers but he welcomed the pain. Reaching down, he fumbled with the rope around his knees, baring his teeth in a vicious grin that quickly faded. Once his feet were free of the ropes, he still had no idea how he was going to reach an opening ten feet overhead, let alone dislodge whatever they'd piled atop its metal cover. Fong's voice came into his head as it often did when he was afraid, "Each journey begin with one step, followed by next step. Worry only about next step."

"I don't know, Mr. Hill. This seems like a real bad night for starting a big fire," said the raspy voiced man. They were sitting at a back table in one of the few saloons still open. Its scattering of customers seemed more intent on taking advantage of the warmth than they were on getting drunk.

Hill glanced sideways to make sure no one had heard before leaning over the table to say, "You let me worry about that. Glicker wants an easy time clearing the land afterward. That means we need to make sure they burn to the ground. So, we need that wind outside to fan the flames into a fast burn, especially since the firehouse's so close."

The raspy voiced man looked unconvinced. "That's a damn hard wind blowing out of the Gorge towards downtown. The fire will jump the street."

"Look, we've got only this job and that new one across the river in Sunnyside. Then we're done for awhile. That Miner fellow was working with Stone and Campbell. Once they discover he's dead, it's for certain they'll find someone else to do their snooping. Hell, he's the third one they've used. We can't keep eliminating their snoops. We're going to get caught."

"But, we don't have to set the fire tonight. Miner's already dead or soon will be. He isn't going anywhere. It'll take time for them to find another spy." The man's hands gripped the table edge, raising the burn scars that puckered their backs.

Anger darkened Hill's face and his fist hit the table, causing others to glance in their direction. He leaned forward to hiss, "When you killed Wally Roberts you lost us that time! The attention has gotten too intense. And, I promised Glicker we'd do it tonight. He's getting antsy and he's already driven all the way out to Oregon City just so he'll have an alibi."

"I didn't mean to kill Roberts," the other man said quietly.

"Then you shouldn't have hit him so damn hard. Besides, it's too late to feel guilty, especially when Miner is dying as we speak," returned Hill.

They advanced achingly slow through the building. Because the barrel factory had been two stories high, they had to contend with rubble from the collapsed second story. With the contents of both floors jumbled together, mounds of debris impeded nearly every step. In less than ten minutes, soot blackened every searcher. The cutting wind froze hands inside gloves and ice puddles sent a penetrating chill through their boot soles. Nevertheless, they kept frantically tossing aside debris and hefting charred timbers.

Tanner and Randolph picked up their pace after spying a distant mountain of debris that looked promising. When they reached it, Tanner put a restraining hand on Randolph. "Hold up a minute. Look at that pile. It doesn't make sense. It's not the kind of stuff we've seen piled together."

Randolph straightened and looked. "You're right, Mr. Tanner. That filing cabinet shouldn't be laying on its side on top of a roof timber. It's a big pile to shift," he added and turned and hollered, "Mr. Solomon, we need your help!"

Seconds later, all four men were lifting and tossing the debris aside.

Sage's fingers froze around the knot he was working. There'd been a scraping noise across the steel plate that covered the opening. The bastards must have come back to make sure he was dead. Fury swept through him—they'd probably already started the fire at Glicker's warehouses.

He imagined the city bell tolling endlessly as the firefighters fought a wind-driven inferno spewing hot embers westward onto downtown rooftops including Mozart's. Ida, Knute, Matthew and all the others in its path—would they flee in time?

Through gritted teeth Sage muttered, "You bastards aren't going to get away with this." His effort turned frantic, skin tearing as he pulled, picked and yanked. "You won't be hauling me out of here without a helluva fight," he vowed aloud.

Once they spotted the flat metal plate beneath the rubble, their excited cries summoned everyone else. Soon all nine of them were flinging aside various bits and pieces. At last, the iron plate was completely exposed. Solomon and Hanke each grabbed an edge and flipped it back.

Everyone crowded to the edge of the pit, raising their lanterns and peering down into the black hole. A filthy, pale white face stared up at them from about ten feet below. The man stood in a pile of loose ropes. He clutched a length of two-by-four in one hand and was scowling ferociously.

Fong was the first to speak. "Mr. Miner, what you doing in that hole?"

THIRTY THREE

His rescuers dropped two long beams into the pit and Sage clambered up their charred slant like a monkey climbing a palm tree. Reaching the top, he turned to Campbell. "Has the fire bell sounded tonight?"

When Campbell shook his head, Sage began staggering toward the street, shouting over his shoulder, "Hurry! We've got to get to the Glicker warehouses along the waterfront. They're going to torch them."

"My god, with this wind, that will take out the whole city. I'll get my buggy," Campbell said, passing Sage at a run.

Sage stopped and turned toward the others. "I can't thank you enough for rescuing me but I don't have time now. We still need your help. Will you stay with us?"

Murmured assents came from between lips stiff with cold. Sage turned to the policeman, "Sergeant Hanke, do you think you can get everyone to the Glicker warehouses? They just have to holler if they see anyone going into one of them. Fong and I need to get there faster with Chief Campbell in case the arsonist is already inside. If he is, we'll try to stop him."

Hanke waved Sage forward. "Yes, yes, get going. We'll head out now. We'll be passing saloons where patrolmen will be sheltering from this weather. I'll send one of them for more help."

Sage looked into his mother's eyes. She gave a little nod and he squeezed her shoulder before moving on past. When he and Fong reached the street, Campbell had already turned his buggy. He said nothing when they climbed in after him—just clicked the horse into a sedate walk on the iced cobbles, frustration evident in the rigid lines of his body.

Safely sandwiched between Campbell and Fong, Sage finally surrendered to the cold, shivering uncontrollably. Campbell reached below the seat and hauled out a travel rug. "Wrap this around you and when your teeth stop chattering, tell us what the hell happened. At this speed, there'll be plenty of time to hear your story."

The streets were virtually empty beneath a solid sheet of ice. Given their excruciatingly slow pace, Sage finished telling his story long before they neared Glicker's warehouses.

"So raspy man may be in warehouse already," Fong said.

"If he's not now, he's soon going to be." Sage turned to Campbell, "I think he's a firefighter or was in a fire because he has burn scars on his hands. I saw them when he took off his gloves to put me in the shipping crate. There's also something wrong with his throat, like he inhaled too much smoke. And, he's over six feet tall. Can you think of who he might be?"

The tightening of Campbell's hands on the reins made clear that he didn't want the arsonist and, maybe murderer of Wally Roberts, to be a firefighter. Still, he mulled the question over before saying, "I can't think of a single firefighter under my command fitting that description. The idea that any one of them would set a fire on a hellish night like this turns my stomach."

"Could he be a volunteer firefighter?"

Campbell grimaced. "Unfortunately, he could be. Half the time, I don't know who they are. They just turn up at the station or fire scene and that's the first time I ever see them. Kind of like you did, Mr. Miner." He sent a teasing grin at Sage and not for the first time, Sage knew why Campbell's men held him in such high regard. It was impossible not to like the man.

Sage turned to Fong. "How did the Sunnyside trap work?"

"Sergeant say we got every rat agent's name. Mrs. Clemens did excellent job."

"So, that means we now have identified all the insurance agents, one firebug for sure, and maybe we'll catch a second one tonight."

Campbell grunted, as if absorbing a blow but he joined in, observing, "And once we get search warrants for those insurance agents' offices and houses, we'll know which building owners profited from the arsons. The city will need to build a new jail just to hold everybody."

Sage pulled the travel rug tighter and said, "The weak links will be the insurance agents. In my experience, the men wearing suits are the first to give each other up. I think it's the shock of discovering themselves in a situation they never imagined they could be in."

Campbell cocked an inquiring eye at Sage. "Well, Mr. Miner I am thinking there's a lot more to your history than you let on. For one thing, I notice you've dropped the countrified accent. And from your diction, I'm guessing you've even got a bit of college under your belt."

"There's a bunch more country in me than there is college," Sage remarked dryly.

They had crossed Burnside Street and were just a block from Glicker's warehouses when Sage said, "We better go on foot from here. Since we're not sure where they are going to be, we might need to sneak into the building. They'd notice a buggy stopping in front."

Campbell reined the buggy to the curb and climbed down to tie Jumper to a horse ring.

Sage looked north. Fong understood the look because he said, "Our army about ten minutes behind. We travel very slow."

The three of them moved up the slippery street without falling. Reaching the front of Glicker's warehouses, Campbell said softly, "If our arsonist is a firefighter, he'll likely start the fire on the river side, using the wind to push it into the building since our lack of a fireboat means we can't spray from that side. He'll also douse the interior with an accelerant. I propose that you each take one end of the dock and work toward meeting in the middle. I'll give you a few minutes start then I'll break in through the front middle door."

He registered their frowns and explained his assignments, "Glicker's warehouses are connected by archways so I'll be able to give the whole complex a swift walk through. I need to be the guy inside because I've been inside before and know how it's arranged. I also know what accelerants smell like and where a fire might be ignited, presuming the fellow is a firefighter. Also, I know how to escape if it blows up—so long as no wall collapses," he added, grimly.

Campbell looked at them. "Do either of you have a gun or other weapon?" At their headshakes he said, "Well, me neither. We better hope he's not armed. Though, I do have these." He held up gloved hands clenched into fists. "I still spar regularly," he added, with a rueful smile that said he knew the futility of using fists against bullets.

On that somber note, the three of them split up. Fong sped down the street toward the south end of the warehouses. Sage ran along the closer north end, reached the dock and began moving swiftly south, searching behind stacked crates and sniffing the air. Seconds later, he saw Fong round the distant corner and begin moving toward him.

The surface of the dock was uneven and sloping. As he went, Sage stepped on more than one dangerously soft board. No wonder Glicker wanted an easy and profitable way out. If the dock needed major repair, the connected warehouses were probably in worse condition. Just as that thought crossed his mind, Sage heard a loud crash, followed by the pop of three gunshots. The noise came from inside. Given that Campbell didn't have a gun, those shots meant the fire chief was in trouble.

He and Fong both ran towards a door set midway in the building's wall and about where the shots had come from. They reached it at the same time. Fong didn't hesitate. His boot flashed out, hip high, right where the lock was. The door crashed open. Momentarily, both of them stood to either side, listening for a response. Then Fong gestured that they should enter low, Fong to the left, Sage to the right. Even though thin clouds draped the half moon, there was still enough light to outline their shape when they entered.

Fong tapped his chest and held up his finger, signaling he'd be first to go. At Sage's agreeing nod, Fong jumped through the door and to one side. Half a second later, Sage did the same. Crouched low, Sage peered into the blackness, waiting for his eyes to adjust. Before they did, another shot rang out, pinging into the wood wall at his side. He dived to the floor. Seconds later he felt a tug on his sleeve and twisted to find Fong's dark eyes shining just inches away.

Fong whispered, "I make noise, draw shooter away. You find chief. Get him out, if he shot."

Sage nodded obediently. "Which direction do you think I should head?"

"Ears say shots came from north of here. Try that way. I draw shooter south. Soon as you hear noise, you go." With that, he noiselessly slipped away. After a long pause, there was the sound of a crate crashing to the floor and running footsteps. Sage immediately moved forward, using wooden crates as cover. He reached the front of the building without finding Campbell. By now, his eyes had adjusted with the skylights overhead letting him see the individual crates, many of them stacked high.

He looked around and noticed an archway between the middle warehouse and the next one. Campbell would have headed for the easiest route into that north warehouse. Sage back tracked and spotted a wide aisle between the stacks. He headed north along it, crouching and moving slowly trying to heighten every one of his senses, the way Fong had taught him.

A gasoline smell strengthened with every step until the odor was overpowering. Nearing the archway, he stopped. A tumbled crate blocked the aisle at a spot where the smell was strongest.

Sage edged forward until glass crunched underfoot. He froze, held his breath and listened. Nothing moved or made a sound nearby. He edged forward a few more feet, squatted and carefully put a finger to the floor and felt wet. He lifted the finger to his nose. Yup, gasoline. He tried to puzzle out what had happened. Maybe the arsonist spotted Campbell and gave chase, knocking the crate over in his haste. Or, maybe, Campbell surprised the fellow by knocking a crate on top of him. That would explain the broken bottle. Did that mean Campbell got away? Sage listened hard, hoping there was just one bad guy and that Fong was keeping him busy in the south warehouse.

His straining ears heard a loud crash and the jingle of breaking glass, followed by a solitary gunshot. For a brief moment, Sage hesitated to make his own noise, not knowing whether there might be two arsonists, then he stood, took a deep breath and called softly, "Campbell, you here?"

For a moment, there was only silence until another crash came from the southern end. As that noise faded, a whisper issued from behind a nearby crate on Sage's right. "Miner, is that you?"

Sage stepped toward the sound, whispering, "Campbell?" In response a big figure rose up from behind a crate—Campbell. "You okay? Did he hit you?" Sage asked

"I'm fine. I managed to bushwhack him with that crate. Broke one of his bottles, but he's carrying one more. He's already thrown gas all over the north warehouse. I suspect Glicker left a supply inside here somewhere. He strikes a match and we've got a very big problem." Campbell's whispers were sharp with urgency. Somehow, they had to stop the arsonist before he struck that match.

"Where's your Mr. Fong?" Campbell asked as he moved to stand in the aisle with Sage. His question was answered by yet another loud crash from the far end of the buildings. This time the crashes went on for awhile.

"I think that's him dumping over crates and leading our arsonist on a merry chase." Another shot rang out. "We better go help him."

"Here," said Campbell, handing him a long crow bar. Campbell had one of his own. "I found these in a pile—they probably use them to open crates."

Crowbars in hand, the two of them crept down the aisle and into the southernmost warehouse. Here too the gasoline smell was overpowering. Ahead of them came the sound of crates falling at a rapid rate. They angled in that direction. Sage was relieved. Whoever was shooting hadn't hit Fong.

They reached an open space surrounded by crates. A number of other crates lay tumbled across the floor. A figure stood in the space, looking away from them and up. Sage followed his gaze and saw Fong crouched atop a stack of crates like a tiger about to spring. The man raised his gun.

Without thinking Sage shouted "Hey" and flung his crowbar in the man's direction. He missed the man, but the action distracted him. Campbell's crowbar had a truer aim and smashed right into the man's gun hand. The gun went flying.

The arsonist didn't hesitate. He ran for the open door on the dock, pulling down crates as he went. Fong leapt down, landing softly like a cat. Sage marveled at the feat, but quickly followed after the racing Fong. Behind him, Campbell's thudding feet brought up the rear. If they could chase the man out of the building, they might prevent the fire. Then Sage remembered. The hand not holding the gun had been clutching a clear glass jug of what had to be gasoline. Ignite that on the dock and still everything would go up.

THIRTY FOUR

Fong reached the open dockside doorway and abruptly stopped on the threshold. Sage peered over his friend's shoulder and saw that it was the raspy man facing them, the jug of gasoline in his hand. He twisted off the cap and tossed it into the river. Sage sensed Campbell behind them—then the fire chief was pushing past.

He stood before the door, his body protecting Fong and Sage. His voice was kind as he said, "Ah, Michael Stuckney, what the devil have you gotten yourself into?" He took a big step forward but halted when the other man retreated closer to the dock's edge. Fong and Sage eased out to stand behind and to either side of Campbell.

Stuckney's words were matter-of-fact, without accusation, when he said, "Couldn't find work after you fired me."

"You know I had no choice. I hated doing it but I had no choice," Campbell sounded genuinely regretful.

"Oh, I know. I'd taken to drinking way too much. The other guys, they were afraid to work with me. I could see it in their eyes every time the firehouse bell rang. You should have fired me sooner."

"We all stumble at fire scenes," Campbell said.

"Naw, the fellas were right. I was drunk when I stumbled against that ladder."

"Bobby's okay now."

Stuckney's bark of laughter was bitter. "Sure, once his broke leg mended."

"You didn't start out drinking. You were a fine firefighter. One of my best. What happened to you?" Campbell asked.

"I loved firefighting, you know?"

"And, you were damn good at it."

"Mary didn't love it. She hated me being gone. She hated the danger. She hated never having enough money for food. She took the kids and went back to her folks. I thought I wouldn't care." This last was said with a kind of wonder.

Heaving a sigh, Stuckney said, "And, then Archie died. He was my best friend."

"You couldn't have done anything more to save him."

Stuckney's tone turned fierce, spurring Fong and Sage into advancing a step. "You didn't see his face when he was lying under that beam. You didn't run away when the roof started falling. You would never have run. We all know that about you."

Campbell said nothing for a minute. "You were in the hospital when we pulled Archie's body out. He looked peaceful. He died of the smoke. He wasn't burnt. He didn't suffer."

Stuckney looked away, upriver, but somehow, Sage was sure the man was remembering how he'd lost his friend.

Campbell tried a different tack, "It took three of us to lift that beam off him. I told you that in the hospital."

"You asked why I started drinking. Now you know. Besides, none of that matters. I killed Wally Roberts. I didn't mean to, but he's dead all the same. But Chief, I never set a single fire. This would have been the first one."

"Who got you into this fix?"

"Hill, the insurance man. He ordered me to set this fire tonight. I should have done it an hour ago. But, I was sitting in there, matches in my hand and I just couldn't do it. I told him over and over that the wind was too strong. That people could die, the whole city could burn. He didn't care." Stuckney stopped talking and shot a glance south.

Sage followed that look and saw that Hanke and Solomon were advancing up the dock from the south and, from the north, Tanner and Randolph were also closing in.

Stuckney turned his attention back to Campbell, his eyes burning. "Hill didn't care, but I did," he said fiercely. He carefully put the glass jug on the dock, straightened and again looked Campbell in the eye. "I cared," he repeated and stepped backward off the dock.

Campbell must have read Stuckney's intent in that look because he was already moving forward, his hand outstretched. But, there was nothing left to grab.

Stone, Campbell and Sage were sitting in Stone's office when the clerk, Roger, arrived for work. Stone heard him and called out, "Roger could you bring me some coffee?"

They heard murmured agreement from behind the closed door and, minutes later, there was a knock and the door opened. The clerk came into the room before he noticed Campbell standing just inside the office. Next he saw Sage and the tray he held crashed to the floor.

"Surprised to see me, Roger?" Sage asked.

The clerk turned white and whirled to escape but Campbell slammed the door shut and stood there with his arms crossed and looking very much like he wanted to punch Roger.

Sage studied the clerk who was not noteworthy in any way. You'd overlook him in a crowd. Hell, Sage hadn't really noticed him even in these small offices. And, that's what had worked for Roger.

"You might as well take a seat, we're going to stay here until we know everything," Sage told the quaking clerk.

Roger felt behind him for a chair and sank into it, somehow shrinking as he did so. He pressed his lips tight together, whether to stop words from pouring out or to stop them from trembling, Sage couldn't tell.

"You see, I couldn't figure out how Hill and his cronies learned so quickly that Andy and I were working with Stone and Campbell. I mean, all I was doing was fighting fires and maybe looking for my missing friend." Sage noticed for the first time that Roger's eyes were just a little buggy. Or maybe that was fear.

"Anyways, while I was thinking on that, as I sat in that black hole of a cellar, gnawing at the ropes and sure I was going to die, I remembered one more thing. That was Mr. Stone here telling me that some insurance companies were being extraordinarily slow in responding to the letters you'd typed and mailed. Letters that should have yielded responses that let Mr. Stone identify "unusual" claims, duplicate claims, high dollar claims, claims coming from the same insurance agents and attested to by the same fire station chiefs. Yet, there were no responses at all."

The man's Adam's apple did a little jump.

Sage continued, "So the three of us got here early this morning and Roger, do you know what we found, shoved far back in your bottom desk drawer?"

The clerk said nothing, just stared at Sage as if he were a mesmerized mouse staring at a swaying cobra.

"We found these, Roger." Sage held up a stack of envelopes. "Letters you had Mr. Stone sign but that you never mailed. And do you know what, Roger? The insurance agents who were arrested early this morning are the very agents that represent the companies to whom these letters are addressed. Isn't that an interesting coincidence?"

Again the man simply stared. Stone broke the silence. "Why, Roger?"

That seemed to loosen the clerk's paralysis. "For the money," he said bitterly. His eyes filled with tears. "I wanted to get married."

A tap sounded on the door. Campbell turned, opened it and let Sergeant Hanke enter.

Sage gestured toward the clerk who he addressed, saying, "Well, Roger. I guess you know that marriage is now unlikely. Instead, I'd like to introduce you properly to Sergeant Hanke since he's about to become your closest acquaintance."

They held the wrap-up gathering in the New Elijah dining room rather than at Mozart's. The John Miner alias had to be preserved and it was important that Campbell, the Coopers, Tanner and Randolph were there. For Solomon, Sage, Mae, Fong and Hanke, these wrap ups had become a tradition.

Hanke started. "As soon as the other patrolmen took over at the warehouse I went to find Chief Hunt. He agreed with me that, once they realized there was no fire, Hill and his pals would destroy all the evidence. So, we woke Judge Berquist up and got the search warrants."

That made Sage smile. Clarence Berquist was renowned as the city's crankiest judge. He was also the most honest—which might explain why he was cranky. It's no fun being the lone wolf in a wilderness of scoundrels.

"Berquist signed the search warrants and at dawn we raided homes and offices all over town, tossing every insurance paper we found into boxes. Folks are sorting through them now. Berquist also signed arrest warrants for Hill and the other four agents. And, we arrested the three

fire station chiefs involved . . . at their homes and not their firehouses."
That courtesy earned Hanke a grateful smile from Campbell.

"All of them are in jail. My testimony, along with the paperwork, will be enough to convict them. We'll be able to keep Mrs. Clemens and the rest of you completely out of it," Hanke said before adding, "Once we've questioned the agents and examined their paperwork, we'll be set to arrest the building owners who submitted fraudulent claims."

Campbell took over. "Michael Stuckney's body was recovered, washed up on Swan Island. I take heart in the fact he never set any fires. Hill apparently torched the barrel factory himself when he couldn't find Stuckney. Otherwise, Orpin's taken credit for every other arson fire in the last eighteen months before his arrest. That means the Glicker warehouses would have been Stuckney's first. In the end, he just couldn't bring himself to do it because when I first saw him he was just sitting on a crate. His conscience probably saved downtown Portland and, maybe, a lot of lives."

"Do you think it was because he'd been a firefighter?" Mae asked.

Campbell's voice softened as he said, "Michael was an excellent firefighter until his life fell apart. He might of survived his wife leaving. She was a hard woman. But, he believed he abandoned his best friend in that fire. No one could convince him otherwise. That's what ate at him. So, like lots of men these days, he drank. And he couldn't seem to stop. He was right. The other men were refusing to work with him. I had no choice but to fire him."

It was clear from the droop in Campbell's shoulders that he would forever regret that decision.

Cooper cleared his throat to get their attention. "It was hard on my family when James and I were arrested but something good came out of it. I learned that conflicts over politics aren't as important as friendship and community."

He turned toward Tanner and Randolph. "I will be forever grateful to you for watching over Frances. Despite the fact we are on opposite sides when it comes to Washington and Du Bois, you two and the others put that difference aside and came to our aid. That will always mean a lot," he swallowed hard and his wife reached over to squeeze his hand. "You go ahead and publish your paper . . . I still won't agree and I still won't like it, but it won't make me angry any more. We're both on the same side in this battle. We're just using different tactics to achieve the same end—economic and social justice for our people."

Cooper turned to look at Hanke, Sage and Fong. "I am also immensely grateful for all that you did. Unfortunately, most men aren't like you. I know that we Negroes face a tough battle and that even tougher times lie ahead. But knowing that there are white people who will take risks for a black person, well, that's also something I won't forget."

It was the next morning when Sage knocked on Violet's door and Andy opened it. The first words out of his mouth were, "Sorry I couldn't come to your meeting but I had to stay to help Violet with Jimmy—he came home last night. Did you catch them all? Can I go back to work?"

At Sage's nod, the young firefighter danced a jig. He called out and the bedroom door opened. A very pregnant Violet waddled into the room, followed by her bandaged and limping husband.

Everyone took a seat and Sage laid out how the fraud scheme had worked and who was involved. Andy shook his head upon learning that his own station chief, Faden, was in jail. "I thought you were wrong when you told me he might be part of it. Leastways, I was hoping you were wrong. I couldn't believe he'd do something like that."

Sage stood to go. "There is one more thing," he said, pulling an envelope from his pocket and handing it to Andy who'd also stood to usher him to the door. "The Underwriters have an arson reward program. Everyone agrees that you should get the reward. If it hadn't been for you, we'd never have solved our problem.

Andy lifted the envelope flap and slowly withdrew a bank check. The amount was enough to cause him to sit back down. "My lord, this is enough for a big down payment on a house," he mumbled. He looked at his sister as joy took hold. "Violet, Jimmy, we can buy us a big house over in Union Town with enough bedrooms for everyone and a fenced yard for Sadie. And maybe I can even get one of those motorcars."

Their rejoicing was cut short when Violet gasped, clutched her belly and bent over. When she straightened, she said through gritted teeth, "Seems like that's not the only reward you'll be getting tonight . . . Uncle Andy."

Late the next morning, Sage climbed the few steps to the house's front door. He knocked softly and a young woman answered. Beside her stood a little girl, her head reaching only as high as her mother's hip. Sage squatted down until he was eye level with the girl. Carefully drawing off the cage's cover, he revealed a snow white bird with a lemon yellow crest. The little girl exclaimed "Joey!" and reached for the cage.

Sage shook his head, saying, "No sweetie, he's not Joey. But maybe he's Joey's brother. I know Joey would want you to take care of him. Can you do that?"

She nodded, somberly telling him, "Joey saved our lifes."

He glanced up at the mother, worried she'd view the gift a burden. Her grateful smile dispelled that worry.

The little girl poked a finger through the cage bars and said softly, "Hello, pretty bird. I'm going to love you, always and always. Just like I do Joey." The creature seemed to understand because his crested head cocked to one side and his curved beak opened. Burbling softly, the bird hopped across the bottom of its cage toward the tiny outstretched finger.

The End

Historical Notes

These notes are offered with the disclaimer that others have conducted far more in-depth research into the history of Portland firefighting. I especially want to acknowledge Brian K. Johnson and Don Porth, who wrote *Portland Fire and Rescue*. Their research and old photographs proved invaluable. Mr. Johnson has been ably in charge of the City of Portland's archives for a number of years. He and his staff do an incredible job of obtaining, cataloguing and preserving Portland's history. They deserve heartfelt gratitude for the work that they do.

That said, there are times when the story's needs required adjustments to the facts. For example, Station 1 was actually one of the better maintained firehouses in the city. The fictional firehouse, with its leaky roof and odiferous conditions, represents an amalgamation of the living conditions firefighters experienced in the city's other firehouses. The City Archives contain David Campbell's written requests to the Common Council for funds to repair the firehouses. His requests referenced various firehouse problems.

Finally, this is a factually complex story that requires a higher number of historical notes which may seem daunting. Please take some comfort from the knowledge that you are being spared at least twice the number that appear below.

Fire Fighting

1. The meaning of various words and labels often change over time. So, although this book refers to the various fire station houses as "Station 1" or "firehouse," in the early 1900's such structures were usually referenced according to the fire apparatus manned by a "company" of firefighters out of that structure, such as "Engine 1, 2, [Steam Engine] Truck 22 [Ladder], Hose 6", etcetera. The story uses simplified labels in order to avoid confusion and allow a smoother story flow. In 1903, there were approximately twenty such "firehouses" in Portland. Today, there are thirty-one but it is a much bigger city.

2. The condition of the firehouse structures was appalling. More than one fire crew abandoned their living quarters during heavy rains because of leaking roofs. Moreover, weather has always significantly impacted the nature and success of Portland's fire-fighting efforts. In particular, ice and wind created dangerous conditions for firefighters, making it much harder to extinguish fires. That remains true today.

3. The description of Sage's first day fighting fires was lifted direct-ly from newspaper accounts of one noteworthy day in March, 1903, when Portland's firefighters responded to one serious fire after another—each worsened by a steady wind. A pet parrot was that day's only fatality.

4. Firsthand accounts and contemporaneous newspaper reports are the source of most of the story's fire descriptions and incidents. For example, there are reports of falling wooden cornices being a deadly danger to firefighters. So much so, that the city code even-tually outlawed cornices with wooden supports. Similarly, there are a number of reports of electrocuted horses, including one that caused the horse to be retired. There is also a report about a hose blast nearly knocking a firefighter off a ladder.

5. Man's initial ignorance of electricity and its potential dangers resulted in many fires, injuries and death. Firefighters were shocked when the ladders or fire escapes they climbed came

in contact with unshielded live wires. They were also shocked when they stepped onto roofs and into buildings. At least one firefighter died from an electrical shock. Initially, the placement and condition of these lines was completely unregulated. And, fierce competition in the business lead to many dangerous situations, such as there being a number of electric companies servicing the same block of buildings and stringing electrical wires every which way.

6. There were numerous instances where fire apparatus collided with other vehicles, most notably trolleys. It is one reason why emergency vehicles were subsequently granted the right of way at all intersections and on all roads. Firefighters were injured and sometimes died in such collisions or when they fell off an apparatus on the way to a fire.

7. Portland's fire horses generally arrived unbroken from Eastern Oregon. They were essential to Portland's fire department from 1882 until 1911, when gasoline powered apparatus began replacing them. In 1920, the last horse drawn apparatus was retired and replaced by a gasoline vehicle. During their service, fire horses were electrocuted, burnt, killed in collisions and sometimes dropped dead after a hard run to a fire. Many of them were famous characters in their own right. Their names are included in early fire department legends—horses named Colonel, Roachy, Jerry, and Blind Dick—the latter lying down and dying when told he'd been auctioned off. Their drivers took pride in the speed at which the animals trotted from their stalls to stand under the harnesses and get buckled in before racing from the firehouse—the record being 13 seconds from the sound of the bell to the horses charging out the door.

8. Dalmatian dogs have long been associated with firefighting as the breed has a known affinity for horses. Historically, Dalmatians had the task of protecting fire horses from charges by other dogs. There is some dispute over whether Portland used firehouse dogs. Some sources report they were participants in Portland's firefighting efforts while other sources state they were never used. At least one early photo shows a dog

sitting with firefighters before a firehouse. Since I like dogs, and have known a loveable Dalmatian, the canine character of Sadie is included in the story.

9. The central fire station, on Fourth Avenue, between Morrison and Yamhill Streets, had a 4,200 pound tower bell that rang whenever there was a fire somewhere in the city. Simultaneously, a message went out over copper wire to every firehouse, pinpointing the location of the callbox raising the alarm. One account states that, on windless days, the huge bell could be heard as far as twelve miles away in Oregon City. It was retired in 1913 and is currently mounted at 19th and West Burnside in the Firefighters' Memorial Park.

10. In 1903, Portland was using a fire alarm callbox system like the one described in this story. To prevent false alarms, the boxes were kept locked with the key held by someone in a nearby house or business. This necessarily slowed response times. Nevertheless, there are numerous documents in the City Archives showing that many neighborhoods petitioned for additional boxes. This system was not changed to an unlocked box system until 1906. By 1935, there were eleven hundred twenty-five boxes installed across the city. Some fire alarm boxes continued in use until the 1970's though the majority were abandoned when telephones became widely available across the city.

11. Firefighting continues to be a dangerous occupation. Not only are many of the dangers described in this story still present but, historically, many firefighters have been disabled or died because of their exposure to toxic chemicals and substances present in fires. Moreover, the stress of the job means that firefighters have higher rates of cardio-vascular related disabilities and deaths. Most states acknowledge these invisible killers through the mechanism of workers compensation laws holding that such illnesses are presumed to have been caused by their firefighting occupation.

Fire Chief David Campbell

12. By any standard, David Campbell was a remarkable and admirable public servant. He was smart, heroic and kind to his men. The story's account of Campbell leaping forward to shove two fire fighters out of danger and the resulting injury to himself is described in a contemporaneous newspaper account. His concern for his firefighters was well-known. He also first gained local notoriety as a popular pugilist. That said, the facts and personality traits attributed to the Campbell character in this story are fictitious except for those set forth in these notes.

13. Contemporaneous accounts indicate that Campbell appeared numerous times before the Portland Common Council (hereinafter "Council") to ask for increased wages and better working conditions for firefighters. He also lobbied against the continuing the use of unpaid volunteers and part time extramen.

14. Shortly after the time in which this story takes place, the Council adopted civil service reforms that were intended to prevent corruption in the form of political patronage. Campbell supported this reform but insisted that all existing firefighters had to retain their jobs. It was quite a political battle that Campbell came close to losing. Once it was over, however, not a single firefighter lost his job.

15. Campbell invented a new type of fire hydrant that was subsequently manufactured in Portland. Newspaper accounts state that the hydrants provided "independent gates" which allowed one stream to be shut off and the hose detached without having to shut down the entire hydrant. This 1903 invention gave firefighters greater flexibility at fire scenes and lessened delays.

16. City Councilman Fred T. Merrill strongly opposed Standard Oil's plan to site additional oil storage tanks on the city's east riverbank. His position ultimately prevailed and all future tanks were installed north of the city near the town of Linnton. This new location has recently been declared a disaster-in-the-making because it sits adjacent to the Willamette (pronounced *Will*

lam it) River on ground that will liquefy in the event of the earthquake that some experts claim is imminent.

17. The already-sited eastside oil tanks, however, did cost Portland its fire chief. On June 26, 1911, the Union Oil storage tanks, at SE Salmon and Water Avenue, caught fire. Although the tanks were enclosed by brick walls and a roof, the fire threatened to trigger a blocks-wide runaway conflagration—especially since they sat right next to Standard Oil's storage tanks. Chief Campbell was on the scene. He concluded that, despite tens of hoses pumping water onto the outside of the building, the fire could not be brought under control unless it was fought from inside the structure. To determine whether that approach was safe for his men, Campbell and two others entered the building. Minutes later there was a gigantic explosion, one that sent people and bricks flying across the street. The roof and walls collapsed inward. The two men with Campbell staggered from the building, injured but alive. He, however, did not survive. On that day, Portland lost its sixteen-year fire chief.

18. Thousands lined the route of David Campbell's funeral procession to pay tribute to a beloved and heroic man. It was likely the largest funeral procession Portland has ever seen. There is a small memorial dedicated to his memory located at the 19th and West Burnside memorial park. It is the scene of annual June 26th ceremonies honoring fallen firefighters.

19. Campbell is credited with having transformed Portland's fire department from a ragtag, ill-equipped, mostly volunteer force into a modern, professional and paid fire department. He also did the research and made the recommendations that brought the first fireboat onto the Willamette in 1904. In 1910, he convinced the city to purchase its first gasoline-powered, firefighting apparatus but may not have lived to see its 1911 delivery.

20. While the wages, working and living conditions of Portland's firefighters were as bad or worse than those described in this story, Portland firefighters did not unionize until after Campbell's death. Campbell is probably the reason why these men delayed unionizing. He lead by example and he demonstrated concern

over their health, safety and financial stability by advocating tirelessly on their behalf.

The National Board of Fire Underwriters

21. The impetus for the fire insurance aspect of this story came from a small 1903 newspaper article reporting that the city's Common Council had voted to plank or gravel the Powell and Milwaukee roads in the Brooklyn neighborhood. The article noted that this improvement took place at the behest of the National Board of Fire Underwriters (hereinafter referred to as "Underwriters") which had threatened to withdraw insurance from that neighborhood unless fire equipment access improved. The article triggered research into the impact this organization had on Portland's development and on the development of cities across the United States.

22. I confess to harboring ill will toward health insurance companies. I am convinced they are rapacious parasites we can do without. I think they should be eliminated and that the U.S. should provide the universal health care enjoyed by people in every other developed nation. That said, I had to re-think my hostility toward insurance companies in general. When I began researching this story, I was ignorant of the crucial and very positive influence fire insurance companies had on our nation's infrastructure and the safety of its citizens.

23. Overall, the research led to the conclusion that, historically, the fire insurance business is one of the few instances where the capitalists' desire for profit and the public's desire for both safety and low premium rates, created a collaboration that yielded long-lasting benefits for almost every community. The arm-twisting tactics employed by the Underwriters in this story come directly from history. Thus, Portland's and other cities' implementation of building and electrical codes, fireboats, passable streets and a host of other public safety measures came about because of pressure exerted by the Underwriters.

24. In the early 1900's, U.S. fire loss far exceeded that found in Europe. In 1865, losses totaled $43 million. By 1899, it stood at $153 million. That marked increase triggered the Underwriters' decision to get into the fire prevention business through inspections, model codes and rewards for information leading to the arrest of arsonists. They also created the Underwriter's Laboratory which certifies the safety of electrical appliances and equipment.

25. The Chicago fire of 1895 wiped out the majority of the city's insuring companies and left its citizens without funds to rebuild. The Underwriters' team of investigators evaluated San Francisco in 1903. Their subsequent report opined that the city's conflagration risk was so great that it was against all odds that the city still stood. That report led the city's insurance companies to significantly raise their premium rates. Subsequently, when the fires associated with the 1905 earthquake nearly destroyed San Francisco, the great majority of insuring companies remained solvent and provided the funds that allowed the city to rebuild at a much faster rate than had Chicago.

26. Under pressure from the Underwriters, the City of Portland designated fire districts wherein there were stricter building codes for remodeled or new commercial buildings. The City Archives contain a number of documents from building owners seeking exemption from these requirements. The Council appeared to usually deny those requests.

27. There is no evidence that the insurance fraud scheme described in the story ever took place in Portland—though there were reports of "arson rings" in the city. The scheme in the story did, however, take place in a number of Midwest states during the story's time period. One of these schemes ended with the conviction of several church members, one banker, one wholesale merchant, fire officials and several insurance agents. Given that the insurance companies were reluctant to share information about customers and claims, it is highly likely that elements of the story's scheme were at play in every American city. The problem was so pervasive that, after years of resisting, the insurance companies finally implemented a shared clearinghouse

in 1915. Its purpose was to identify double insurers, suspicious claim patterns and other such elements of fraud. The industry also successfully lobbied to change state laws so that payouts reflected actual losses, rather than insured losses.

28. The character of Edward Orpin is based on a real person of the same name. The real Edward Orpin confessed to multiple arsons and armed robbery in 1903. His physical description comes from a line drawing that was published in the newspapers at that time. That said, the facts and personality traits attributed to the Orpin character in this story are fictitious except for those set forth in this note.

Racism in Portland

29. In the early 1900's most African-Americans lived on the west side of the Willamette. They began moving to the eastside after the erection of the Enterprise Lodge of Masons near Larrabee and Clackamas streets. The Enterprise Lodge's membership included many social leaders of Portland's black community. This vibrant eastside community was subsequently demolished, in the late 1950's, by a developer-led urban renewal program that sought to build an event venue called the Memorial Coliseum.

30. In 1903, Portland's African-Americans were better educated than Southern African-Americans and poor Euro-Americans. As stated previously, in the historical notes attached to earlier Sage Adair stories, the black men employed by the Portland Hotel played a crucial and ongoing role in the development of Portland and its African-American community.

31. In the early 1900's Oregon had a number of "black laws." Because of the federal Bill of Rights, these laws were unenforceable except for the one that outlawed inter-racial marriage. That law was not repealed until 1949 when the lure of World War II shipyard work had significantly increased the population of Portland's African-American community.

32. In practice, Portland was somewhat unique at the turn of the twentieth century. Black men voted and served on juries. Portland's district attorney, however, refused to let blacks serve as jurors in trials where the defendant was black and the accuser was white. He claimed blacks were incapable of rendering a fair decision against one of their own. Of course, he had no such concerns about white jurors in cases where the accuser was black and the defendant white.

33. Portland public schools were racially integrated. This was not because the white majority believed black children deserved an equal education but because they found maintaining segregated schools too expensive. There were no black teachers and black children rarely stayed in school past the sixth grade.

34. As the 20th century progressed, discrimination worsened for all African-Americans. The nascent racism of white Portlanders was fed by the steady racist drumbeat coming from the South and Midwestern states. Much of this growing racism was repeated by Portland's Euro-American-owned newspapers in the guise of merely reporting. An example of this is the following 1903 Portland newspaper article which states:

> W. E. King, editor of a black newspaper down in Galveston, Tex., takes a sensible view of the race question and lectures his people in the columns of his paper. He admonishes them that no one will respect them [African American] so long as the bulk of them are "lazy, shiftless, characterless, and inclined to copy the vices of the whites while ignoring their virtues."

35. Attorney McCants Stewart, briefly mentioned in the story, was Oregon's first black attorney. He quickly won grudging respect from his white colleagues for his superior lawyering skills. Unfortunately, Portland's black community was too small and poor to support a full time lawyer and whites would not hire him. He eventually moved to San Francisco and died shortly thereafter.

36. In 1952, William Carr was hired as the first full time black member of Portland's Fire Department.

A.D. Griffin

37. The character of B.J. Cooper takes as its inspiration, a real person, Adolphus Dyonisius ("A.D.") Griffin. Griffin was the editor of Portland's first black-owned weekly newspaper, *The New Age*. He published the newspaper from 1896 to 1907. Very little is known about Griffin. Some historians report that he was married to the daughter of Blanche Bruce, the first black senator in the U.S. Congress. The Griffin's home was located at the current site of the Blue Moon Tavern in the Nob Hill neighborhood. Griffin left Portland in 1907, eventually settling in Kansas City where he worked as a detective and as a newspaper editor. Mrs. Griffin remained in Portland, reportedly operating a hair salon from her home. The facts and personality traits attributed to the Griffin-like character in this story are fictitious except for those set forth in these notes.

38. Using the threat that his newspaper would discourage a blanket black vote for republicans, Griffin pressured the Republican Party of Oregon into making him a convention delegate. And, as in the story, they appointed him to the newly created position of convention "doorkeeper." His subsequent editorials encouraged blacks to vote their conscience, rather than for a particular party. He eventually became a democrat.

39. A.D. Griffin was a member and provided a portion of the funds used to establish the Enterprise Lodge. The fraternal organization shared space with the Enterprise Investment Firm of which Griffin was a founding member. This investment organization was the first one organized and operated by men of the black community.

40. Griffin had an on-going feud with the white editor of the *Oregonian*, Harvey Scott who often wrote editorials contrary to those appearing in the *New Age*. At one point Scott opined:

> The *Oregonian* . . . believes this race [African Americans] capable of improvement, and it knows that improvement is going on all the time. At the same time it knows. And every

person of judgment knows, that social equality and racial amalgamation of blacks and whites is impossible.

41. Griffin published approximately 400 issues of Portland's *New Age* newspaper, focusing on the activities and news important to Portland's black community. In his well-written editorials Griffin was conciliatory towards whites, relying on reason and example to convince them that African-Americans were equal to whites. It likely explains why many of his advertisers were white-owned businesses that served blacks as well as whites.

42. For most of the paper's issues, Griffin editorialized in favor of Booker T. Washington's views while being critical of W. E. B. Du Bois' position. That changed as time passed and the South's virulent racism began to infect the North, including Oregon. Refuse to Serve signs began appearing. Unions wouldn't accept black members and growing white prejudice reduced employment opportunities.

43. In 1902, Griffin wrote an editorial entitled "Crime and Punishment." In that piece and other editorials he decried the continual and obvious disparity in the rates of arrest and levels of punishment. He used police department data to support his assertions. He also chastised the *Oregonian* newspaper for sensationalizing negative stories about blacks and always assuming the blacks were guilty as charged. He decried the fact that it published markedly more negative coverage than the coverage about white suspects in similar situations.

44. In September 1902, a black man was lynched in Marshfield, Oregon, now Coos Bay. Griffin opined that the crime was heinous, without stating what it was, but he objected to the lawlessness of the lynching.

Booker T. Washington and W.E.B. Du Bois

45. The story attempts to portray the changing attitudes African-Americans began to have toward white racism at the beginning of the twentieth century. A schism developed in black communities all across the country, including in Portland, over the Booker T. Washington approach to winning racial equality and that of W. E. B. Du Bois. In Portland it yielded, in 1903, a second newspaper when African-American men employed by the Portland Hotel and others, aided by black attorney McCants Stewart, launched *The Advocate,* which rivaled A.D. Griffin's *New Age.*

46. As time passed, Griffin's editorials moved closer toward the Du Bois viewpoint. He also "walked his talk" by publically rebelling against Portland's segregation. This assertion is supported by two *Oregonian* news articles which give a flavor of Portland racism in the first decade of the twentieth century and reveals how Griffin's position appears to have changed.

> *Morning Oregonian,* 4/21/1905: Editor A. D. Griffin, of the Portland New Age, entered the Pullman saloon on Fifth street last night and asked for a drink of whisky. It is against the rules of the Pullman saloon to sell drinks to colored men. And the bartender refused to take Griffin's money. Griffin insisted that the man treat him the same as his white brethren, and argued the matter for fully half an hour. Finally the bartender consented and gave Griffin a drink of whisky, at the same time taking the ten-dollar bill which the negro had been flourishing in the air when declaring his rights. The bartender rang up $10 on the cash register and refused to give the negro any change. A free-for-all between the negro, the bartender and the proprietor ensued. The white men were too much for Griffin, who soon found himself sprawling outside the door on the sidewalk, minus his $10.

> *Morning Oregonian* 9/29/1906: REFUSES TO SERVE NEGRO Bartender Then Has Colored Editor Arrested for Disorderly Conduct. Because the bartender at Vigneux's' saloon drew the color line and would not serve A. D. Griffin, editor of the

Portland's *New Age*, the latter called for an explanation and was arrested for disorderly conduct. "We serve no coons here," the barkeep is alleged to have said when Griffin asked him to "draw one." "As it happens, I am not a 'coon', retorted the colored editor. "We don't serve niggers, either," quoth the beerjerker. "I am not a nigger, either," said Griffin. "Well, what are you,? Was asked. "I am a negro," was the reply. "We don't serve coons, niggers or negroes," said the presiding genius at Vigneux's. "Get out." Griffin says he then asked for an explanation, and this led to his arrest by a convenient policeman, who led the colored man to the police station, where he was booked on a charge of disorderly conduct.

Miscellaneous Bits

47. The county's Hillside Poor Farm was located three miles west of the city on Jefferson Street. It housed about 100 people at a cost of approximately $7 per month, per "inmate."

48. The character of Fred T. Merrill is loosely based on the real Fred T. Merrill who made his fortune selling safety bicycles in Portland. In 1898, he sparked an interest in the safety bicycle by challenging teams of horses to races that he won. He also served as a commissioner on the Common Council and was known for representing the interests of his working class constituents and for taking stands against corruption and monied interests. He did, indeed, do much to stop Standard Oil from building more oil tanks on the east bank of the Willamette across from downtown. He was also an incessant advocate for legalizing prostitution. The other facts and personality traits attributed to the story's Merrill character are fictitious.

49. The fact of a general strike taking place in New Orleans is true. It took place, however, a few years earlier than suggested in this story. In 1892, 20,000 workers, represented by forty-two unions, united in a city-wide general strike. After three days, management agreed to higher wages and more hours of work.

50. While Portland's firefighters were slow to unionize, Portland had a relatively high rate of unionization in the early 1900's. The Labor Day Parade & Picnic was the city's biggest civic event. This level of unionization yielded higher than average wages and shorter work hours citywide—as well as more leisure time. These changes, in turn, created a relatively larger middleclass and substantial working class neighborhoods. The union impact was so significant that today's inner eastside neighborhoods, with their big foursquare houses, were once known as "Union Town."

ACKNOWLEDGMENTS

ONCE AGAIN, I WANT TO start by thanking the readers of this series. Their enthusiasm and support has encouraged Sage to keep fighting the good fight. I hope his adventure stories return the favor by encouraging and supporting their individual efforts to make the world a better place.

To the extent this series accurately reflects history, that is due to those who have done their best to preserve the past. In particular, I want to thank the staff of the Portland City Archives who are dedicated and enthusiastic about preserving their city's past. And, as always a thank you goes to the staff of the Oregon Historical Society and to the voters of Portland who decided the organization deserved financial support. May that continue.

This book in the series received special reviewing assistance from retired firefighter Brian Runyan who provided valuable corrections and additions, one being that firefighters never leave a smoking fire scene. Claudine Paris provided many helpful suggestions and corrections as did Sally Stoner who offered the final detailed fixes that made the story more understandable and fluid. Any remaining clunky bits or errors belong entirely to me.

I also want to especially acknowledge author Caroline Miller whose encouragement, wit and wisdom have provided immeasurable comfort on this journey.

A special thank also goes to KBOO radio's Labor Radio show and its host Lane Poncy who has given the series exposure and an ear.

And finally, as always, I must acknowledge my husband, George Slanina. His unwavering support, kindness and always pithy, right-on observations continue to make this series and my happiness possible. One can never acknowledge wonderful husbands too often or too much.

*Thank you for reading **Slow Burn***

We invite you to share your thoughts and reactions with your library and on Goodreads as well as on your favorite social media and retail platforms.

We appreciate your support!

Other Mystery Novels in the Sage Adair Historical Mystery Series
by S. L. Stoner

Timber Beasts

A secret operative in America's 1902 labor movement, leading a double life that balances precariously on the knife-edge of discovery, finds his mission entangled with the fate of a young man accused of murder.

Land Sharks

Two men have disappeared, sending Sage Adair on a desperate search that leads him into the Stygian blackness of Portland's underground to confront murderous shanghaiers, a lost friendship and his own dark fears.

Dry Rot

A losing labor strike, a dead construction boss, a union leader framed for murder, a rag-picker poet, and collapsing bridges, all compete for Sage Adair's attention as he slogs through the Pacific Northwest's rain and mud to find answers before someone else dies.

Black Drop

In this ripping yarn, President Theodore Roosevelt has left Washington D.C., embarking on his historic train trip through the American West. Little does he know that assassination awaits him in Portland, Oregon. The words of a dying prostitute warn Sage Adair and his allies that they will be blamed for Roosevelt's murder. Since life is never simple, Sage also learns of young boys who need rescuing from a fate worse than death. As the presidential train and the boys' doom rush ever closer, every crucial answer remains elusive. Who is enslaving the boys? Who plans to kill the president? Can either tragedy be stopped?

Dead Line

Sage Adair encounters murder and mayhem midst the sagebrush and pine trees of Central Oregon's high desert. This captivating land of big skies, golden light and deadly secrets is the home of hardy and hard people–some of whom intend to kill him.

The Mangle

During a blistering 1903 summer, Portland's steam laundry women are working ten hellish hours a day. Exhausted and ill, they demand a nine-hour workday. Sage Adair, and his mother, Mae, join their fight until women begin disappearing. Desperately searching for the missing women, Sage and Mae face grave danger midst suffragettes, prostitutes, social workers, white slavers, arsonists and heartless bosses. Inspired by actual historical events, this is the sixth book in the award-winning Sage Adair mystery series.

Request for Pre-Publication Notice

If you would like to receive notice of the publication dates of the eight Sage Adair historical mystery novel, please complete and return the form below or contact Yamhill Press at www.yamhillpress.net.

Your Name: ________________________________

Street Address: ________________________________

City: __________ State: ____________ Zip: ________

E-mail Address: ____________________________

Yamhill Press
www.yamhillpress.net

NOTES